THE TALE OF HERMOD

Tale of One Year

January 1092 - November 1092

Published by the Author:
Dr Jo Chapman Campbell
Milnacraig of Kilry
Alyth
Perthshire
PH11 8HS

ISBN 978-0-9935504-0-9

Printed and bound by Robertson Printers, Forfar

FOREWORD

This story is the first of a series of five Tales, based around the author's Ph.D. thesis, completed in 2008. The title of this thesis is 'The Stone Sculpture of Cumberland and Westmorland from c. 1080 – c. 1130 in a social and historical context.' The Tale of Hermod is set in the year 1092 and introduces both real and imaginary characters which are woven into a poetic tale of magic and intrigue, introducing Celtic and Norse mythology. Historical figures, facts and places are used to establish a framework for the Tales. Many of the characters introduced here feature in all four Tales to follow: The Tale of Lokin (set in 1100), The Tale of Ketel (1106), The Tale of Bueth (1112) and the Tale of Rikarth (1115).

The front and back covers are paintings by Edward Chapman Campbell, a professional artist, author and musician, who lives in Dumfriesshire.

'Come to Bassenthwaite.
The time is nigh.
The secrets are to be told,
for in the telling,
the legends will be saved.
Come.'

CHAPTER ONE
Bassenthwaite (January 1092)
Lokin

The stone chipped off in sharp flakes as Lokin worked his chisel across the rough surface. It was still early and the winter sun was rising reluctantly from behind the eastern hills, promising a bright but chilly day. There was a bite in the air and the boy shivered, moving the wax candle a little closer. Snow lay like a snug winter coat across the hills and intricate, feathery gloves of frost covered the thickets of broom beyond the stony wall of the church-yard. Lokin shivered again and realised he was hungry. An hour earlier, he had crept from the little hut he shared with his father and three young brothers. The fire was out. The cold congealed broth in the clay pot on the black hearth, the remnants of supper, looked unappetising in the grey light. Yes, he was hungry.

The colourless dawn stepped back to allow the yellow day to alight on the winter ground. Lokin looked expectantly across the yard. Soon, Roberto, the master-mason, would arrive and he always brought something for Lokin to eat, a hunk of rough bread or perhaps a baked egg or two. The previous autumn, in the year 1091, Roberto had arrived in Bassenthwaite, sent by the Norman lord, Ivo de Taillebois, to organise the building and decorating of a new stone church. Lokin remembered well his first sight of his new master. He looked as ancient as the grey stones of the hillside with long grey hair and a straggly grey and white beard which, when deep in thought, he twisted into funny shapes, making Lokin and his friends laugh. His smile was as broad and crinkled as the open sea, his eyes dark, ladled with humour. Speaking a sort of Italian mixed with Norman-French that was difficult at first to understand, he told Lokin and his friends stories of foreign lands and of his early life in the northern hills of Lombardy, near a city called Firenze. His face lit up each time he spoke the word. 'Firenze'. Just the name sounded magical to Lokin.

Lokin stared at the pale yellow sky stretching across the wide

1

morning. It was at moments such as these, alone, a little hungry and very cold, he thought of his mother. At almost thirteen years of age, the oldest of the four brothers, he remembered her most clearly. Ketel, his next brother was a year younger. He, too, remembered her gentle touch and the soft songs she sang nightly as the boys settled down to sleep. Ketel, a good storyteller, told of his mother riding a beautiful white horse. To him, she was the Queen of the Fairies, radiating light in the dappled shadows of the green, green forest. Her face was not faded but fresh and new as if life had only just touched her soul for a brief moment. She lived in the deep glades and across the high fells, where shadows darkened mossy dells and where westerly winds gaily tossed the tall grasses. 'She is always with us. Just close your eyes', Ketel would say, 'close your eyes and think of her.' Bueth was the third brother. Just three years old when their mother died he, too, remembered her face. Now seven, he screwed up his small nose and imagined her beside the winter hearth or picking herbs in the dense hedges of the summer hillside. As for the baby, Rikarth, now almost four, he sometimes stopped, quite suddenly, near the thorns by the village bounds. Sniffing the warm, damp air of the summer evening he would call 'Mama' and point to the hedgerows where butterflies lazed in the late sunshine and bees spent busy hours, saturating the afternoon with the buzz of tiny wings. Tugging at his father's long tunic, he repeated, 'Mama'.

On this cold January morning thoughts of his mother were fresh in Lokin's mind. Now, in the lightening of the day, chisel in hand and his craft in his heart, he remembered her with joy. She had sung and danced through her short life, leaving no trace of bitterness. She went without tear or complaint. Lokin remembered the first day she had coughed, with Rikarth only a baby, clinging to her breast. The cough took over for such a short time. Then she was gone, with her family around her, by the red fire of a white freezing January. Now she was with the spirits of the wood, their mother, Helewisa.

The grief following her death echoed through the village and beyond, over the hills into neighbouring valleys. Anketil, their father, a skilful and renowned wood-carver, threw himself into his farming and his craft. Sorrow sat upon his shoulders and harrowed his handsome face as he worked throughout the long summer days, tending goats, pigs and chickens, collecting wood and berries, hunting rabbits, field mice and hedgehogs deep in the forest glades. In the late summer evenings, he stared across the colourful hedgerows into the forest beyond, waiting perhaps for a glimpse of her face or the gentle touch as her brushing past him in the fading sunlight. Throughout the long nights of the northern winter, he stared silently for hours at the black lake, watching the dark water sway mysteriously beneath the wind and the waves stroking the shore, licking the sodden rocks with their relentless tongues. Neighbours brought broth, herbs and hunks of meat which were thrown into the pot above the fire. Anketil's sister, Aunt Gretil, who lived in a village called Isel, a few miles down the river, cooked and scrubbed the hut and the boys. Uncle Chetel, his brother, was a fisherman on the great river Eden that wound north of the black mountain, before turning west to a sea which stretched to the farthest edge of the world. He brought them fresh fish: trout, perch and, occasionally, a salmon. Thus, with the help of family and neighbours and each other, life slowly returned to some sort of normality.

Lokin was thinking on these things as he chipped patiently the pinkish grey sandstone. He looked out across the lake beyond the village. The white robes of another winter morning lay across its unwrinkled surface and golden sunbeams danced to and fro touching the mountains of Allerdale. Now, after many months of toil, the church building was almost finished. Work had recently begun on the decoration of the doorway arches and the arch above the chancel. Finally, and most important of all, Lokin must carve the font, to be placed at the eastern end of the nave. On this morning, Lokin was copying a drawing of a monstrous snake with swollen belly, large evil eyes and a long, curling tail that suffocated a tender plant in its unforgiving grasp. He chiselled its features, etching out the shadows behind the terrifying teeth and carefully depicting, with the finest of lines, the snarl of its jaw. As he carved, he imagined the creature's hot and smouldering breath. Lokin smiled to humself. 'Of course, dragons

3

don't really breathe.' Suddenly, a cold finger of the north wind tapped his face and he shivered. The yellow morning was now pale blue as the winter sun slipped from sight and grey clouds rose above the mountains to the east. Lokin recognised their familiar dance. 'A storm from the north,' he thought, returning to his work, unaware that, from the shadows beyond the fence, a pair of dark eyes watched intently. Lokin carved and etched, blowing away the stony dust as he did so. The dragon emerged from the ancient rock as if awaking from a long sleep. The sun suddenly reappeared, strangely bright, hanging above the pale horizon and blue daylight spread across the mason's yard. Lokin's solitude and the silence of the sun would soon be interrupted. Others, including his aged master, Roberto, would arrive to ply their stony toil and the yard by the church would fill with noisy tools and voices. The day would pass quickly, Lokin knew, until the pale sun set beyond the western mountains, slipping down beyond the sea into an unknown and mysterious cavern. He hummed to himself and concentrated on his dragon of stone. Beyond the fence, beneath the thicket branches, the eyes were still. Lokin hummed and etched and saw nothing. The dark eyes watched, unblinking, and saw everything.

CHAPTER TWO
Allerdale and Greystoke, 1092

Allerdale, once the ancient kingdom of Rheged, stretched from the western sea to the great mountains in the east and was carpeted with forest. To the south lay the lordship of Copeland, to the east the small lordship of Greystoke. For over two hundred years, Northmen had come to these valleys and forests, from the lands of ice and deep fjords beyond the relentless rhythms of the black sea. They came not as invaders but as farmers, tradesmen and craftsmen, mixing with the Anglian races of old Cumbria and the ancient and mysterious Celtic communities of the forest glades. They brought with them skills of war and of peace, of sword and tool as well as the gift of story-telling. In their long, long boats, they brought their sagas, their legends and their heroes across the sea to these green, mountainous lands.

Allerdale was a vibrant and mysterious land, rooted in tradition, inhabited by people with many languages, many beliefs, singing a song of fierce independence. The village of Bassenthwaite lay on the southern edge of this ancient kingdom, huddled east of the long, black lake. To the north, the land rose and fell with mountain, forest and dell and villages were scattered across green slopes and along shadowed valleys. Settlements nestled in the remote glens, hidden from the world by winter snows and by golden summer forests. To the west of the mountains, the twisted shoreline with deep, sandy inlets and treacherous, marshy banks lined the lush rolling hills. Impenetrable thorn thickets lay beneath giant oak and beechnut. Deep, meandering rivers ran blue with gold and silver fish. This was a land of summer plenty for man and beast but also a land of winter storms and long darkness, a land of ancient mystery, myth and legend, strange creatures, an untamed land of unfathomed fables and secrets.

In this year, 1092, it was beyond Allerdale's southern edge that the Norman mantle now enwrapped the land. At the ancient settlement of Appleby, the powerful Norman, Ivo de Taillebois, was constructing an enormous white castle above the plains, a vast and threatening place. To the south, the land was lush with green pastures and forests overflowed with wild game and people and animals thrived. But now the Normans had assumed control and every man and beast, every hectare of grazing and scrub, every building was to be counted. All the information was assembled in a book, called by the people of these lands the 'Book of Doom'. But to the north, in Allerdale, they remained free. Here, in Westmoringeland, on the outer reaches of the new Norman kingdom, Ivo de Taillebois was respected, feared, yes, but respected. It seemed he wished for harmony with the people of Allerdale who had inhabited and farmed these lands for generations. The 'Book of Doom' did not cover the mountains of Allerdale or the western sea marshes of Copeland or the villages of the deep, hidden valleys of Greystoke. Bassenthwaite, by the black lake, lay beyond the tentacles of Norman power and Ivo left these lands alone.

Lord Gospatric governed Allerdale. Descended from the legendary ruler of the ancient kingdom of Rheged, Urien, he was generous and wise. He grew up amid the turmoil of the Cumbric people's struggle against the marauding Scots and was touched by tragedy at a young age when his mother and young sister, Ethwin, were murdered by marauders. Later, as his father fought ahead of him in battle, amid the screams of the fallen, Gospatric had learned of courage. He had learned also of love through his marriage to Ellesse, with whom he bore four children. Now, in this winter of 1092, it was the autumn of his long life. He was grey-bearded, grey-haired, his face wrinkled from the constancy of the westerly winds, but his eyes were dark, his manner deceptively gentle and his mind as sharp as the flint axe strapped to the saddle of his small pony. Waltheof, his youngest son and a fine young man, would assume the responsibility of Allerdale and all within its bounds upon his father's death.

Greystoke was a small lordship to the south-east of Allerdale, surrounded on three sides by towering mountains. The southern boundary lay along the watery ribbon of the Ulls and its ancient castle was constructed on the east-west route through the mountains, guarding the western lands of Copeland from invaders. The Lord Sigulf governed this kingdom, inherited from his father, Liulph, a Saxon lord who lived so long ago that nobody could remember him. Sigulf was, like Gospatric, an old man and much respected. They had fought together in war and enjoyed each other's friendship in peaceful times. Their subjects were free men, not serfs, whose duty was to fight whenever the peace of this ancient realm was threatened. Sigulf's son, Forne, like Waltheof, a young man of about twenty years old, would inherit the title and the responsibilities upon his death.

The pastures and fells of Allerdale and Greystoke were common lands and villagers had licence to graze their flocks, pick berries and gather firewood and, of course, to hunt through the forests. They fished, too, the small, mountain streams and across the black lake. Recently, however, across this remote world, rumours hung in the mountain air and the word 'Norman' was often whispered in the village huts and along the lakeside shores.

CHAPTER THREE
Anketil

The boys' father was born in Bassenthwaite in about the year 1060. His father, Aegir, and his grandfather, Snorri, came from the northern lands of ice and crossed the eastern mountains into Allerdale when the summer harvest was almost complete. Snorri and Aegir were carpenters and, after sailing south over the restless sea, they had settled for a time on a grey and misty island called Lindisfarne. Here, a band of monks inhabited an ancient, dilapidated monastery, eking a meagre living from the few grey sheep that clung miserably to the grey rocks above the grey stormy sea. Once, this had been a great centre of worship. It was rumoured a marvellous Book of Gospels was created here, inscribed with gold and lapis lazuli and studded with precious stones. Now, however, the fields were bare, the monks poor and there was little work. Snorri and his son thus had departed this forsaken place to travel west across the ravaged dales of middle England where recent war had torn to shreds a land of plenty. They walked for many days through this desecrated land and reached the mountains of the north-west cradling the deep valleys that stretched down towards a silver sea. Sparkling lakes were scattered among these mountains, glistening in the autumn sunshine. From the mountain crests, they looked down for a long while on these valleys basking in the fruits of the harvest, replete with colour. Snorri turned to Aegir and spoke in a quiet voice.

'This is where I must leave you. This is where you will settle and find joy. Take my stories with you and pass them on to all who listen. There are those who must learn of the hero Sigurd and the tales of the north. Tell of his courage, his valour and of his betrayal. The chosen ones will find purpose and a guiding light will show them the way. Sigurd lives. This I know. Tell his story to your sons and their sons to save Allerdale, the ancient kingdom of Rheged. More I cannot tell you, but your son and his sons must know of Sigurd. It is the ancient land of Allerdale you now see before you, stretching to the westering shores. Allerdale. Go down into these golden valleys and find an ancient place named Bassenthwaite. There, you will stay. My path leads me far from here but bear no burden of grief. My life will continue within the tales of Sigurd and in the stones carved with great skill that carry his story. Do not be afraid. We will, I promise, in this world or in another, meet again.'

Snorri turned, and without looking back, wrapped his long grey cloak about him and walked swiftly away into the trees. Aegir was alone in the clearing, the sun slanting down through laden branches touching the grass at his feet. He felt its gentle warmth and reached out his hand to touch the yellow glow. He looked again at the trees where his father had disappeared. There was no footstep, only silence. Turning westward, he saw a valley beneath the forest where a long black lake glistened in the autumn sunshine. On its banks sat a cluster of huts surrounded by neat wicket fences. Children ran in all directions, happy in the sunlight, and, in the cool shadows, animals grazed and slept. Aegir gazed at the scene and he knew. This was Bassenthwaite and this was where he would settle. He descended the steep stony path that led down to the village.

And this is where he stayed. He spoke the language of the Norse villagers who had once travelled from the same distant lands. He also understood their ancient form of writing scratched in spiky, runic letters on the damp earth or on pieces of bark or stone. He was thus made welcome and presented with a small piece of land to raise his own animals and build a hut. The gentle calmness of this tall fair stranger endeared him to all. Soon he was building fences and enclosures by day and, by night, carving wooden handles for swords, tools, ornaments and jewellery. Aegir carved many creatures from the broken stumps he found in the woods: red deer, wolves, hounds and eagles, two-headed snakes, ugly trolls and twisting dragons, characters of the fireside sagas. His skill was widely recognised and, through Aegir, son of Snorri, the tales of Sigurd reached these ancient lands.

Many villagers believed in God and in his son, Jesus, whose stories were found in the Bible and brought by missionaries from Irish lands many centuries earlier. Monks had travelled also from the far south,

9

from Italy, Egypt and from the distant eastern lands. These holy men instructed the communities in the power of this God, to punish but also to forgive, promising redemption from sins but also warning of the terrors of a world beyond death where the damned were tortured for all eternity. Most folk, who learned of this God, accepted these terrifying truths and worshipped in little churches and chapels, built in God's name, scattered across the hills and narrow valleys. They married their sweethearts and buried their dead in forlorn, remote and windswept church-yards. But Celtic and Norse blood ran deep in their veins and in their hearts and, through the long winter nights and in late spring evenings, on the highest peaks and among leaf-bound forest glades, more ancient beliefs were honoured. They danced by woodland streams, bathed in ice-cold springs and sacrificed young lambs to the myriad of deities of the deep, dark earth. They farmed and sang the long year through, raising children, cutting hay and tending animals. But their spirits were free, running with the wind and listening to the song of the mountain streams. They worshipped God, yes, within the walls of their small, wooden Christian buildings, but they also revered the sun, stars, forests and the racing clouds, praying to the gods and goddesses of ice-blue streams and deep, dark lakes. It was these beliefs that provided hope and joy in their brief and tenuous lives.

One autumn day, a little time after Aegir's arrival, a family returned to Bassenthwaite after a pilgrimage to York. A new abbey, dedicated to the Virgin Mary, had been founded there by the Conqueror and had become a place of pilgrimage. The building was reputed to be of extraordinary beauty and elegance, designed in the latest fashion and decorated with many painted statues. The father of this family was a Christian man who disapproved of the old Celtic beliefs and tales of magic and sorcery. Two daughters, both about Aegir's age, had travelled with their mother and father to this holy place and now returned home after a long and difficult journey. Aegir first saw the younger daughter, Matilda, emerging from the woods, leading her tired, brown pony, fair hair falling to her waist, her eyes as blue as forest rock pools, her skin as clear as the bluest northern sky and a smile, although tired, that spoke of kindness and courage. It was love at first sight and within a few weeks they were married. Aegir agreed to convert to her father's Christian religion but he kept the secrets of his Norse heritage quietly in his soul. Indeed, he and Matilda shared this love of Celtic myth and Norse saga. A year later, in early summer, Lokin's father, Anketil, was born. The family thrived. They baptised their son in the wooden chapel and told stories of the miracles of Jesus, of saints and of angels. Under the wide summer sky or by the winter fire, however, they spoke and sang of different tales, of magic, of strange animals and trees, changing and shifting, enticing all into their mysterious world. They told also of the adventures of Sigurd and his horse of magic. Anketil grew up in awe of this hero, carving his story in wood and on bone as weapons, tools and ornaments for the village folk.

Helewisa was a child of the uplands. Her grandfather, Ulfin, like Aegir, had arrived from the northern sea and married a girl from the fells, the youngest of a poor family of crofters. They had scraped a poor but contented living among the high fells above Bassenthwaite. Here, the winters took a terrible toll on man and beast but the summers bathed the mountains with warm light and the children ran among the purple, heathery slopes. Their eldest daughter, Gunrild, married a man from Strathclyde called MacGille or Mac for short. He spoke only raw Gaelic and his manner was rough but he was a good man whose skill was in hunting wild animals and he was readily accepted in the community. He and Gunruld were broken-hearted at the death of their firstborn son. Helewisa was born the following summer and grew into a strong and beautiful creature, blond and tall like her mother, with the dark eyes of her father. She was the apple of his eye. Through these early years, she learned the secrets of the woods, hidden life of the animals, changing seasons, the passage of moon and stars, signs of approaching storms and the smell of dew on damp, October mornings.

Several years passed and it was decided to send Helewisa, as the oldest child, across the forested slopes to Bassenthwaite, to find work to provide for her family. Mac took her to the village and asked for Aegir, Anketil's father. These two men had known each for many years and had hunted together often, ending the long days huddled by camp fires, shrouded by the forest shadows, sharing songs and stories. Mac

11

trusted Aegir with his life and with his daughter, and it was Aegir and Matilda who took the ragged but beautiful child into their home, providing food and warm blankets in return for scrubbing, collecting wood from the thickets and mending the torn clothes of the little ones. Anketil was of a similar age and they at once found a deep friendship. They grew together, first as brother and sister, then as friends, then as lovers. They married in the last days of December in the year 1078 in the small wooden church, kneeling before the altar beneath the graceful cross carved by Aegir with ribbons of decoration, with serpents, dragons and birds. An aged priest from the monastery of St Bethoc called Columba performed the ceremony which was followed by days of merriment.

Anketil and Helewisa built a hut, lined with thick ferns and grasses, near the dark green forest where the pigs rustled. They talked and sang of magical lands beyond the western skies and how, one day, they would sail away across this silver sea to discover the secrets beyond the horizon. In the summer months, amid great rejoicing, the first child, Lokin, was born. Helewisa's family came down from the fells to celebrate. The long days were full of damp August heat, the heavy air alive with insects, the earth carpeted green and yellow with grasses and flowers. The baby thrived among this land of summer plenty and crawled among the ducks and hens, scratching across the dusty yard. Soon, a second son, Ketel, was born and, within four years, two more, Bueth and Rikarth. Anketil entertained all with tales of Norse heroes, of Sigurd and Lokin, of Christian gods and local saints, of Saint Bethoc and Saint Brigit, of mysterious Saints Kentigern and Ninian and of woodland fairies and nymphs from a magic and a secret world. Lokin sensed always the pure joy his mother and father had found in each other and recognised a special love within their humble walls.

In the winter evenings, as the shadows lengthened and the lights of the village fires flickered across the night sky, the family ate their simple meal. Their father told stories of a world far out of ordinary sight, much to the delight of the four boys, who listened, wide-eyed in the half-light. He spoke of distant shores beyond the blue horizon, of mountains standing high against the silver skies of ice, tales of deep,

12

dark fjords diving far beneath the grey-gold sun-kissed waves, a land where winter was perpetual darkness and summer shone with unwavering, yellow light. Through his words, the ancient but not-forgotten heroes rose like silent giants from the sea and came down from those distant mountains. Anketil had learned many stories from his own father, Aegir, whose memory of the northern lands was as clear as the ice beneath the steep fiords. Aegir spoke of his own family, of his father, Snorri, of his mother, brothers and of the loss of friends in war and on the deep, black ocean. Anketil told of ancient legends of the north where the sun never rose and where perpetual night ruled the earth beneath a frozen heaven. Of all the stories, those of Sigurd were the favourite. Lokin and his brothers sat, transfixed, by the glowing fire, as Anketil spoke of his valour and courage, but also tales of deceit, cowardice and hatred. Snorri's words, spoken to Aegir on that distant summer's day, were passed down to Anketil.

When he spoke, however, of white, stone churches and intricate carvings, Lokin listened eagerly. These carvings would speak in a mysterious language and only the chosen few would understand. The message through the ancient stones would save Allerdale and gather its secrets in a place where evil could not reach. Hearing these words, Lokin knew his own life was being touched in some mysterious way.

'Upon arches, above doorways, windows and chancels and on fonts, stone is carved with a myriad of patterns, masks, dragons and strange beasts. The creatures and monsters inhabiting this stony world belong to a time shrouded in mystery, revealed in the sagas of fireside and forest. Deep within the caves beneath the mountains, the rocks know the journey of life and death and the life beyond death. The ancient rocks, carrying the memory of these tales, are transformed into carvings that write their own language. This language, however, is available only to those who listen, who hear the stories and understand the message. To these chosen few, the decoration speaks of life's mystery and the quest to uncover its secrets.'

Thus, the tales of Sigurd sifted through the smoky darkness of their hut-home, catching the young boys unawares, drifting above the black shroud beyond the door. Anketil's words stayed with them through the winter nights, haunting their dreams.

13

CHAPTER FOUR
Bassenthwaite, January 1092
Lucy de Taillebois

Two autumns previously, in the year 1090, Anketil had taken his four sons to Isel where his sister Aunt Gretil, her husband, Uncle Thorro, and Lokin's cousin, Gille, lived. It was a thriving village by the banks of the great river Derwent flowing west to the wide sea beyond Copeland. The purpose of their visit was to baptise little Rikarth, now almost two years old. The church of grey and white stone was newly completed and was causing quite a stir across Allerdale. It replaced the old, dilapidated wooden chapel, built in the time of Rheged, and had been ordered, it was said, by Ivo de Taillebois, Baron of Kentdale. The church shone white in the late summer sunshine. Exquisite, crisp decoration covered the arch above the southern doorway, on the chancel arch within and around the tops of the stone piers along the nave, all painted in red, green, ochre, blue and gold. Lokin stared at the painted faces with their staring eyes and wondered if they could talk, and, if so, in what language? He reached out to touch the delicate shaft of the doorway but was quickly reprimanded by Aunt Gretil who, carrying Rikarth, ushered him and his brothers through the doorway into the dark nave, dimly lit by tall narrow windows. 'Don't touch', she whispered. Lokin glanced back at the faces and dark eyes followed him. What were they saying from their stony world?

Soon, rumours spread that a similar church was planned for Bassenthwaite. It was during the following spring, in the year 1091, a Norman lord had indeed arrived, dressed in red and silver ermine, mounted on a white horse of great stature, accompanied by his wife, also dressed in red and riding on a small grey horse of exquisite beauty. Several smartly dressed attendants rode with them and, at the rear, at least a dozen armed knights astride powerful horses with gleaming bridles. Anketil and the boys stood in the door of their hut, staring, bewildered. They had never seen horses like these before. Although it was early April and the summer lay just over the hills, there remained a cold shiver in the air. Lokin drew his cloak around him. Ivo de Taillebois spoke of his intention to build a stone church in God's name, similar to the one at Isel, dedicated to the ancient saint called Bethoc. He gazed beyond the array of curious faces to the black lake shimmering in the winter sun. These are God-fearing people, Ivo thought, and also good farmers, evident from the fat animals and fowl in the yard. The children with their dirty faces wore thick cloth and the fine-looking women had long, fair hair and blue, blue eyes. Ivo turned to Lucy.

'I think we will enjoy the task of building a church here.'

'It is beautiful', Lucy replied, looking up at the dark hills surrounding the village like a velvet mantle, touched by yellow rays of the dipping evening sun. As she looked, a forgotten memory stirred for a moment in Lucy's heart. Then it was gone. Something had touched her but she could not reach it in the deep recesses of her soul. She patted her mare, reassured by her peaceful presence. Ivo had often spoken of hidden danger lurking in these dark hills, beneath the deep lakes and among the moody, uncompromising forests. Lucy, however, did not share her husband's fears. She loved these lands and wished she could share her feelings with her ageing husband. She glanced across at him but Ivo was looking at a tall, fair man standing in a shadowy doorway, surrounded by four young boys, the smallest clutching his rough coat. Lucy saw the tall figure etched against the doorway. Then he was gone, merging with the darkness of his hut. The doorway was empty. Ivo and Lucy left soon afterwards, assuring the village folk that masons would arrive in the late summer, about harvest-time, to begin constructing the church. They rode away towards the south-east, along the lakeside, towards Appleby. From the doorway of his home, Anketil watched for a long while after the riders had vanished into the evening.

For several weeks, the village buzzed with talk of the church and of Ivo and his lady but no messenger came. The warm spring months brought new life and energy to the lands of Allerdale. Then, one day in early summer, a messenger arrived with news that the church was, indeed, to be built. Masons and quarrymen were expected at harvest-time and stone would be gathered from the hills above the village. Great excitement rippled across the village and across the fells. Ivo had kept his word. For Anketil, three years after Helewisa's death, the news acted like a magic wand. His face glowed with anticipation as he listened to the discussions of the new building and its decoration, the stone carvings above the doorway and the delicate ivory and wooden objects within. He was to design the magnificent cross of beech wood to be placed above the altar and the stories on the stone font beneath the chancel. For Anketil, the crucifix and font became his way of touching Helewisa. He immersed himself in the creatures inhabiting the swirling decoration, the dragons, wolves, strange birds, snakes and beasts of all description. Within this world, through his charcoal and his chisel, he reached out to touch his lost beloved as she flew high among the eagles and dived with the pink salmon beneath the frothy burns. Life returned to Anketil.

CHAPTER FIVE
Bassenthwaite, January 1092
Piero and Rainaldo

Rainaldo and his father, Piero, had arrived the previous summer. They had been in the company of a noble Norman lady, Margaret, travelling from the Norman lands north to a place called Dunfermline. A great white cathedral was to be erected here, carved from ancient rock and some said this lady, of royal descent, was to be married to the King of the Scots. Margaret enjoyed Piero's stories and liked the two grubby, brown-skinned travellers. She carried with her an embroidered picture given to her by a merchant who had travelled from distant Byzantium. Rainaldo, skilled with a pen, was intrigued by the creatures embroidered on this piece of cloth; two snarling two-headed dragons with long, twisting, flowering tails and creeping serpents with tails like mermaids. Scratching on leather and stone, he avidly copied these fantastic beings. Piero discussed many things with this noble and enlightened lady, including ideas for her new building. He spoke of his native Tuscany, of Pisa, Lucca and Firenze, where the ancient Roman way of building churches with columns and arches persisted. Margaret was fascinated and spent many an hour in Piero's company.

Rainaldo and his father would gladly have travelled north with this lady but, among her band was a jealous man, a southerner called Adam, who resented the attention Piero and his young son commanded. One night, he planted some coins in their sacks and, as the sun rose, gave the alarm that money had been stolen from his purse. It was, of course, found in Rainaldo's possession. Margaret, instead of seeing them punished, ordered them to leave and head westwards and not return. She was sad and also a little surprised but Piero knew that pleading innocence would lead to further trouble. Thus they left, guided by the rising sun. Margaret watched them leave but was sure they would one day meet again.

Piero had heard of a valley beyond the mountains where lay a deep lake, where people spoke in strange tongues and where forests echoed with ancient song. It was said trees danced and spring water healed all manner of ailments and sky and sea met in a torrent of water from which rose sea-gods and goddesses with unearthly powers.

'Father, I think you are making up these tales', laughed Rainaldo, light-hearted for the first time since their sad departure. Trudging along the forest path late into the afternoon, they stopped to pick berries and chew on puffy white mushrooms.

'How do you know all this is true? Have you ever met one of these goddesses?' He smiled at his small, red-faced father.

'I think you are just hoping it is true so you can be swept away by such a creature and live in paradise! Anyway, what would Jesus think about dragons?'

Piero, a little out of breath, turned to his son.

'Rainaldo, there are many things in this world we cannot explain. And, I might add, Jesus is one of them. I know I have raised you to believe in him, pray to him, to follow the Bible readings, but, if you think about it, nobody actually ever saw Jesus. So, the same goes for the gods and heroes of our tales. Just because nobody has ever seen them does not prove they do not exist.'

Rainaldo laughed again, tugging at his father's long grey beard.

'You have an answer for everything. Our stories must be based on something, surely? Perhaps our imagination?'

Piero looked intently at his son.

'You have much imagination, my son, too much and sometimes I am afraid for you. There are those who are stuck in their way of thinking and have no imagination. These are dangerous people. We have just encountered such a man and nearly lost our lives. So, have imagination for yourself, as much as you wish, but be careful with whom you share it because in sharing the hidden secrets of your mind you lose a little piece of your own self. You must be careful of this.' His eyes darkened and his brow furrowed. 'Believe me, this I know'. They walked on in silence towards the sun now setting on this ancient land.

Two days later, after climbing and descending and climbing again, Piero and his son reached the lands of Allerdale. The August sun shone in the late afternoon and shadows danced among the leaves above their wooded path. Emerging from this world of green, gold and sparkling light they saw a small village, lying far below by a long, dark lake. Bassenthwaite. They knew this was the place of which Piero had been told. Here, they would stay and, in time, would discover the reason for their journey. They stood and looked for several minutes, then, descending among the gorse thickets, scattering goats and chickens, were warmly welcomed by several members of the village who appeared from their huts, offering food and shelter.

The friendship between Rainaldo and Lokin was instant. They spent many hours that first autumn playing among hay stacks, running through forest glades, splashing in streams of cold mountain water that bubbled down to the silent, serious lake. They learned each other's language and soon Lokin's Italian tongue became quite respectable. Rainaldo, on the other hand, found the Norse dialect mixed with Cumbric and ancient Celtic words more of a challenge. He often scratched his head, struggling with pronunciation. With his clear voice and aptitude for gestures, however, he easily made friends among the children of the village and 'Rainaldo's lingo' made folk smile. Through their friendship the boys gradually learned, not only each other's language, but also their stories, of Italy and Normandy and of the distant northern lands. Their tales were of heroes and villains and adventures over the golden sea to the setting sun. Why wasn't life exciting like it used to be? Where are the monsters now? What happened to the heroes of the northern sagas and the wicked dragons of the magnificent eastern cities? The two boys often lay in the smoky darkness of the hut listening to their fathers, Anketil and Piero, speak of valour, truth, of treachery and cowardice. But, as this summer of 1091 moved inexorably into autumn, Piero's sight dimmed and his speech sometimes faltered. He sat for many hours in the doorway of his hut, wrapped in rabbit furs, protecting him from the devouring winds. He was an old man.

On this day in the autumn of 1091 the masons and their apprentices arrived and the village buzzed with excitement. New huts were hastily erected and everyone helped. The older boys collected strips of willow and branches of pine to place across the wooden roofs. Rikarth and

Bueth gleefully chased the village chickens, hurling pine cones at each other and the poor fowl. Ketel and Lokin followed Anketil to the forest, checking rabbit snares and pulling long threads of bracken to line the hut floors. Piero watched from the door of his hut, smiling to himself, acknowledging the villagers as they passed and watching the glow on Anketil's face as he pulled up yet another wall of a new hut. Everyone was talking about the new church.

A few days later a tall man with long white hair arrived in the village. He had no pony and must have walked many a mile but did not appear tired. This was Roberto, the master-mason from beyond the white mountains. He was to instruct the masons in the art of building the new church and oversee the decoration within. Some said he was of Italian birth, others that he descended from the Celtic tribes of the east but nobody really knew where he had come from. Anketil and other village elders greeted him and Lokin saw his gentle smile and heard his strange Italian words. He wanted to speak to him but Roberto turned from the crowd and looked towards the site chosen for the new church. Meeting this quiet mysterious man would have to wait.

That was many months ago and the autumn had fallen away into a cold and frosty winter. Roberto became, not only Lokin's master, but his friend. They sat for many hours, discussing the church and the carvings and Lokin found something almost magical in Roberto's presence. He was a strange man and seemed to know everything. He taught Lokin about building a church, how to plan, measure and construct walls strong enough to stand for a thousand years, how to lay roof timbers and to leave spaces for windows. He showed him plans and drawings of buildings in the south of England, in Normandy and in his native Lombardy, beyond the white mountains. They sat for hours on the frosty ground discussing the carvings to be placed above the south doorway and above the chancel arch. The masons worked tirelessly, day after day, but the winter was kind and progress uninterrupted. The church and its decoration gave a purpose to everyone, most of all, to Anketil and his eldest son.

Now it was January, in the year 1092. The late winter day was idling to a close and the bleary sun wiped the earth with a watery promise of spring. Lokin was intently studying one of Rainaldo's drawings, a dragon's face with dark oval eyes and sinuous body. Suddenly, his friend's head appeared from behind the wall.

'Lost in thought, were you, my friend?' Rainaldo said, 'Where were you just then? Let me see, up the mountain or across the sea or perhaps in the forest?' He chuckled, then leaped nimbly over the mossy stones and sat down beside Lokin who smiled but said nothing. Rainaldo continued in a hushed voice.

'I have heard strangers are in the forest.' He paused and looked at Lokin mischievously. 'Shall we have a look, once the sun is down?'

Lokin looked away for a moment or two. He knew his father's strict instructions to stay within the village confines, especially now with these rumours of strange folk but he was tempted.

'Rainaldo, I cannot go against my father, you know that. But', he paused, 'if we just go a short way, just to edge of the forest, where it rises towards Borrowdale. First, I must finish here. I'm starving, too. Let's get something to eat. What are you doing about your father's meal?'

Rainaldo picked up a small piece of grey stone, turning it over in his hand and rubbing the smooth surface. He moved away from his friend and his shoulders stiffened. Something was on his mind.

'Piero was sleeping just now. He has been resting a lot these past few days. I am afraid. He is my father and best friend and I have no other family except you, of course, and your father and brothers.' He turned to Lokin. There was a brief flash of fear in his eyes. Then he laughed.

'Quick. Let's go now before you go home for food. Once you are full of stew and pie, you will lose your sense of adventure'.

'We must be home before dark, promise?'

'I promise', replied Rainaldo, already running away towards the forested slope above the village.

CHAPTER SIX
The Legend of Sigurd

Anketil often recited the tales of Sigurd, Lord of the Lands of Ice. The boys knew every mesmerising word of their favourite stories. Lokin remembered one winter night in particular when his father told of Fafnir, the dragon's conquest. It was a wet night and the wind whistled and whined across the soaking mountains, racing down into the village and around their little home. The animals huddled from the storm beneath any shelter they could find. Even wild deer on the fells and slippery otters beneath the icy waters of the lake had taken refuge. Lokin remembered this night, not just for the storm, but because of the strange message uttered to him by the wind. His father spoke softly at first but, as the story progressed, his voice grew in strength and became unrecognisable. Wide-eyed and wide-mouthed, the boys listened and Rikarth shuffled a little closer to his brothers. The wind whistled his father's words.

'Sigurd was the son of Sigmund, the famous warrior killed in battle by the God Odin long before Sigurd was born. His mother, who was named Hiordis, reared him in a lonely cave, high on the rocky slopes of a forgotten land. On his death, Sigmund's sword had broken and the pieces were carried back to his mother by a young prince, whose name was Alf. On seeing Sigurd's mother with her new baby, he decided to marry her and immediately took them to his castle in the mountains. Here, the young Sigurd grew up, amid splendour and comfort, without a care in the world. He was a well behaved and easy-going lad, quick to learn and forgiving of his half-brothes, who often tried to deceive him with tricks and lies. He had no envy in his blood and was not jealous when their father gave his brothers fine horses and jewels and nothing to him.

He fell under the influence of the evil Regin, son of Hreidmar, the magician. Regin and his two brothers, Otr and Fafnir, had magical powers. One day, Fafnir murdered his father and stole all the gold that belonged to him. The God Odin, who had killed Sigmund and regretted this act, disguised himself and gave Sigurd a beautiful black horse called Grani, son of his own horse, Sleipnir. Regin asked Sigurd to find Fafnir and to kill him and he moulded a sword out of the shattered remnants of his father's, a sword which now had the powers of magic within.

Anketil, lost in his thoughts, paused for several moments. When he continued, his voice was very soft. Lokin moved towards the fire in the grate to hear his words.

Sigurd lured Fafnir over a pit and killed him with this sword by stabbing him under his belly. As he died, Sigurd drank his blood and, in so doing, learned the language of all the birds, who told him immediately of Regin's treachery and deceit. Sigurd then ate from Fafnir's heart which gave him the wisdom of all knowledge and the courage to uphold this wisdom until the end.

This wisdom and its secrts remain with us and must be passed on to those who follow. If not, all will be lost and the world of Allerdale will pass into a mythical place. We must tell the stories to our descendents but also must carve in ancient stone the stories of Sigurd across the land, in wood and in bone also, so that many can learn for themselves the wisdom and the courage of this hero. Remember, those who listen here tonight, remember this. The story of Sigurd must be carved in stone, in stone from these ancient hills. Trust me, for I am the messenger. Listen to my words. You are to carve this message in the ancient stones.

Anketil stopped speaking and stood by the fire for a long time. Little Rikarth closed his tired eyes and stretched out on his rough hemp blanket, Bueth beside him. Lokin and Ketel stared into the orange embers, the words washing through their minds. Their father seemed preoccupied and said nothing. The wind blew furiously around the hut, snapping twigs and branches from the trees and trying to lift the fences from their stony foundations. Lokin listened to its song, in awe of its strength. Then, just for a moment, he heard someone speaking through the wind, with words at first he could not understand. He glanced at Ketel, but he and Anketil appeared unaware of this strange voice. Lokin listened again but heard only the screaming gale as it tore across the land and up into the mountains. Where had this storm come from? Where was its home? He imagined its journey across black seas and over the steep, black northern cliffs. Did it speak to him? Had it come to him with a message? Crossing to the heavy, wooden door, Lokin opened it slowly. The night world was awash with water and battered with wind. Lokin opened the door just enough to push through, closing it behind him. He stood, in the shelter of the eaves, watching in awe at the sudden transformation of his familiar world. Suddenly, a voice spoke to him, this time with words he did not know but yet understood. It was a calm voice and deep and spoke clearly amid the roaring of the storm.

I am Grani, horse of the great hero, Sigurd.
I am also the wind
The silver wolf.
The black swan.
You will know. You will see.
You already do.
Listen for me in the wind
Watch the skyline in the moonlight for the swan's flight.
Run in the forest with the silver wolf.
You already understand the language of the wind.
You can hear me now.

Lokin hugged the shelter of the doorway.

Soon, you will understand the language of the swan and the wolf.
I will speak to you.
The black swan will bring you his message.
The silver wolf will lead you to safety.
You have been chosen.
Watch the moon, the wind and the sun.
The silver wolf.
The black swan.
The great black horse.
It is Grani.
The song is to be sung.
Wait. Listen.
Wait for the song.
You have been chosen.
Listen.

The voice faded as the wind tossed and danced away across the trees above the village. It swirled above him one more time and then rose beyond the forest and up on to the highest fells. Lokin watched its force rise above the mountains among the racing clouds in a tormented sky. Then, it was gone. All was quiet. The trees breathed relief in quiet shudders around the village. Lokin had heard the words. He was certain. And the words stayed close to his heart. 'You have been chosen.'

CHAPTER SEVEN
Kentdale, January 1092
Hugh and Herluin

Hugh and Herluin, his brother, rode side by side along a muddy trail through the forest. They were heading for the small settlement of Kentdale to meet with Ivo de Taillebois. The path narrowed ominously as they passed a rocky, rain-soaked crag but the two riders were well used to such journeys and rode their nervous horses without fear. The skies darkened and a winter chill crept into the creases of their heavy garments. Hugh glanced at his younger brother and saw the familiar look of defiance on his brow. He wondered what the outcome of this meeting would be. A little later, and sooner than expected, they saw light ahead and sent a knight ahead to warn the wooden fortress of their arrival.

So, this was Allerdale. Hugh had heard many tales of these remote lands beyond the conquered fields of Mercia to the south. Through his upbringing in the monastery at Bec he had become acquainted with stories of the Celtic peoples that inhabited these farthest reaches and of the Nordic folk who came from beyond the freezing sea to settle here. In the great library of the monastery he had read many books on these lands and stories of the saints that once lived here. Although Norman, he felt uneasy about conquering such lands and subduing these ancient kingdoms. He had felt not a little shame as they travelled through parts of the conquered lands to see the changes wrought by their conquest and not all for the good, it seemed. No wonder people resented these foreigners and he was one of them. Many people had been displaced and many had lost land and kin. Hugh looked across at his brother and wondered what he was thinking. It was difficult to know with him as he said little but he feared that his angry brow harboured thoughts of revenge. And Hugh knew that revenge was seldom what it seemed and never brought peace to a troubled soul. Herluin blamed Ivo de Taillebois for the death of their parents and young brother. He knew this. Herluin had often stated this. But, there was no proof and the suspicion was eating him up. Herluin hated Ivo and there was nothing Hugh could say to lessen this poison in his heart. As for Ivo's brothers, Ralph, recently been appointed Sheriff of Bedford, and William, seeking high office in Lincoln, well, even Hugh considered these men to be trouble. They were greedy and untrustworthy but this did not make them murderers. Well, not quite, he thought. As for Ivo, Hugh respected the man and appreciated his honour and his integrity.

They reached the lights of the wooden portals and the horses gladly entered into the safety of the keep, yet another symbol of the encroaching Norman fingers of control. The two brothers dismounted and stood for a moment or two watching the heavy gate close behind them, both deep within their own thoughts. They did not speak again that night. Beyond the wooden walls, with the gate now firmly closed, the creatures of the winter night and the shadows of the forest watched and were alone once more.

CHAPTER EIGHT
Bassenthwaite, January 1092
The Black Horse

A little later, when Lokin had finished his work, the two boys sprinted away from the mason's yard with its carpet of neatly ordered grey, white and pink stones. They disappeared between the stunted birch trees on the edge of the village, scattering a large family of resting pigs. Assorted fowl, startled, rose into the darkening air with loud, indignant squawking. The boys ran even faster in case the sound had alarmed the watchman at the village gate, but all was quiet as they reached the larger trees. They stopped to catch their breath and, puffing with the sudden exertion, looked about them. Just then they heard the snap of a twig in the darkness. They peered into the shadows. Lokin felt a twinge of fear tingle down his spine and up to the top of his head and he prayed to the saint, Bethoc, the saint of Bethoc. 'Please save us, let it just be a deer or a lost fawn, or even a fox'. Silence hung in the twilight. Then, Rainaldo touched his arm. Slowly, inch by inch, as if drawn by a magic thread, the bushes ahead parted. The boys sank to the leafy floor and held their breath. A few yards across the damp moss stood a tall figure, robed in black. His face was hidden in shadow silhouetted against the greying forest evening. Behind him stood a huge horse, etched in black. The boys' bare knees stuck to the moist ground and silence engulfed the forest like a web. An owl hooted some way off and a half moon emerged momentarily in the deepening blue sky. Then, without warning, the figure turned and, with his horse, disappeared into the almost black trees beyond the clearing. Lokin saw a fleeting glint of silver on the horse's head and the bridle made a sort of quiet, metallic click. The bushes fell back into place. The forest was silent.

The boys knelt in silence for several minutes. Then, rising slowly to their feet, they stared at the darkness enfolding the forest. Their legs were heavy and Lokin shivered in the damp cold.

'Who or what was that?' Rainaldo spoke first. 'What a horse. Lokin, he was the biggest horse in the world.'

Lokin did not reply but stepped gingerly across the clearing to the mossy ground where the figure had stood. He knelt and ran his hand across the soft earth. He whispered, under his breath, 'He has left no mark. Where are the marks of his boots and the hoof-prints of his horse?'

Rainaldo knelt beside him.

'Perhaps we dreamed him', he said. 'Yes, of course, we did.'

Far away in the shadowy night, a distant sound of a horse galloping echoed from the forest. Then, silence.

'No', said Lokin, quietly, 'It was not a dream.'

They turned and walked thoughtfully back to the village. Piero still slept, huddled in a woollen blanket. His breathing was even and Rainaldo turned to his friend, speaking in a hushed and serious voice. 'He sleeps peacefully. I will see you in the morning. Say nothing of what we have seen to anyone.'

Lokin found Anketil anxiously awaiting him. Ketel was standing by the fireside, his face hidden in shadow. The two little brothers were sleeping soundly. As Lokin entered, Anketil stood up and faced his son, noticing in that moment that the boy was almost as tall as him. He had grown up quickly these past few months.

'I suppose you were with Rainaldo?' he asked slowly but without anger.

'Yes, father,' replied the boy, 'we went to the edge of the forest'. He hesitated, uncertain whether to tell what they had seen but remembered Rainaldo's words.

'It was alright. We did not go beyond the clearing'.

'I will only say this once to you. The thwaites are safe and even where the pigs graze among the thickets, but never go alone beyond their bounds. There is talk of unexplained events in the forest and above the fells. A stranger has been seen and it is not known whether his intentions are good or evil. I do not wish to frighten you but I must insist on this. Do not stray. Is that clear?'

Lokin dropped his head but said nothing. For some reason, he could not tell his father of this stranger and his black horse. Pulling back the thick blanket beside Rikarth, he snuggled against the warm sleeping body. Ketel lay down just a few feet away.

'Where were you?' he whispered. 'Please tell. What were you and Rainaldo up to?'

'Shut up, Ketel. Go to sleep. I will tell you when I have had time to think about everything. Promise. Now, go to sleep.'

Lokin closed his eyes but did not sleep. His mind was racing this way and that. Anketil stood for some time beside the dying fire. His eldest son, lying awake in the smoky darkness, realised that for the first time he had not shared something with his father. Eventually, as the first threads of light flickered across the forest, he fell asleep and dreamed of a huge, black horse with a silver bridle and of a dark tall rider etched against a yellow moon. The figure beckoned to him to follow. Lokin stepped across the shadows and turned to call Rainaldo. But there was nobody behind him. He was alone.

The next morning was bright and unexpectedly sunny. Anketil had to rouse the young sculptor and it was long after sunrise when Lokin reached the masons's yard. Roberto was already moving among the carved stones, inspecting the work from the day before, tugging at his long, grey beard.

'What happened to you, young man?' he asked, with a twinkle. 'I hear that you and Rainaldo were beyond the bounds last evening. What did your father have to say?'

Lokin looked sheepishly at him but said nothing.

'Oh, I see', went on his master. 'It is like that, is it? Secret stuff. Oh well, never mind. I am sure you will tell me when the time is right.'

He looked directly at Lokin with a sudden seriousness and his eyes sparkled blue.

'In fact, I know you will.'

Roberto turned towards the church. 'Now, let's get to work.' Lokin stopped. How did Roberto know of their adventure? He wanted to ask but something kept his silence. He walked slowly towards the church, following the tall, slightly bent old man who seemed to know everything.

CHAPTER NINE
Bassenthwaite, January 1092
The Font

A few days later, Lokin sat alone with his chisels. Perched on his worn leather mat, he was carving a dragon from a roughly hewn block of pinkish grey stone. The eyes and nose emerged from the timeless rock, hewn from the fells above the village, stone born too long ago for any man to recall. When Anketil had explained this Lokin tried to imagine something even older than Octrida, his great grandmother, whose wizened face resembled the crags hanging high above the mountain passes. Staring at the chunks of rock, and caressing them with his cold hands, he wondered if they would share their secrets, telling their own stories of a forgotten time. He whispered, 'Who are you?' Feeling a little silly he looked around to see who was about. He stroked the pink, chalky stone. 'Who are you?' he whispered again. 'Can you hear me?' He looked round again. 'Can you say anything?' The stone lay cold in his hands. Winter air touched his cheek. Then, for a fleeting second, he felt a tiny whisper of heat beneath his fingers. He was certain. He touched it again but this time the stone lay cold in his hands. 'My imagination', he thought.

He thought then of his brothers, of Rikarth telling his stories with dark eyes flashing, speaking his own small boy language which nobody understood. His frustration often bubbled to the surface as he struggled for words and he would stamp his tiny foot against the soft earth. His gestures spoke a thousand words. Rikarth was his mother's spirit and his life would be an adventurous one, for certain and Ketel, almost ten now, with his quiet good sense. He just seemed to know what was right and what was wrong and, often, what to do about it. Lokin smiled remembering last summer and the home-made raft Anketil had made to sail on the lochan above the village. Lokin, Ketel and Rikarth rowed out over the black surface, leaving Anketil and Bueth watching from the shore. The smallest boy suddenly stood up and, without warning, fell out of the boat into the cold, dark water.

31

For a moment, nobody moved. It happened so quickly. Then Ketel, waiting for the little head to reappear above the murky water, calmly stretched down and lifted him from the blackness. Anketil shouted with relief.

'Thank you, Ketel. I thought I was going to have to get very wet.'

'It was just common sense, father. He had to come up again. Everything does, except stones, of course.' They all laughed, except Rikarth who was shivering with cold and very cross. As for Bueth, he loved to wander among the thickets, listening to birds, counting butterflies, sitting alone in the late summer sun. He was happy just to listen and seldom gave an opinion. He certainly never told a story. Their mother's loss had perhaps affected him most of all. Lokin decided he must keep watch over this brother. Ketel and Rikarth were strong in body and spirit. It was Bueth who would need him.

Suddenly, Roberto's voice interrupted his thoughts. Lokin had not noticed the old man approaching and was a little startled. Roberto spoke.

'The dragon matches the other stone perfectly. It could almost be breathing. What do you think?' He chuckled. Lokin said nothing.

Later, they sat beneath the arches of the new doorway, studying sketches by Anketil of dragons, snakes and sea monsters, creatures to be carved on the font. Roberto spoke.

'We will start work on the font in a day or two. Oh, by the way, your uncles Thorro and Chetel found a discarded stone on the road near Isel. It is square and quite large and was perhaps an altar long ago. Four faint figures are carved on the surface but otherwise it is undamaged. I have arranged for a cart to go and collect it. It is the perfect stone for a font.'

Lokin was anxious about the responsibility of the font, but excited too. Suddenly, however, a sharp cry cut the air and his thoughts. Far above the forest an eagle hung in the wind like a blown sail on a blue and white sea. It cried again. Lokin wished he could understand its words. Then, he remembered, he had been told to wait. He peered into the sky but the eagle had disappeared into its lonely world where he could not follow. Lokin then spoke words that just seemed to flow from his mouth.

'Roberto, I think we should include the story of Sigurd on the font, with Fafnir, the dragon, his horse, Grani, and the birds. Perhaps an eagle? What do you think?'

The master rubbed his chin thoughtfully. A secret smile spread across his face and Lokin wondered what he was thinking.

Roberto spoke in a low voice.

'I wonder if Ivo de Taillebois knows the tales of Sigurd.'

He watched Lokin stand and stretch, thinking about this question. What, indeed, would the Norman know? Roberto saw the boy stand tall and fair like his father.

'Anyway, when is the great lord Ivo coming back to see our work?' asked Lokin, with a slight edge in his voice.

'Before the arrival of spring, so I hear. The church will be finished, the font, too.' Roberto looked at Lokin and they smiled.

'Of course, it will be finished', said the boy with confidence but Roberto knew there was something on his mind.

'I wonder who first invented dragons,' said Lokin slowly, almost under his breath, idly picking up a tiny sharp-pointed tool.

'I have often wondered the same question. Dragons belong to all time. They are everywhere. They are the stories of day and of night, stories for fathers and also for sons. My ancestors in Lombardy spoke of dragons, so, too, did the herders of the steppes, the merchants of the eastern mountains beyond the road of silk, the boatmen of the icy north, even those who lived here in our lands of Allerdale in the time of Urien. Every story includes a dragon.'

The boy looked at the old man as he tugged his beard. Their breath hung in the cold morning like puffs of chilled, moist smoke, like dragons' breath.

'I think,' Roberto continued, 'I think dragons belong deep in the hearts of all people. They conjure up our innermost fears but they also give us mystery in our lives. We need mystery, don't you think? Things we cannot explain. Whether they exist or not, actually, does not matter. They belong to a distant but not forgotten time and in unknown places. This time and these places are kept alive in our stories and in the tales told by a thousand firesides. If they once lived above the black mountains, across the jewelled eastern hills or beyond the white southern deserts, they have passed into legend and these legends are merely an extension of our own lives. One day, this life, our lives, too, will become legend. For us, dragons are real in our stories and so in our hearts. We need them to understand both good and evil in this world. We cannot recognise evil without good. To understand beauty, we need ugliness. To understand truth, we must know falsehood. To understand and experience joy, we need sorrow also. It is all a balance. But, to understand anything at all, it seems we need dragons.'

He paused, looking intently at the boy.

'Dragons are in us and around us all the time. We have, I believe the choice, to believe in them, or not.'

Lokin scratched the ground thoughtfully, creating little circles and diamonds with his tools. He then started to draw the eye of such a creature, outlining its furrowed brow.

'I think,' he said, slowly, 'I think there are moments when dragons are very real. They come of their own accord.' He thought of the dark figure and the black horse. Fear bristled on the back of his neck. 'Oh yes', he continued, 'they come at any time and assume any guise.'

Roberto spoke quietly.

'Because I have come from southern lands, Lokin, beyond the white mountains, a land of warm sun and balmy breezes, perhaps you see me as different to your people. But, think about this, my father's father and his father before him came from the northern lands, just as your grandfather did. We are all descended from the same men of the North beyond the ice-cold sea. We just have different words and writing and my skin has been burnt by the hot sun. But the stories and dragons we have in common.'

Lokin, thinking of Roberto's words, idly scratched the sandy earth drying in the watery sunshine. He wondered if Ivo de Taillebois or Lucy, his lady, believed in dragons.

'What does this say?' Lokin asked, smiling with a sudden glint of mischief. A message in runic letters lay scratched in the dust.

'This object....' began Roberto slowly, 'this object was made....' He hesitated again. 'This font was made by Lokin and brought to great splendour.'

Roberto laughed. 'That is very bold of you, Lokin,' he said. 'Shouldn't we say, 'by Lord Ivo?'

'Why? You, Roberto, are the master of the whole building. My father designed the font and I will have carved it. We also have to mention Rainaldo and his drawings too. How could I have made these dragons without his help?'

'So, we must include Rainaldo, too, and, I suppose, all the masons and stone-cutters, the carters and the men at the quarry? And Sigurd, too, I suppose!'

They laughed and Lokin brushed away the runes with his foot. He stood up.

'Time to eat. I will see you tomorrow, young lad. Not too much thinking now!'

Roberto looked at the tall boy walking briskly away and then up at the arches above him. It was going to be magnificent, a real spectacle. He smiled, broadly. It was almost time.

CHAPTER TEN
The Forest, January 1092
The Black Swan

Anketil waited in the clearing for several minutes. He had run fast across the fell and was a little breathless. He knew there was an old stag just ahead of him but he had yet to catch up with the nimble, cunning beast. He glanced around the wintery world. It was cold but no heavy snow had fallen for many days and the earth was a patchwork of white, grey, brown and pale yellow. Only the crests of the mountains were iced in white. Anketil was aware of silence across the forest. The wind was at rest and no bird called from the brown depths beneath him or from the silver crags above. He listened but could hear nothing. Where had the old stag gone? He was about to set off again, heading north, beneath Randal crag, hoping to pick up his trail. As he turned, however, his attention was caught by a movement far above the towering rock face. Anketil caught his breath. A huge bird hung in the heavens, silhouetted against the pale sky, a great black shape slowly circling the summit. He had never seen such a bird before. The swans that lived on the black lake were as white as snow as were the smaller birds visiting the water from the frozen north. What was this creature?

The swan slowly flew closer to the forest, circling and gliding in the winter air. Anketil could almost see its eyes now as it floated in its world above him. With the occasional flap of its mechencial wings it was mesmerising and Anketil stared in wonder. He strained his eyes to see every detail. Then a strange thing happened. A sudden wind blew from the north and tore around the corner of the fells, hitting the slumbering trees with unexpected glee. The world was shaken awake and the silence pushed away across the southern valleys. Anketil tugged his woollen coat about him and tightened his scarf. He looked once again to the sky, now angry with darting clouds. He peered into the storm but the black bird had disappeared. There was no sign and he wondered if in fact he had imagined the creature. Picking up his short spear, he headed north, home towards Bassenthwaite and ran as fast as he could. His thoughts of hunting had gone but perhaps he might pick up a rabbit or two as he went. Far above him, set against the crag stood the old stag, his mossy antlers disguised by the knarled alders. The creature watched the man running towards the north. He saw the wind tear across the pines beneath. He saw the empty sky where the great black bird had lingered for a moment and turned back to his forest home.

CHAPTER ELEVEN
The Road to Kentdale, January 1092
Ivo de Taillebois

The horses' bridles and saddle trappings jangled as the small group of riders walked wearily through the darkening forest. The light of day was slipping away and Ivo de Taillebois was anxious to reach the keep at Kentdale before nightfall. The following day he planned to ride east to Appleby where Lucy awaited him. Two years previously, on his accession to the throne of this new Norman kingdom, the Red King had ordered Ivo to move northwards, establish bases at Kirkby Lonsdale, Kentdale and Appleby and to protect the realm from the peoples of the mountainous lands of the Scotii. This new king, the Conqueror's brother, was respected by few. His appetite for hunting and drinking was well known and he had little time for affairs of government. Only time would tell if the king would prove a wise ruler of his disparate kingdom.

They had travelled over many days from the Lincolnshire castle inherited by Lucy from her father and Ivo and his men were weary. He intended to meet with Hugh of Bec and his brother Herluin to discuss matters relating to the establishment of churches and perhaps a religious house in these northern regions. Hugh was a respected member of the monastery at Bec, a village close to Ivo's home and he knew the man well. He had much experience in these matters. As for Herluin, well, he was unsure of his part in these affairs but Hugh had suggested his presence and Ivo did not object. Herluin he did not like and he knew well the reason why. But here in the farthest reaches of the Norman kingdom, the distant past seemed far, far away and Ivo had no wish to fear it.

Recently, in this remote region, accounts of mysterious happenings were spreading and rumours told of queer folk seen among the wooded hills and beneath the high crags. Ivo's men listened to these tales around their campfires but their lord dismissed disdainfully this scare-mongering. As they travelled through the forest to Kentdale, however, he found himself watching the dark trees with uncharacteristic suspicion. Ivo had witnessed war and death often and little surprised or alarmed him. Here, however, in these strange lands, he felt uneasy as Eagle, his great white horse, jogged the uneven path through the gloomy evening. The unseen forest eyes watched. Dark shapes merged with the tall, angled pines and stooped beneath the bent oak and misshapen ash. Unfriendly thorns reached out to scratch at the unwary from the bedraggled undergrowth. The horses moved nervously. With their destination almost in sight, Ivo pushed his tired stallion forward and men and horses gladly followed. On reaching the crest of the rising ground, Ivo glimpsed the light of the wooden keep of Kentdal, their refuge from the forest night. He breathed a silent sigh of relief and cantered down the gentle slope. The sentries at the strong wooden gates shouted and a flurry of activity sounded from within the walls. Ivo turned to his sergeant, his faithful Turgis, and laughed.

'Well, so much for your bad feelings about this journey! We haven't seen or heard as much as a rabbit or a hare. I could have done with a fresh one of those for supper.' Laughing, he turned his horse to the open gate, aware of Turgis's anxious words.

'The journey is not over yet. Tomorrow, the path leads us over the black heights. The forests are thick and the land is steep. I have heard there are folk who wish us harm. We need more support and a further supply of archers.'

'You and your archers, Turgis. Because they were successful on the fields of Normandy does not mean they are of use in these forests. And who, exactly, do you think we are fighting? There have been no uprisings in this region. None.'

Turgis was silent. He did not like to argue with Ivo but could not dispel this uneasy feeling which had intensified on leaving England and approaching the ancient Cumbric lands. They were being watched, of this he was certain. Ivo turned in the saddle and called back to the company of horsemen.

'Fires and food await us. Take care of your horses and then make yourselves comfortable. Let's eat and be cheerful and cheer up poor old Turgis! Anyone for a good story?'

A cheer went up and the party passed through the gate, which closed firmly behind them, leaving the darkening forest to the invisible night creatures and seeing but unseen eyes.

Dawn broke with a pale, yellow sun. Ivo woke refreshed and called Turgis to prepare the horses for the final part of the journey to Appleby. As the winter sun stretched its arms across the forest, the Normans departed, riding across marshy hillsides and thickly forested slopes. The journey proved uneventful and Turgis's fears unfounded. They arrived at Appleby early in the evening and Lucy greeted her husband in the courtyard of the white castle. The weather was cold and quiet over the following days and Ivo, Turgis and Lucy rode beyond the confines of the great walls, across rolling hills and broad valleys. Teams of masons worked tirelessly, preparing stone and erecting the fortress. Others dug the wide moat, dammed with oaks from the forest above the Eden. It was a bustling world and Lucy watched with delight as the buildings rose from the green plain.

Lucy's father was a wealthy Lincolnshire landowner, Thorold, who, although an Englishman, had faired well under the new Norman regime. Her mother was Beatrice de Malet, from the farmlands of northern Normandy. When Ivo had first met Lucy, almost eight years previously, she was betrothed to a Norman knight she had never seen, a match arranged by her father to secure her prosperous future in this conquered land. Ivo remembered her anguish as she described her misgivings at such a match. Her future husband had supported the Conqueror in his quest to subdue Normandy and had proved his valour. In return, he would receive a wealthy bride to provide comfort and heirs, payment, in fact, for his loyal service.

'But what if I hate him on sight', Lucy had sighed, 'and what about love?' She moved across the garden, bright in the spring sun. 'What shall I do, Ivo, if I really am unhappy?'

'I cannot answer you, Lucy, but if you were my daughter, I would wish only for your happiness. When you meet this man perhaps you will be content after all. Let's hope so.'

They took each other's hands and danced across the dewy grass. Ivo looked at this girl growing into a lovely young woman. Although much older, he saw her beauty and in the glistening sunlight on that morning felt a surge of jealousy at the thought of some rough diamond taking this precious jewel for himself.

That was the spring of 1083. Eight years on, he still could not believe the turn of events that had led him to take the child as his own bride. The death of her betrothed, drowned on a sea crossing, closely followed by the death of her own father, Thorold, had left Lucy vulnerable and alone. One afternoon later that summer, in the same garden, Ivo asked if she would accept his hand in marriage in the realisation that his age was at least twice hers and that his life was half over and hers just beginning. Lucy had accepted with gratitude and glee. She laughed and called him 'her naughty uncle'. They clasped hands and, gradually, as time passed, she became more comfortable with his touch. They were married on a cold day in February in the following year, 1084, in a small church close to Lincoln, recently rebuilt in the new Norman style but dedicated to the old English saint, Frideswade. Ivo and Lucy said their vows in Latin and in Anglo-Saxon, standing together beneath a stone arch newly carved with flowers and dragons and staring faces. Before a small congregation they became man and wife. They left the church watched by dark stone eyes and Lucy shivered as she stepped into the warm sunlight.

Initially, they lived at Lucy's father's castle, a small wooden tower, built ten years previously. Ivo realised the necessity of transforming the structure into stone for Lucy's safety and stones were quarried and dragged across the marshes in heavy carts to begin the alterations. Lucy loved the activity of the mason's yard and spent her days wandering among the labourers chipping with their tools, always ready to stop and explain their craft. Ivo watched from the windows of the tower and wondered what the future held. Across the newly conquered kingdom new churches were rising up from the fields, often replacing those of wood and stone or built where only wooden or stone crosses had stood, on the roadside or at the edge of the village. Stone was quarried from surrounding hills and a whole industry moved across the countryside.

Then, one cold morning at the beginning of March 1085, a

messenger from the Red King arrived, demanding Ivo's attendance at Gloucester. He wished to compile a great book, assessing the ownership of his new kingdom. Ivo gathered the required information from ancient Westmoringeland and the lands surrounding Kentdale. In return he was granted new titles, Baron of Kentdale, Lord of the manors within, Kirkby Lonsdale, Casterton, Barbon, Mansergh, Lupton, Hutton Roof and Thirnby. Within months, Ivo had moved masons to Kentdale to construct fortresses and churches of stone. There were murmurs of discontent as under this Norman yoke many folk had lost lands and ancient rights. Ivo's thoughts about the Norman invasion were mixed. The king had instructed him merely to create a secure and efficient border. The lands beyond this, Allerdale and Copeland, Greystoke and Carlisle, Cardew, Cumdivock and Cummersdale were to remain free and the King had no present plans to invade this ancient Cumbric kingdom.

Two years passed and, by the winter of 1091, the castle at Appleby was almost finished. Here, Ivo established the northern bastion against the Scottish marauders. The great white castle lay beneath the mountains of Allerdale and the people of Allerdale watched uneasily as the fingers of Norman power stretched inexorably towards their fells and valleys.

CHAPTER TWELVE
Appleby, February 1092
Morcar

It was evening. Within the great white fortress of Appleby, Lucy sat in the small parlour with Morcar, her young sister. Since their mother and father's death, they had become constant companions. Ada was with them, orphaned at a young age and, now alone, she had found refuge and companionship with the two older women.

'Lucy, I hear horses in the courtyard.' Morcar stepped across the candlelit room to the narrow window, peering into the gloom.

'Yes, it is Ivo and his men, and Turgis too'. She caught sight of the tall, bearded figure standing beside Ivo's white horse, Eagle, and knew it was Ivo's unsmiling sergeant. She felt a little nervous. Lucy dropped her needlework and skipped down the narrow stone steps, out into the damp evening. Ivo climbed down wearily from his saddle.

'Ivo, I am so glad to see you home. We have been hearing stories of strange things happening in the forest. Did you meet anyone? See anyone?' She watched her husband's face as he stepped from his horse and then glanced at Turgis, his face bowed in the shadows, but he turned away towards the stables. Lucy turned back to Ivo with a questioning look.

'Don't alarm yourself, Lucy. No, we saw nothing of interest, a few beggars, many deer and hundreds of wild birds. I wish I could have taken time to hunt but you were more enticing.' He laughed and took her in his arms, hugging her small frame to him and savouring her sweet smell.

They turned and with arms linked entered the shadowy doorway where wine, bread and sweet biscuits lay on the table. Ivo looked at Lucy with unashamed affection. Morcar turned away, remembering Alain, her first love, her childhood sweetheart. She recalled the resolute expression on his face as he left to fight across the sea. She could still hear the sharp clatter of hooves on the cobbles as he rode away. She remembered his soft kiss goodbye. Alain never returned and,

43

many months later, a messenger arrived with news of his death from the plague in a town called Ravenna, in some far off land where the sun always shone and where a vibrant sea sparkled blue to the horizon. In recent weeks, however, she had seen another face in her dreams in the secret night, a face with dark eyes and an earnest expression. She had watched him from the windows of the castle at Lincoln as he rode away with the lord Ivo and he was in her thoughts constantly. Turgis. On this winter night, in this northern outpost, the snow thick on the hills, for the first time since Alain rode away from her, she knew she could love again. Ivo's voice interrupted her thoughts.

'Morcar, Lucy and I are away to bed. It has been a long day for all of us.' Ivo looked at the small, white face of his wife's sister. She lacked the sparkling beauty of Lucy but her face was kind, her eyes large and very blue. He must ask Lucy about Turgis and this small girl.

'Thank you for the meal. We want to be alone now.' Morcar silently withdrew, pulling the heavy door shut. At last, she slept as the threads of dawn moved across the ceiling above her.

The following morning, Morcar was woken by the noisy cackle of chickens in the yard below and the shouts of the cook chasing small ragged boys away from the bread ovens. She roused herself and with some relief saw Ivo and her sister still slept beyond the oak door. She quickly washed and scurried down the stone steps to fetch water. The cold air smacked her face as she pulled back the heavy door on to a snowy world. A small, shadowed figure slipped away across the icy cobbles but she could not see his face. For some reason, she felt uneasy. She did not recognise the figure. Then a voice called from the kitchen, a deep and reassuring voice.

'Let me help you, Morcar.' A tall figure stepped towards her. 'Let me carry the water. It is heavy and you must be cold.' Morcar's tongue was tied to her mouth and she was quite unable to speak.

'Thank you, Turgis', was all she could muster in reply.

'So you do know my name. I hoped, but was not sure.' He looked down at her with a kindness that was strangely surprising. He always seemed so grim and serious. Turgis took the heavy buckets and they climbed the steps to the upper chamber where Ivo and Lucy had not stirred. He looked at Morcar for a long moment but said nothing, leaving her in a flurry of emotion. Her hands were still shaking as Ivo appeared at the door.

'Something to eat, I think, Morcar. Today, Turgis and I are riding to a settlement called Salkeld to decide where best to construct another bridge. It is too cold for Lucy. We will return before the sun sets.'

Later, Morcar watched Ivo striding across the courtyard where Turgis held two horses, one a bright red, the other grey, the great Eagle. Minutes later, the familiar sound of heavy hooves on the cobbles filled the air. She heard Turgis shout an order and then the men were gone, away into the winter morning across the snowy landscape.

CHAPTER THIRTEEN
Bassenthwaite, February 1092
Hermod

It was early February, the year 1092. The day had arrived for Ivo and Lucy to return to Bassenthwaite to witness the progress of this new church beside the black lake. Ivo had received word from Roberto that the walls were almost finished and the decoration of the stonework was progressing well. Roof timbers were hewn and prepared and Anketil had carved from an old forest willow the tall, elegant wooden crucifix to be placed above the altar. Ivo and Lucy, accompanied by Turgis and two knights, rode away from Appleby in the late winter sunshine and headed north-west across the open moor. Morcar remained to prepare for their return the following evening. She watched the riders leave the safety of the courtyard and then scampered up the winding stairway to the turret to see them disappear beyond the crest of the distant skyline. She thought she saw Turgis stop and turn, just for a moment, before they were lost to sight. Although the road was not considered dangerous, there was continuing talk of strangers and Morcar had heard these whisperings. 'Come safely home,' she said quietly to the cold wind as it blew from the castle towers.

As Ivo and Lucy rode away from the hectic industry of Appleby towards the black fells, Lucy felt the faint warmth of the rising sun on her back. Spring was still several weeks away but the path ahead shone with a pale light gently touching the earth. Lucy was excited and yet, for some reason, nervous too. She wondered whether her decision to ride this long journey was wise as, in the first light of day, she had briefly felt a little faint. She thought nothing of this now as they rode towards the hills. They planned to reach Crag Castle at Mardale on the edge of the heath by eventide although crossing the surging rivers Lyvernet and Lowther, frequently impassable with winter snow, might hold them up. As it was, their journey proved uneventful. They crossed the Lowther by the impressive tower at Rosgill shap and descended towards the small wooden structure of Thornthwaite castle. Such fortresses reminded Ivo of the growing Norman presence in this region. He felt comforted but still wary of the darkening forests to either side of the rough track. Suddenly, a spectre emerged from the shadows ahead. The riders halted. In the twilight stood a stone cross, its delicate patterns flickering in the fading half light fingering through the branches of the forest. Lucy and Ivo stared at this unexpected apparition, captivated by its beauty. Carved creatures danced their stories across the surface of the stone and roaring dragons and their unearthly opponents fought their ancient battles. Lucy recognised among the figures those of Sigurd, of the God Odin, of Fafnir, the wicked dragon and others. As they rode away down the empty track, she looked back. The cross, merging with the forest shadow, had disappeared. Had she imagined it? She peered into the blue shadows. Chanterelle suddenly shied and Lucy glanced into the tangled thickets beside the path. Just then, the castle came into view.

'It is going to rain,' called Ivo.

'Just a shower, I think,' replied Turgis. There was something strange about this place. Lucy was not afraid but Chanterelle tensed beneath her. She looked up at the blackening hills, entranced by the angry beauty of the deep blue and purple sky. The pale sun had disappeared, replaced by a curtain of glowering water scudding across the sky with long, spectre-like beams. Ivo glanced over his shoulder at Turgis and shouted 'Hurry, let's go'. His two hounds, Radal and Lenef, sped away in front and Ivo, leaning across Eagle's glistening neck, saw the dogs vanish into the grey thickets ahead. Suddenly, the rain came down in torrents. Lucy threw back her head and laughed, urging Chanterelle forward with her easy grace.

Ivo and Lucy cantered abreast, their horses' bridles almost touching. Lucy saw the unease on her husband's face and there was a sense of urgency in his shoulders lowered over the white, steaming neck. Suddenly, not far ahead but out of the sight, a short scream cut the air. Ivo urged Eagle faster and, on rounding the corner, he saw Lenef on the wet grass, trying to raise her head. Turgis jumped to the ground and crouched next to the animal. There was no sign of Radal. Lucy reached them, Chanterelle puffing with the sudden exertion. Ivo spoke sharply. 'Quickly, Turgis, we'll take her to the castle. She needs warmth and rest. Turgis, cover her with your cloak. She must not get cold. Where is her father? Where is Radal?' Ivo glanced into the shadows.

He went on. 'Turgis, take the men and ride the high pass to find him. Hurry. He may be chasing whatever attacked her. We must find him before he too is injured, or worse. Place her on Chanterelle who has carried many hounds withouth complaint.'

Lucy saw a strange expression on her husband's face. Turgis lifted Lenef and placed her carefully across Lucy's coloured saddle cloth, placing his cloak over the dog. The torrent had ceased but the air was heavy with the threat of another. Chanterelle shied at the sudden weight but the hound did not struggle as Lucy held her close with one hand, guiding her horse with the other. Turgis and his two companions sped away through the soaking trees. In an instant, they were gone into a watery world. Rain streamed down Lucy's face and her hair hung in wet threads. Ivo stopped.

'Listen, what do you hear? I have not heard that sound before. It could be a wolf or a fox, but I don't think so. Listen.'

The wind whirled across the oak-brown slopes and blue mists of water enveloped the world around them.

'I can't hear it, Ivo. Perhaps it was the wind through the trees or the river. We are almost at the crossing.'

'You must be right. I cannot hear it now. We must find Radal.'

Lucy clutched Lenef and Chanterelle splashed and slipped in the fresh mud. The path descended steeply to the river, where the banks were low enough to allow the horses to cross the rough waters. Recent rain had swelled the rapids, already raging with melting snow and water swirled through the gorge below. 'Yes', thought Ivo, 'the noise I heard could have been the river'. There was no sign of the dog, however, as they forded the strong current in single file. Lucy's small figure sat straight in her saddle, holding tightly her precious load. Thankfully, in a few minutes, the towers of Crag Castle emerged from the grey mists. The bailiff greeted them as Ivo took the hound from Lucy's horse and laid her on the soft matting of the hall. Her wound did not appear to be life-threatening but the dog was dazed and her eyes were dull.

'She has had a shock of some sort', said Ivo.

'What strange thing could she have seen? Not a wolf or a fox, these hold no fear for her or her father. I wonder where Radal is', said Lucy, with a worried frown on her rain-soaked face.

'We must rest now', said Ivo. 'Turgis will find him. He cannot have gone far. We will leave at first light to reach Bassenthwaite by the middle of the day. Lenef must remain here until we return tomorrow night.'

Soon, shouts announced the return of Turgis and his two companions. Lucy and Ivo waited by the fire in the great hall. Turgis strode in.

'Not a sign anywhere. We rode to the top of the oak forest and along the hill. There were calls of many wild fowl, buzzards and owls, but nothing suggesting the whereabouts of the hound. One of the men, however, thought he saw a wolf like a silver shadow running amidst the rain, disappearing into the wet mists. He described it as 'unearthly' but I did not see this apparition.'

'Thank you, Turgis. Now rest. The rain has already stopped and the sky is clear. Be prepared for an early departure.'

The following morning was very cold but dry. Snow hovered above the northern mountains and winter's icy fingers clung to the forest. Lucy shivered as they rode from the castle but pale threads of sunlight stretched down through the trees lighting the sparkles of lingering moisture and touching the silver buckles of the bridles. Leaving Lenef in the quiet safety of the keep, the riders headed through the forest towards Bassenthwaite. There was no sign of Radal. Ivo knew the path and the journey passed quickly through the winter landscape. They made good progress and soon emerged from a wooded slope of oak and ash. Down below them, the huts of Bassenthwaite clustered in groups on gentle brown slopes. Long tendrils of smoke rose lazily and pigs, goats and chickens nosed their happy way through the tawny grasses. Beyond them lay the lake, snaking into the blue distance, lapping the fells with its long black tongue. Nestled in the thickets, close to the

49

huts, the half-finished church lazed like a strange white creature in the strengthening sun.

'It is a wonderful sight,' said Lucy quietly, her worries about the hound forgotten in that moment. Mesmerised, she held Chanterelle still for several moments. She saw the village, the huts, animals, small children and the lake with its misty swirls. She saw the mountains beyond, touched with snowy caps, lifting into a sky that spoke of a different, unknown world. Ivo watched her thoughtfully and they rode without speaking down the slope, through the thicker trees and across the grassy slopes. In minutes, men, women and children spilled out into the winter sunshine and ran towards the approaching company.

A few days earlier, a messenger named Hakon had brought news of their impending visit. The young man seemed tired and shaken. When the excitement of his news had died down, he spoke without drama with Anketil and the village elders of a strange atmosphere in the forest as if something or someone was following him. He had stopped several times to drink from the deep, brown burns but saw nothing. Anketil listened. Perhaps it was just Hakon's imagination as the afternoon shadows lengthened and the trees took on different shapes, resembling the spirits of the night hours. Lokin and Rainaldo, standing quietly together in the shadow of Piero's hut, looked at each other. They had not mentioned their strange encounter to anyone but when Lokin saw his father staring thoughtfully at him he quickly looked away.

Now, on this bright winter day, the concerns of Hakon were forgotten as Roberto stepped forward to greet Ivo and Lucy. Ivo looked around him at the motley faces staring at the visitors. Then he looked at the church lying peacefully, almost finished, in the sunshine.

'I am pleased with progress, Roberto. Very pleased.' said Ivo. Lucy, astride her horse, gazed at the white building rising from the dusty ground.

'It is beautiful', she spoke, in a half whisper. 'Beautiful'.

Ivo looked at the small, dark-skinned mason who returned his stare with calm and steady eyes.

'I am impressed with the speed of the building. You have done well.'

Roberto bowed. Lucy dismounted, handing Chanterelle to Turgis. She walked slowly past her husband and Roberto towards the building.

'My lord Ivo', said Roberto, 'this task and all its decoration will be completed in a matter of weeks, and the font, of course. There is a renowned woodcarver in the village named Anketil who has designed a unique decorative scheme for this. His son, Lokin, already a talented carver in stone, is to carve the stone font.'

Ivo watched Lucy move with effortless grace towards the church, her long fair hair tumbling to her waist. Without taking his eyes from her slim figure in its red and white ermine covers, he replied.

'Go ahead, Roberto,' he said in a loud voice for all to hear. 'This font will be known throughout Allerdale. Young Lokin must carve the surface with great beauty and with reverence to saint Bethoc, to whom I wish to dedicate this church. It is to be covered with mysterious legends and stories, perhaps with heroes of other worlds. He can choose any tale he wishes to tell.' Ivo looked at the expectant faces in front of him as a murmur of approval rumbled through the crowd. Roberto took hold of a hand in the shadows of the hut behind him, the hand of a boy but also the hand of a young man. Lokin stepped forward into the sunlight, standing tall, his slight frame contrasting with the plump Italian beside him. Then, from the darkness of the same doorway a second figure, tall and fair-haired, very tall and very fair, emerged. He stood by his eldest son.

'This is Anketil, my lord, who will carve the wooden crucifix to be placed above the altar. And this is his son, Lokin, my young sculptor.' Anketil and Lokin bowed low. Ivo nodded and smiled at father and son. Something in the tall man's steady stare unsettled him. Anketil's eyes met his with a directness which was unusual in its intensity. The farmer had no fear of this powerful Norman and the tall, fair-haired man did not smile. He had no wish for friendship. Respect, this was enough.

Walking back from the half-finished church, Lucy rejoined her husband. Then, she saw the tall unsmiling man, standing in front of the dark doorway of his home. His shoulders were straight and his faded hair, bleached with the mountain sun, was touched by the breeze from the dark lake beyond. She stopped. Gazing directly into the deep, blue eyes Lucy's breath was sucked from her body. She tried to smile but her face froze. She saw, in that moment, a thousand years of mystery and heard a story of an ice-cold distant sea upon which no boat could sail, of mountains so high they reached beyond the sky. Anketil looked calmly at her and their story was told in a thousand huts across the land, in a thousand forest glades, in a thousand eastern cities. This was the story of love, of searching and loss, of courage and of betrayal. Lucy tried to breathe. Anketil's steady eyes watched her. She blushed and looked quickly away. Then, suddenly, she smiled, her fresh skin sparkling in the sunlight and turned from the hut. Anketil watched her from the shadows of his doorway. How she reminded him of Helewisa, an extraordinary likeness. Despite the sparkle, however, her eyes were not the same. These eyes before him now were light and carefree, while Helewisa's were full of mystery, telling of a journey that would not end, where no rest would come, eyes that carried not only joys of the day but also night's sadness. These eyes before him had still to cry with pain, the pain of childbirth or of longing for a lost beloved. The boys' mother had lived a thousand years and found truth and love in one short lifetime with him. Then she had continued her journey beyond his reach away above the stars. Anketil felt a pang of desperate longing as he watched the young woman in the sun. He read her soft eyes and understood her sudden shyness at his instant knowledge of her. Lucy glanced towards her husband, chatting easily with Roberto. She lifted her long gown conscious of Anketil's gaze upon her back as she walked back towards the church. She did not look back.

A shout disrupted this quiet scene and Lucy's mind was torn from the man in the doorway. Emerging from the thickets a tall figure strode towards the gathering, his clothes bedraggled, his hair falling beneath his shoulders. He was carrying a heavy bundle, slung across his chest. Lucy realised with horror it was the body of the lost hound, Radal, head swinging gently to and fro. Ivo stepped towards him.

'Where did you find the hound?' he asked the man who stood, with eyes of the deepest black, watching the Norman lord with an air of intense dislike.

'I came upon him in the forest, high above a deep ravine and revived him with some woodland herbs. He was not hurt but was very afraid. Of what, I do not know. '

'Thank you for saving him. What is your name so I can pay you in silver.'

'I don't want payment for saving your hound. I did it for him, not for you or any other of your foreign band.'

There was an uncomfortable silence. All eyes were on Ivo to watch his reaction. He merely smiled broadly and turned to Lucy.

'We must leave now if we are to reach Crag Castle this evening.' He stretched out his hand. Lucy stepped towards him uncertain of how to react to the man and the sleeping hound slumped in his arms. She spoke quietly, looking directly at him.

'Please look after the dog and if he recovers perhaps you will return him to me. I trust you to take the greatest care of him'.

'You have no need to trust me. That is my problem. You must only trust yourself. Another man's trust is not your burden. As for the hound, he will find you again if that is his journey. If not, rest assured, his journey is worthwhile.'

As Ivo and Lucy rode away into the forest above the village, Ivo pondered his words. The man called Hermod watched with a strange detachment as they vanished beyond the darkening skyline. Lucy, however, only thought of the tall farmer with fathomless blue eyes which had peered into her soul. She felt strangely at peace with her thoughts and for the first time in all their years together a separate being from her husband.

CHAPTER FOURTEEN
Cardew, February, 1092
Thorfinn of Cardew, son of Thore

Thorfinn was angry, very angry. He had argued with Thore of Cardew, his father, that morning and still felt aggrieved. He paced up and down the path by the River Caldew and watched the restless clouds settle over the mountains to the south. The air was cold and the winter still gripped this northern world of Cummersdale. The river raced through a steep gorge and leapt over rocks in and out of shadowed caves beneath the sodden banks. Thorfinn stared hard at the raging torrent but his mind was elsewhere. The differences between this young man and his father had begun some weeks ago. Thorfinn wished to extend their territory south towards the edges of Greystoke. The aged Thore of Cardew, descended from the Gaels from over the water to the north considered Sigulf of Greystoke one of his compatriots and trusted his judgement and his honour. Forne, his eldest son, had grown up with Thorfinn and the families were considered loyal members of the lands of Cumbria. But deceit was in the air. Thorfinn and Forne were conspiring together to expand the boundaries of not only Cardew but also Greystoke.

One day, deep in the forest, their treacherous conversation had been overheard. They had stood together by the ancient oak above Cardew and did not notice a small figure in the shadows beyond the glade. Although their voices were hushed, the words had floated across the winter air like notes on a breeze and the little man had heard every word. Soon afterwards, he had arrived at Thore's small but sturdy castle at Cardew and told him of his son's plans. Thore stared at this strange messenger with his beady eyes and bright green cloak, listening in horror to the words he spoke. He moved away to the window and wondered what had happened for his son to become a traitor. The old man turned to question further but as he did so the messenger vanished into the winter air. Thore was left with his thoughts and fears. He had heard talk of a figure seen in the forest and knew the tale of his son's treachery to be true as this messenger was surely this little man of magic that some had talked of. The following morning, when questioned, of course Thorfinn had at first denied all knowledge of such things. Thore knew his son was lying and challenged him in anger and in sadness. Sigulf was his friend.

Thorfinn considered all this as he watched the torrent beneath him. Suddenly, he turned sharply and muttered loudly to himself.

'The Normans, of course, the Normans.' He moved away from the noisy clamour of water and paced to and fro.

'Ivo de Taillebois and his merry band, of cours, that is how we will achieve this. I must seek Forne and make plans. We will befriend these conquerors and their power and weapons.'

He climbed back up through the forest and turned south towards Thursby and his father's castle. Then he hesitated. Perhaps he should head towards Greystoke. His held his pony still for some minutes as indecision crossed his mind, then turned south, towards the mountains and the grey castle of Sigulf and his son, Forne. As he left the clearing, he did not see a tall man with a stick and a patch over his eye step from the shadows. Tucking the stick beneath his arm, the man turned and strode in the opposition direction, towards the city of Carlisle.

CHAPTER FIFTEEN
Bassenthwaite, February 1092
Kugi

During the previous autumn huge chunks of sandstone were quarried from the slopes above the village. Heavy carts, hauled by grumpy bullocks, rumbled over the rough ground to the village. When the snows came the week before the celebration of Jesus's birth, transporting this stone became impossible as the tracks deteriorated into pools of icy mud. The oxen were left to fend for themselves in the woods above the village. Far above them, on the steep slopes above Borrowdale, grazed the little mountain ponies of these lands. They spent the months of summer around the village but, as autumn approached, they left the village and climbed up to shelter in the forest glades and forage in the deep dells of this remote world. They were hardy and needed little nourishment to survive the winter months. It was said that woodland folk gave them food and that elfin riders flew with them across the starry nights. Lokin loved these stories and wanted to believe them but Rainaldo was always a little sceptical.

'Lokin, think about it. Nobody has ever seen an elf riding a white pony, have they? Have you?'

'Not yet,' replied his friend quietly, as if to himself. 'Not yet.'

Lokin loved these ponies for their sharp intelligence and proud steps. One in particular was his favourite, a small white pony with black eyes that reminded him of the mysterious rock pools beneath the oak glades. Looking into these eyes a new world opened up, a world of watery dells and of a forgotten time when all ponies ran fearless and free. Lokin named him Kugi which was a character in one of his father's stories where Kugi was a boy, not a pony but equally small and brave. Lokin watched with a heavy heart as one autumn day the little white pony had sped away to the windswept heights.

'He will be fine', said his father. 'They know better than any how to survive up there. That is their home. That is the land from whence they have come.'

Lokin did not feel particularly reassured.

'He will come back. I know he will,' he said to himself. As if in answer, the pony turned at the top of the meadow, standing white against the dark forest, with streams of golden dawn across his body. His dark eyes looked back at Lokin. He whinnied loudly once, tossed his proud head and was gone. Now, as the feast of Saint Bethoc approached and the days lengthened, the ponies would return.

CHAPTER SIXTEEN
Greystoke, February 1092
Forne and Thorfinn

Thorfinn drank from a large, heavy goblet, a silver goblet. It was beautifully crafted and he wondered where old Sigulf had found such an object and how many more he possessed. Forne had said little of his father's wealth and Thorfinn was a little suspicious.

'Excellent mead, don't you think?'

Forne appeared through the large doorway of the hall that led to the castle courtyard.

'Are you joining me?' replied his friend, feeling the cold seductive metal in his hands.

'Yes, in a little while. I must, first, see to my horse. As you know, I plan to journey to Salkeld to meet with Dolfin and Gospatric.'

Thorfinn bristled. He had not been invited to join this group and wondered why? Forne answered his thoughts, betrayed by the expression on his face.

'Oh, don't worry. This is just the beginning. If I don't turn up, Gospatric will start questioning my father and I don't want that. Not yet. You just have to be patient, my friend. Patient. He turned back to the door and hesitated.

'By the way, there are several more goblets such as this one in your hand. Patience.'

Forne left the hall and Thorfinn was alone with the roaring fire, the silent servant and his heavy goblet of fine silver.'

CHAPTER SEVENTEEN
Bassenthwaite, February 1092
The Font

The font was to be placed beneath the chancel arch of the new church which, on Ivo's orders, was to be dedicated to Saint Bethoc. Carved by Lokin it would be covered with a variety of ornament and with Bible and Norse stories from Anketil's designs. Included were scenes with the saint defending her honour, the young Jesus standing in the river Jordan with Saint John the Baptist and the hero Sigurd in combat with a two-headed dragon, its tail curling into a myriad of flowers. Anketil had also included a small figure running through the forest with his hound at his heels, carrying his chisel and hammer, his son, Lokin. Roberto merely raised his eyebrows a little but said nothing, to Anketil's surprise. He had expected him to object to the inclusion of both Sigurd and Lokin within the decoration but he did not.

On this cold day in early February Lokin began to carve the font design on a discarded stone found by Uncle Chetel on the road to Isel. The square stone had lain out in the winter wind and summer rain for many lifetimes and only the merest trace of a few long forgotten figures remained. Lokin rubbed the surface to eradicate all faint traces of the Roman world and, as the ancient people disappeared beneath his hand, he thought of the inevitable passing of life. He wished he had known these people. Who were the Romans who had journeyed from a land baked by the sun, a land of black olive bushes and wiry goats, a land of ancient stone buildings and statues? What was their life like in the lands of Rheged before the coming of the people from the north? The slab was smooth now and any trace of these ancient figures once adorning its surface was gone. Lokin drew new outlines with his sharp charcoal stick and Roberto watched in admiration as he covered the bare stone with his father's designs.

During the following days, crisp, clear detail was etched against the smooth ground and rounded figures emerged. Lokin spoke to nobody during this time. He ate and slept little, pausing only to consider the detail and to stand and stretch his long legs. Radal lay nearby. They were now inseparable. One day, just as the winter sun dipped beyond the fells, Lokin stood up. The carving was finished. As he stretched, he heard a voice from inside the ancient stone. He listened. The stone was speaking to him in a quiet but clear voice. Lokin felt no surprise or alarm. It was as if he had been expecting this. What is more, he understood the meaning of the words although the language was not his own.

'I am now complete. Your job as sculptor is done. Your next task is just beginning. You will know what to do and who to trust. Now paint me in bright colours and gild my words in gold. Tell all Allerdale the carving is complete. From far and wide, those who must see me will come, those who understand my message and also those who do not. Let them come. Let them all come. Then, we will know, we will know.'

Lokin stared at the figures, flowers, long stems of vegetation, little stars and curling dragons. This time there was no mistake. He understood the words that were spoken to him. Then, as he looked, Sigurd moved, just for a moment. Lokin had brought him into his world through his chisel and, as he looked directly into the stone eyes which stared back at him from the ancient rock, something stirred in the boy's soul. He stared at the stone face, at the eyes he had carved but, once again, all was still. But the boy knew this was not his imagination. He knelt down and touched the cold surface, gently caressing the ornament. The enormity of his task lay heavily on his shoulders. He sat with his carving and with his thoughts.

Some time later, he walked down the nave, through the south door, out into the bright afternoon sun. Roberto came across the yard.

'The carving is finished,' said Lokin, in a flat and rather tired voice. He and his master turned and entered the church. The grey font lay in the grey shadows. Roberto spoke slowly and Lokin was surprised at his words.

'The stone has spoken to you. I know this. Few understand this language. You, Lokin, are one. Do not be afraid.' He paused.

'It is the most beautiful carving I have seen. You are not yet thirteen years of age and yet you have a skill beyond your years. This skill is sent from the forests, from the mountain passes and from the creatures that live there. It is sent from God, whichever one you choose to believe in. You are blessed but also cursed as there is danger ahead for you but great rewards also. Your quest is to save the lands of Allerdale. This I have known for a long time. Listen to the message, Lokin, and then obey.'

Lokin considered these words.

'How do you know these things, Roberto? You seem to read my mind.'

Roberto chuckled.

'Oh, I just have the art of an old man! We are all busy bodies, you know, nothing more.'

Lokin went on.

'I heard the message clearly but I am not afraid. When I began to carve the decoration, there were times when my hands were not my own and the figures just appeared. The tools moved across the surface and the figures of St Bethoc, Sigurd and Jesus stepped out from the stone. Are you saying they were already inside the stone and my hands simply released them?'

Roberto nodded and spoke slowly.

'All is well, Lokin. You will soon be a man and a famous one. Many will envy you. Choose carefully those you can trust. Anketil travels a different path and will stay close to the spirit of your mother in the forests. Ketel and Bueth have yet to know their purpose. Rikarth, too, will learn the language of the stones. Tomorrow, as dusk fades, come with me to Piero's hut to hear the story. It is time now for you to understand the message contained within these timeless rocks and to learn the identity of the messenger.'

Lokin thought of his father. Did he already know of this?

'Have you spoken to my father, Roberto? There has been a distance between us these past weeks.' He paused, remembering the black horse and its strange rider in the wood. The old mason did not answer immediately but looked away towards the dark lake, deep in thought.

'Your father knows that his sons do not belong to him. The secret of the carving is carried through you, Lokin, and the process has begun. There is no stopping now. You are blessed and also cursed as with this knowledge you face many dangers but also will find joy and peace. You will discover many mysteries, but, first, fear must be conquered. Fear holds us all in its grip and holds us back. Fear not, my son, you are and will be protected, always, and in unexpected ways.'

The old man, bent with years, left the church, leaving Lokin alone by the raw stonework. Soon, Rainaldo's light and skilful hand would cover the surface with bright colours and what a spectacle it would be. He stared at the oval eyes of the dragon and for a second he was certain they blinked. He touched the stone and felt a tiny thread of warmth. He sat for several moments and then with trepidation touched the stone again. This time the unblinking dragon remained ice-cold. He glanced around the church in the gathering darkness and strained his ears in the silence. It seemed the building with its grace and beauty had fallen asleep. Lokin rose and left once more by the south porch, pulling the heavy oak door behind him, leaving the dreaming shadows and the font figures to return to their stony world. He did not see the eyes watching from the darkness beyond the doorway nor did he not see the small figure leave the murky dusk to follow him.

That evening the family spoke little over their simple meal. Afterwards, by the fire, Anketil told his sons a long tale of a northern land where a boy, lost in a black forest, discovered a cave and, on entering, began to speak an unknown language. His voice rose and fell with words unknown to the boys, a language they had never heard. The strange words flowed easily from his father's mouth as he recited the tale. Suddenly, he stopped. He stood in the shadowed doorway and did not speak again. The brothers, one by one, fell asleep but his eldest son called him softly once or twice but Anketil never moved. Finally, Lokin also slept, uneasily, with his father's strange language in his heart and Roberto's words in his head.

On waking, he remembered Roberto's words, the warmth of the stones and the silent church. What did it all mean? His father's covers by the fireside had not been touched and he was nowhere to be seen. Lokin gazed out into the dawn. The mist lay in a heavy blanket over the sleeping village, caressing the little church. Nothing moved. Even the chickens slept. Then, suddenly, just for a fleeting moment, the grey wall lifted. Lokin's heart stopped. By the church, standing tall and absolutely still, was a man, dressed in black, holding a black horse whose head was touched by a glint of silver. Then, the mist closed in again. Lokin stared at the thick, grey cloud, straining his eyes. The boy stood in the doorway and listened. Far away in the forest, he heard the distant sound of a horse galloping. Suddenly, a chicken in the eaves above his head clucked noisily. Relief flooded over the boy's cold body. He smiled up at the bossy eyes above him. The hen fluttered clumsily to earth and started her daily round of pecking and scratching across the yard. Lokin laughed at the normality. Calling Radal from the shadows, he left the hut, stepping into the mist. He must find Rainaldo. The lone horseman was, this time, no figment of his imagination.

Crossing the yard to his hut, he heard a shout from beyond the thickets and recognised Ketel's excited tones. Another shout. This time, it was Rainaldo, running through a sea of chickens and ducks.

'The ponies. Lokin. Quick. Come with me. The ponies are back.'

They ran through the scrubby trees and into the glades beyond. Ahead they saw the ponies darting among the trees, happy to be home. Lokin watched for Kugi's dark eyes. Where were those eyes that told a thousand stories? A sudden and very loud whinny behind him made him jump.

'Wow, what was that?' shouted Ketel.

Lokin knew exactly what it was. He turned and saw Kugi, standing white and still against the dark corner of the forest. He stared at the boy for many moments. Lokin stared back. Then, with a toss of his little head, the pony galloped towards the safety of the village, followed by the rest of the herd. Kugi was home. Spring was just beyond the hill.

CHAPTER EIGHTEEN
Salkeld, February 1092
Forne of Greystoke

On this late winter's day, dressed with a sky as blue as the distant ocean, Gospatric and Waltheof, his son, had arranged to meet Ivo de Taillebois at the vill of Salkeld, on the banks of the River Eden. Present also were Sigulf, Lord of Greystoke, and his son, Forne. They had talked of the Red King's intention to move his troops north to Luguvallum, also called Carlisle, an ancient place on the estuary of the Eden where the broad river curled and rolled westward towards the restless often treacherous sea. Ivo had assured Gospatric and Sigulf their lands were not threatened, stressing the King's aim merely to establish Carlisle as a defence against the growing threat from Strathclyde and from the borderlands beyond Liddesdale. Gospatric had ridden away from the meeting deep in thought. He respected Ivo de Taillebois and believed him to be an honourable man and he was seldom mistaken. As the clear day with its endless blue sky cooled the orange forests on the hillsides, all Allerdale awaited with anticipation news of the Norman plans.

Gospatric's castle at Papcastle was built on the ruins of an ancient Roman fort. The massive blocks of light grey sandstone which once formed the walls and ramparts had been re-used in its construction. Embedded within the south wall was a small chapel, beautifully decorated with carved stone, painted walls and finely woven tapestries. Here, the family worshipped God, Jesus and the saints. They were a Christian family but the blood of the pagan north and Celtic east also ran in their veins. Around the forest campfires were recited tales of heroes, dragons and birds who understood all languages, of love, courage, intrigue and revenge. Magic and alchemy stalked these tales and the dark forests of these fabled lands held many secrets. Among the favourites were the stories of Sigurd, the dragon-slayer, and Gospatric felt this heroic life touch his own. Other tales were told, of Olaf, Lokin and of Weland, of the king called Fornjot, of the mysterious Saemund Sigfusson from the Land of Ice, Njal's Saga and the Saga of Eyrbyggja. These tales and others filled the black winter nights and the long evenings of the endless, white summer days.

Three days after the meeting at Salkeld, late in the afternoon, Gospatric was reading from the Life of Bethoc, the legendary Irish saint, famed for her miracles and her compassion. The manuscript with its colourful illustrations of episodes of her life had been made across the sea in the lands of the Scotii, or the Irish as they were later called, in one of the monasteries there. Gospatric had been gifted this precious book by Olaf, the King of Man, a prosperous island off the western shore of Allerdale. A sudden shout echoed from the parapet of the massive stone wall and pulled his eyes reluctantly from the neat Latin writing. He glanced through the narrow window into the courtyard below and saw Forne, son of Sigulf, attired in black, standing beside his enormous black horse. Gospatric studied the young man for several moments. He could not hear Forne's words but clearly he was concerned for his animal that stood patiently while one of his great black legs was inspected. The horse was led away, walking gingerly across the rough stone cobbles. A moment later Gospatric's heart surged with pride as his own son, Waltheof, emerged from a dark doorway into the yard. Together, the two young men turned, deep in conversation, and walked towards the castle hall. Gospatric left the window and awaited their arrival.

'Forne, welcome', he said, as they entered through the arched doorway. A faint glimmer of alarm flickered in the dark eyes of the visitor.

'Welcome to Papcastle. Where is your father, lord Sigulf?'

Forne's grey eyes looked tired.

'My father is unwell and is being cared for at Greystoke. I have come alone to tell you this news. The messenger sent to you from Appleby by Ivo de Taillebois was killed as he rode through the forest above Greystoke Castle. His horse was unharmed but distressed and came alone to our gates. My father sent a search party and they found the young man lying by the ford across the great river. He had not a mark on him. A passing traveller found the body and he spoke to me in confidence, suggesting the man had died of fright. Certainly, his eyes were set hard with terror and his body rigid. I do not know what to make of it. There has been talk of unexplained happenings in Allerdale and in our lands also.'

Forne looked away from the shrewd eyes of his friend's ageing father, his face partially hidden by shadow. Waltheof shifted uneasily. Forne continued.

'I must return home at once but my horse has picked up a stone. May I leave him here for the night? Waltheof has given instructions to bathe his leg to prevent swelling.'

'Yes, of course, we will take care of the horse well. You must borrow old Greyalf. He will care for you along the rough forest tracks.'

He studied the young man, trying to identify the cause of his discomfort. Something in this young man's demeanour made him uneasy.

'Thank you', replied Forne, moving towards the heavy door. 'I will return with your horse tomorrow but must attend my father tonight. I will also send a messenger south to Appleby to announce the death of the news bearer.'

Forne looked sharply across at Waltheof, leaning against the doorway but he said nothing as he turned and left the hall. Gospatric and his son stood in shadowed silence for several minutes. Waltheof looked inquiringly at his father but did not speak. Long after the sound of Greyalf's hooves upon the stony path was swallowed by the winter night they stood together by the fireside. Then, much later, Gospatric slowly climbed the stone steps to his chamber and his books, leaving his son by the flickering flames, deep in thought.

CHAPTER NINETEEN
St Bethoc, February 1092
Eltred, son of Ivo

Eltred stared at the sea beyond the wide sandy beach, his horse resting beneath him. They were alone except for the westerly wind on his face and a multitude of grey birds sweeping through the winter sky above. Twisting and tumbling, this way and that, they filled the heavens with their graceful argument. Eltred watched in awe at the rhythm and accuracy of their flight.

'They have purpose, direction and control', he thought to himself.

'Unlike us.' He spoke to the wind and repeated the words, 'Unlike me.' His threw his head back to the wind and called loudly to the birds above.

'Unlike me'. His horse moved uneasily.

He turned from the sea and waded slowly through the shallow cold ripples touching the shore. He and his horse walked for some time, surrounded by sea, by tumbling birds and by the grey unforgiving winter sky. Suddenly, Eltred's attention was caught by a movement on the grassy hill beyond the dunes. He stopped. He was certain something or someone moved among the swaying grasses but only the seabirds's cries filled the morning. He must have been mistaken. He turned his horse back towards the small village along the shore beneath the rocky headland.

The area surrounding the small settlement was a broad soaking swathe of peaty marsh. The streams ran towards the sea, their banks thick with alder crouching along the mossy slopes, stretching inland towards the forests of Allerdale. These marshlands surrounding St Bethoc cradled the village in their treacherous arms and separated the village from the barrier of mountains to the east. Eltred glanced back along the shore once or twice but saw nothing. He knew that strange sights had been reported in the forests of Allerdale and across the fells of Copeland but it was just talk, just the odd grey wolf or black swan. He had heard mention of a silver wolf among the crags above

Bassenthwaite and just did not believe it. And, as for the horse that was seen above Greystoke that left no mark in the moss, well, this was nonsense. Of course.

But now, as he approached St Bethoc, he found himself glancing back along the shore. He sensed a presence but could not explain it. His horse jogged a few steps. Eltred slowed to a walk and considered his options.

'Do I support my father, the great Ivo de Taillebois, and oppose the king's invasion of the Cumbric lands? Or do I betray my father and follow my own fortunes in this dangerous game we are playing. The invaders are Normans and after all, I am half Norman, son of the great Lord Ivo. They are inevitably moving north to take control of Carlisle. No doubt about this.' He approached the village and knew in his heart which way he must go. He had for many years followed his father and fought with him in battle and listened to his opinions on many subjects. He respected him, there was no doubt, but did not love him. In fact, he sometimes hated him for abandoning his mother all those years ago. He had returned only to collect his son upon her death. For this, Eltred hated him. For this, he must feel no guilt at his betrayal.

He reached the small wooden gate. A tall monk appeared, robed in brown wool which fell to the dusty ground. A hood covered his eyes and Eltred could not see his expression. A long-fingered, long-veined hand stretched out thinly to take the rein as the young man, Eltred, son of Ivo, dismounted and turned towards the refectory where food and wine awaited him. Then he would ride east across the marsh to Egremont and there make his plans. As he entered the narrow door and disappeared into the shadows, the tall monk lifted his hood for a moment and smiled. Hermod patted the horse and rubbed its soft nose. He spoke to the animal in quiet unknown words which none could hear except the sharp pricked ears of black.

'Keep him safe and I will follow you. Tell me where he goes at all times.' The horse merely dropped its great head as if in reply and closed its eyes.

CHAPTER TWENTY
Carlisle, February 1092
Dolfin

A week later, Dolfin was sitting in the upper chamber of his stone tower. Above the city, long tendrils of smoke from the city's winter fires rose into the cold air. Logs smouldered in every cottage as the afternoon winds spiralled gently down from the north. People and animals shivered as they hurried home to fireside and stable. It was a rambling town, settled by many peoples throughout its long history, people with different customs, traditions, languages and legends. It was a town of constant activity, with folk coming and going, some to stay, others to pass through. From the north, east and south, from the western islands and beyond, they arrived in this hectic place. The harbour was a busy scene and ships brought merchants and travellers, soldiers and craftsmen, artists and poets. Men and boys unloaded fish and animals and fine goods from the east. The quayside bustled with activity as wool from the uplands, salt from the mines along the shore and cut stone from the fells were loaded upon the ships. Dolfin loved this unique place. An alarming soldier figure he was certainly not. A short young man and not at all glamorous, he bore no resemblance to his younger brother, Waltheof, the armoured knight admired by all. Dolfin was, however, a clever man. He had no misconceptions about himself. This was his strength.

Dolfin moved away from the window and picked up a large weighty book, the story of the Irish saint Brigit. Written in Latin in a monastery in the lands of the Scotii, the book was brought to Carlisle with Patric, a monk, who had arrived many years previously. Fluent in Latin and in Norman-French, Patric became part of Dolfin's household and soon his faithful servant. He was a Christian but his native land was also, like Allerdale, a land of fable and mystery and all things were possible in this unpredictable life. On this day, Dolfin expected five visitors; Gospatric and Waltheof, Sigulf of Greystoke and his son, Forne, and the Norman, Ivo de Taillebois. The discussion would inevitably revolve around the Red King's plans. Dolfin called Gerluff, his manservant, to clear the table of writing materials and to place the precious manuscript away from sight. This tall, one sharp-eyed old man had been with Dolfin for many years. He had walked into the courtyard one day and started to cook the most delicious broth ever tasted, much to the cook's annoyance. All had agreed that he must stay and stay he did. He never spoke a single word and Dolfin sometimes wondered whether he actually had a tongue. Thus, they never conversed, but, then, they had no need. They knew each other's thoughts and Dolfin saw in this man everything he wished to be himself. Gerluff's silent wisdom inspired Dolfin throughout his days and stayed in his sleeping heart.

Ivo, Turgis and young Theo, the stable lad, arrived late in the day. Riding through the busy lanes, they heard many languages and saw different faces, some dark-skinned, some with light, pink complexions and, of course, many tall, blue-eyed, fair-haired icemen. They saw bedraggled beggars, ragged and torn. They saw dapper, finely-dressed men, stepping haughtily around the mud, talking in high-pitched voices from Spain. There were knights riding a variety of mounts from great chargers to little wiry ponies. There were children, old folk, bent and broken, farmers, merchants, fishermen and craftsmen and artists and poets discussed and argued. On arrival, the three Normans were watched by numerous castle eyes as they dismounted in the courtyard of Dolfin's keep. Eagle moved uneasily in this strange environment and Theo led him away to a stable beyond the archway beneath Dolfin's window. Ivo glanced up at Dolfin, awaiting his arrival and raised his hand in greeting. Turgis followed him into the substantial stone building with its fine floor of marble taken, it was rumoured, from the Roman fort of Maryport along the coast. Dolfin stood by the fireplace at the far end of the hall and watched the two Normans enter the room, one a tall young man, the other already bent and grey with years. The Lord of Carlisle stepped forward and welcomed them warmly. Gerluff watched from the doorway. Dolfin and Ivo spoke together in Norman French, of the city, of the people and of the coming spring.

A little later, Gospatric and Sigulf, together with their sons, joined them. Gerluff laid a substantial meal and the men talked long into the night. Now the talk was of the Red King's plans for the kingdom of Allerdale and for its city. Dolfin, Gospatric and Sigulf were, once again, amazed at Ivo's impartiality. This powerful man appeared neither greedy nor ambitious and did not support any Norman move against Carlisle. Gerluff, hidden in the shadows of the book-lined chamber, studied Ivo's ageing face in the hesitant flickering firelight for signs of deception but found none. Ivo spoke with a sincere conviction. Waltheof and Forne sat at the end of the heavy oak table, listening intently. Waltheof occasionally glanced at his friend's dark profile but could not see his expression.

They drank ale made in the rich orchards by the Eden water and ate hunks of venison from the southern forests of Copeland. It was a wholesome evening that all would remember. The different beliefs, customs and aspirations were lost in a spell of good humour, honest opinion and, by the end of the evening, excellent story-telling. Dolfin told at length of the beautiful Queen of Galloway across the Solway water, carried away by a monster and imprisoned for a hundred years until the arrival of her prince. As he described her, he looked intently at Ivo. Just for a moment a flicker of recognition in the dark eyes suggested perhaps Ivo was thinking of Lucy. It was late when they retired to rest but Dolfin stayed in the library, smoking his long, curved pipe. He wished he could hear Gerluff's thoughts, tonight of all nights. The servant moved like a spectre around the room until his master fell asleep. Then, a strange expression touched his face and he disappeared down the dark, stone steps leading to the shadowed courtyard.

The following day, Gospatric and Waltheof rode west to Papcastle. Sigulf and Forne headed south to their forest fortress of Greystoke beyond the domed hills. Ivo and Dolfin sat for many hours, discussing Dolfin's collection of books and writings. Ivo was fascinated by the extent of Dolfin's knowledge of classical authors, of philosophy and of current thinking in the church. He knew many languages also, of the east, of the ancient Celtic world and of the incoming northerners and Gaelic people. He knew of the monks at Bec and, although had never travelled to the east, talked of the wonders of the Byzantine world and glorious Constantinople, the city of a thousand tall towers, glittering in the eastern sun and adorned with sparkling jewels. He spoke also of dark Arabs who came across the sunlit sea to southern Spain and built huge castles across the southern deserts. He spoke of their strange language and their knowledge of sun and stars, earth and heaven, of time, of numbers and of medicine and philosophy. He talked of Sicily, the island kingdom of the Normans, taken from the Fatamids of Egypt, where the two worlds of Jesus and Mohammed merged in a court of extraordinary wealth and culture. He told of the lands of Catalonia and the white mountains of Spain, telling of their poetry and their art and their dramatic and colourful way of life. He talked also of the northern lands, beyond the white winter sun where dragons ruled and where heroes fought against impossible odds upon the dark earth, inhabited by even darker spirits. He talked of a forested land called Finland and another known as Kvenland, stretching snow-covered and icy beyond the White Sea. He knew of their rulers, a king called Fornjot, and his sons, Aegir, Lokin, and Kari. He understood the calendar of the pagans and how the inhabitants of the Land of Ice believed in many gods, those of this world and those of the worlds beyond. He talked of the lands of the North, the islands of Orkneyinge and of summer expeditions in the fine, narrow craft of the Norsemen beyond the edge of the earth. He even talked of distant Novgorod, of King Jaroslav and the Earl Eilif.

Ivo wished many times during that day that Lucy had met this extraordinary man, with the fat and jolly Irish poet called Patric and his silent manservant, Gerluff, gliding through the dark shadows. He was sad to leave in the late afternoon but wished to return to Appleby to hear news of the king. The question on his mind as he rode towards the valley of the Eden was not if the Red King would turn his attention to the Cumbric lands and the strange, magical city of Carlisle with its charismatic leader, Dolfin, but **when**.

CHAPTER TWENTY-ONE
Cardew, February 1092
The Silver Wolf

It was late in the afternoon. Thorfinn of Cardew stood by the stone wall that ran up the steep slope above the castle. Nobody knew who had once laid the heavy stones but this ancient line had stood sentry over the valley for many lifetimes. Now, moss and lichen covered the wall and long grasses grew amongst the dark damp recesses. Thorfinn fingered the soft feathers of brown and green impatiently. He was waiting for someone and his face was anxious. He turned and walked up the steep hillside, following the line of the wall. His step was quick and agile, his shoulders forward as he climbed. All of a sudden, a tall figure appeared above him, dressed in black. It was Forne, son of Sigulf, who raised a hand in brief greeting.

'Where have you been?' asked Thorfinn, a little breathless.

'I left my horse at the road beyond the fell and climbed. It was too steep for him and he seemed a little lame.'

'Did you see anyone?'

'No, I don't think so.'

Forne hesitated.

'But', he said slowly, 'I did have a strange feeling of being watched. There was no sign of anyone, however, and I suppose my imagination took over in the shadows.'

Thorfinn looked anxiously about him.

'There are many rumours about but nobody has actually seen anything. I have sent a message to Eltred to meet us at the church of St Bride, beyond Isel. I have yet to hear a reply. I believe he is at Egremont.'

The two men stood in silence for a few moments. Glancing uneasily up and down the hill, they moved nervously into the shadows of the scrubby alder and ash.

'Let me know when you have a definite plan.' Forne spoke quietly. 'I must return to Greystoke to avoid raising suspicion.' He moved away and Thorfinn started his descent back to the clearings below. Stepping between the scattered boulders, he suddenly stopped and stared at the edge of the forest. There, standing beneath an ancient oak, partly concealed by its branches laden with the damp of winter, stood a huge hound. It looked like a wolf and its colour was almost silver. It stared, un-moving, at Thorfinn with eyes as black as the river deep. Neither man nor beast moved. Several minutes passed and Thorfinn wanted to shout but could not. He wanted to run but was rooted like the oak. Slowly, the creature turned away into the dense undergrowth like a night shadow and disappeared. Thorfinn watched for any sign of movement but saw nothing. He turned and, without looking back, ran swiftly down the hill to the castle.

CHAPTER TWENTY-TWO
Bassenthwaite, March 1st 1092
Lucy and the Message

The March day was being sucked into inevitable darkness beneath the heavy clouds. The late winter skies were darkening above the mountains and a lone curlew called from its distant haunt, heralding the arrival of spring. It was still cold. Lokin sat alone in his hut. Radal lay sleeping by the fire and the boy watched his gentle breathing and wondered at his good fortune at having such a creature in his life. A few days earlier at dusk, Hermod and Kugi had left the village, causing quite a stir. Nobody yet knew why he had come to Bassenthwaite and rumours were beginning to spread. Lokin listened for a long time for sounds of little hooves striking the hard stones of the hill paths but heard nothing. It was as if Kugi and his rider had completely vanished.

Lokin and Rainaldo missed Hermod. They liked this quiet and unsmiling man who spent many hours with the brothers in the woods beyond the village, sharpening sticks and making snares for rabbits and hares. He had built a raft from rushes and bracken and when the frozen ice of winter melted, they sailed across the black lake. He had taught them how to swim beyond the shallows without filling up with the cold, black water beneath their splashing legs. He had played with Bueth and Rikarth in the late winter mornings, running and hiding amongst the thick bushes, laying trails of nuts and berries, shells and rabbit ears for the boys to follow. Hermod refused Anketil's invitation to sleep inside their hut. Instead, he lay beneath the outer eaves in a hammock of wool and hemp which swung its lullaby in the lengthening evenings. Lokin hoped to catch him asleep in this loftybed but he was awake long after the boys finally slept and up again before they awoke. The hammock was always empty.

Lokin and Radal were now inseparable. He had longed for a dog of his own but Anketil disapproved of becoming too fond of any animal. 'Life and death are just two ends of a short tether', he used to say, 'never far away and inexorably tied.' As a youth, Anketil had lost his own dog, a little terrier-like creature, whose bark and bite were well renowned in the village. He loved her and mourned her loss for many months after a wolf took her on the heights above Borrowdale. Now, watching his son with Radal, he was concerned. The animal belonged to the Norman lord and soon he would return to claim him. The hound was a valuable breed from the eastern empire of the Turks, where dogs and horses were bred for speed, beauty, courage and also ferocity. But Lokin found nothing but gentleness in Radal and, as he recovered from his strange malady, the dog looked increasingly to him for companionship. He remained reluctant, however, to run beyond the boundaries of the thicket. He sat down when they reached the forest and as much as Lokin tried to persuade him to move into the trees the dog stayed in the sunlight. He watched the dark shadows and looked steadily at his young master.

'No,' his dark, dog eyes spoke. 'I am not going into those unknown shades. I am staying here in the light, where the sows graze without fear and where the small birds fly amongst the grasses with gay abandon.'

Lokin laughed at his laziness. Or was it fear? There had never been an explanation for his strange sickness. During these days, boy and dog sat together as the sun set beyond the western hills. They hid in the thickets from the sudden squalls of cold rain soaking the earth. They went together to the yard where Lokin chipped and carved his stones and Radal trotted home beside him when the light failed and candles fluttered in the evening glow. They slept close together, often with Rikarth tucked between them, in the warm cocoon of the hut.

One evening, just after Hermod had left on his unknown quest, Uncle Chetel told a long tale of Sigurd. Radal, lying close to Lokin, tensed. Lokin was sure the hound understood every word. He lay quietly but his eyes were alert, his ears, too. Chetel was a fine story-teller and, his voice rising with the dramatic conclusion of the tale, every ear listened in anticipation. Now, as the fire died in the embers, Lokin felt tiredness overwhelm him. He loved the stories of Sigurd, his hero of the cold, grey lands beyond the black sea, from whence his grandfather had come. Sigurd's love for his horse, Grani, and all the animals and birds gave his raw valour a gentle touch and Lokin wished to meet and serve such a man as this. He pondered on the sudden departure of Hermod and the little white pony and remembered the words softly spoken as they left.

'I am just borrowing him. I will feed him fine corn and sweet hay. We will return before long. Have no fear for your beloved pony.'

Lokin did not ask where he might acquire this fine feeding but at least he felt some comfort. Long after his uncle had finished his story and his brothers had fallen into a deep late winter sleep, Lokin sat staring at the embers and thinking of all that had happened in the village over the past few months. The church was a source of pride to all the villagers but Lokin knew that their lives had changed and the mystery of the carvings was only just beginning. He must be patient. But who was Hermod and why had he come? At last he slept, dreaming of Sigurd and Hermod, of Grani and Kugi but Radal lay awake, watching the ebb and flow of the long night.

The next day, young Theo rode in haste from the forest, astride a small pony. He announced importantly that Lord Ivo de Taillebois and Lady Lucy would arrive the following day to inspect the completed church, its carvings and decoration. The villagers went into a frenzy of activity. Rushes were laid across the floor and woollen tapestries, woven with colourful saints and legendary figures, were hung upon the walls. The tall crucifix, carved by Anketil from an ancient willow, was placed upon the altar. Candlesticks of wood and bone were placed around the nave and within the chancel. Lokin's square font of white sandstone, now coloured with bright jewels and painted in hues of red, blue and purple, lay just beneath the step into the chancel. The gold lettering of the inscription was etched in runic letters, from the language of the Norse lands, lands of his ancestors. It read 'Lord Ivo commissioned me, Anketil designed me and Lokin hath brought me to this splendour.' What a proud moment it would be for the villagers. What would Ivo de Taillebois think?

The following morning, the sky darkened with the promise of late snow. Huts were prepared and makeshift stables for the horses. Ivo and Lucy arrived in the late afternoon, emerging from the sulky black trees above the village. They rode side by side on two grey horses, one huge, the other really quite small. Two figures rode behind the couple, a tall man on a red horse and a girl, her slim figure perched on a little brown pony. Behind them, attired in grey armour, were three knights, watching with cautious eyes. Ivo and Lucy dismounted and the tall man took their horses. They walked slowly to the entrance of the church which rose like a spectre against the evening sky. The path was bedecked with candles and lit with numerous lanterns, scattered across the black sky like woodland fairies dancing attendance on these visitors. The south porch glowed with candles and Ivo and Lucy gazed at the carvings above the arched doorway. The painted faces, some with monstrous features, returned their gaze with staring eyes. Vegetation, entwined with flowers, leaves and berries, reminded Lucy of the stark, lonely cross of the forest they had encountered on that rainy day. Inside the church they were astounded by the sheer opulence and variety of decoration. Shadows danced across the painted, wooden roof and tapestry figures leapt from their woven walls, touching the spectators with long, fibrous fingers. It was a marvellous sight.

Ivo chatted easily with Roberto, expressing his admiration for the skilful craftsmanship.

'It seems as if a magic wand has touched this place', said Ivo.

Roberto said nothing. Leaving them in the doorway, Lucy walked alone up the narrow nave to the candlelit chancel steps. She glanced up at the arch stretching across the chancel, carved with a myriad of ornamental designs and staring faces who demanded her attention. Then, in the corner, beneath the pulpit, she saw the font. It was quite small but stood with a quiet grandeur that captivated her. She stood for a few moments and then knelt on the matted floor, gazing at the stories and patterns carved across the coloured stone surface. She saw the two-headed dragon with its huge curling tail, patterns of trees and flowers, strange creatures and tiny figures hidden amongst the foliage. She saw the story of Jesus and Saint John the Baptist and the cross of his death, the story of the miracle of St Bethoc and her magic bracelet. She saw the story of the great Norse hero, Sigurd, in his final battle with the great dragon, Fafnir. Then, she looked closely at the golden inscription, written in runic letters and etched with fine white lines. Lucy drew her breath sharply. The words, she knew them. The letters glowed in the flickering light of the candles and she was pulled towards them, drawn into their world. As she read the words, the carving spoke, softly but clearly.

'Lokin he hath made me and brought me to this splendour. Read me and read the story of this stone.'

She stood up slowly and turned to Ivo, a few yards behind her, her face as white as a spectre of the night. She spoke and the words she uttered were in a voice not her own. Her astonished husband looked at her.

'He is here. The time is now. The stones have spoken.'

She looked so strange and Ivo did not know the voice that spoke to him. He stepped forward with alarm and, as he did so, Lucy collapsed on the rushes strewn beneath her feet.

CHAPTER TWENTY-THREE
The Forest, March 1092
Hermod's Tale

After leaving Bassenthwaite, Hermod spent many nights above the black lake. He remained close to the village but hidden from sight. Early one dawn, eating his meal of oats and honey, he heard a faint whistling cry from the dense thickets beneath the black crag above him. Kugi lifted his head. Silence, once again, washed over the forest. It seemed this world of wet morning branches was frozen in time. Then a second whistle sounded in the valley below, not a call of fear or distress but a signal. Hermod listened, the woodland world suspended in the morning air. Suddenly, a branch swayed to one side and into the clearing walked a small figure, too small to be a man, but bigger than a dwarf and also a little fat. His head was uncovered and a red cloak hung from his narrow shoulders. Carrying a small green sack in his right hand, he was alone. He stopped just a few feet from Hermod.

'Hermod. We meet again. I am Tallis of Tandrallion, son of Dedrulf, Lord of Dehallion. You may not remember or you may. It does not matter. I have many disguises, faces, colours. I am what you see now, today. Tomorrow is another time. It is important you trust me, today and tomorrow. Our task ahead is difficult and dangerous but there are many who will help us in our quest. The players are assembling. Allerdale is stirring. Like you, I come from the world beyond this and I live in another time and another place but I see all times and all places. I see your past as I see your future as you travel through this story. For this is but a story, a story of this world and beyond, a story of all time. Trust in me, in the story and most of all in yourself. You have great powers. These can be used for good or for evil. It is for you to choose.'

The little man called Tallis fell silent. He dropped his head and looked at the ground. Nothing moved in the forest. No bird called or leaf stirred in the breeze. The world stopped. Hermod lifted his head and replied in a deep clear voice.

'I remember well our meeting and have been waiting for you to come. I have been waiting for the signal. I have listened. There is both treachery and valour. There are hearts of truth in these lands of Allerdale but also hearts of falsehood.' Tallis studied the sadness etched on the man's face. He spoke softly,

'Tell me your tale, Hermod, for in the telling, your spirit will be freed.'

Hermod fingered Kugi's ruffled mane and looked to the distant hills. He took a deep breath and began his story, slowly at first, then gathering speed. At last he could speak.

I have come, Tallis, from a land far from here. My father was Sigurd, the hero of the Norse sagas and all the stories of the world. We lived far away in the mountains, beyond the icy fiords. My father spent long months and years away and my mother raised my brother and me alone through the long, black winters. She told us stories of my father's voyages into the arctic wildernesses and south to the blistered, desert sands and these I have kept close to my heart. My brother, Siyulph, died when I was young. He drowned in a great storm in the fiord although it was said the silkies of the seashore took him. Many times, by the rocks, I heard cries from the icy waters below but found no trace of him. My mother never recovered from his death and she died before I reached my twelfth year. I lived with her brother and helped on the farm and fished with my cousins but I wanted, above all, to find my father. On reaching the age of eighteen, I put down my farm tools and left the valley for ever to find him.

For years, I journeyed the northern lands, encountering many dangers but I always knew something was keeping watch. It is difficult to explain but perhaps, to you, there is no need. I sailed cold, dark seas, climbed high steep valleys and crossed white frozen wastes. I travelled alone for many years but I never felt alone. I was often hungry but food was always provided. I was attacked many times but rescue was always at hand, often in the most unlikely guises. I found no trace of my father. One day, in the late spring, I came upon a group of hunters, travelling south from the lands of the reindeer to their lowland farms. They invited me to accompany them, sharing their fare, their warm huts and their stories. Amongst them was an old man, grey and wizened, who seemed somewhat aloof from the rest. He sat apart and

81

seldom spoke. He did not smile and yet had a gentleness about him which was very comforting. At last, late one evening, he spoke to me. We were alone, standing some distance from the huts and he looked straight into my eyes. I could not believe the words I heard.

'Hermod, it is you. I am Sigurd. I am your father. I know you have searched for many years to find me but I could not reveal my identity until my own journey was complete. Now it is. Soon, I will leave this world but there are things you must know, knowledge to be passed to you. You are to carry on my quest and will travel far from this land to do this. There will be danger and treachery, but also friendship and love. Tomorrow, we will leave these fine hunters and travel to the western shore. For now, welcome, my son. I have loved you long. Your mother is in my heart daily and I know we will be together in another place. Your brother lives also. You cannot see him but you will meet with him again, in the most unexpected guise. Trust me in this. We are all together, as one, although in this world we cannot see one another. Forget place and time, Hermod, forget these prisons we place upon ourselves. There is much beyond and much behind which we cannot see but in our hearts we know. Why do you think we tell our stories and honour our heroes? We need to return to our true selves, to our true lands of our birth and of our death. Life is but a spectre, a moment of imagination, a brief glimpse into the unknown.'

Sigurd stopped speaking and looked away to the sea where the sun was setting across the golden waves. Hermod, his son, remained silent. They stood together in harmony, as one, father and son, although time and distance had separated them for many years. These rolled away as their love spread across the evening light and touched each other.

'There, to the west, is the way you must go.' Sigurd did not turn his gaze from the golden sky. 'There is a land called Allerdale, deep in the mountains and far from this place. The land and its people are in great danger and must be saved. Evil threatens to destroy the heart of this ancient land.' He was silent again for a long while. When he continued, his voice was softer. 'I will live on in the stories and legends of these people, by firesides, in summer evenings, by dark lakes, in deep, red forests of oak and beech. I will live for ever in these places and will be remembered in the stone carvings, on the painted crosses of the roadsides and in the delicate books of the learned. My *story will be told in stone, Hermod, and you and the chosen few will read and understand this language and find my story carved in unexpected places. You will know who to trust and who must join you in your quest to save Allerdale and to save the legends that live within the mountains. If these die, then the love that binds us all together also dies and we will lose all hope of eternal peace together.'*

He hesitated for several moments and turned to face his son, standing tall and silent.

'I will always be at your side, although you will not always recognise me. But you will know when it is me. I will keep you safe and those you love but my powers are limited in this world of hatred and deceit and may sometimes falter. Be prepared for this. Even your father, the great Sigurd, cannot overcome all evil.' He turned back to the sea. *'You are to leave me now, even though you have just found me. Leave this place and with courage travel west and your heart will bring you to the place where the story begins. One day, and this I promise, we will meet again.'*

Hermod finished speaking and was silent for a long time. At last, he continued.

'This is my story, Tallis. I am Hermod, son of Sigurd. I have come to save the secrets of Allerdale, to save the legend of Sigurd and to bring peace to the hearts of these lands. I was brought to Bassenthwaite by Radal, the hound of my father. Bassenthwaite is the beginning of my quest. Here, in this place, are those whose hearts are part of the story. There is good and also evil in the hearts of Allerdale. I have much to do.' He suddenly and unexpectedly smiled. 'I think it is you who have been watching from the shadows.'

'Put it this way, Hermod, I was just keeping an eye on things.' Tallis laughed a merry laugh like bells tinkling in the winter frosts. His eyes twinkled in the sun. Hermod looked at him seriously once more.

'Tallis, you have heard my tale. Tell me why you are here and what part you must play within this story.'

Tallis spoke in a quiet voice. 'My part in this tale will be made clear to you in the language of the stones. Take comfort. You are in the right place and everything is as it should be. You know already those you can trust in Bassenthwaite and the creatures who will assist you. Now, to business. Take these messages to Papcastle, tell Gospatric and his son of the meeting at Bassenthwaite. Then, to Dolfin, Lord of the castle in Carlisle. Then, south to Sigulf at Greystoke. The message is simple and reads '*Come to Bassenthwaite. The time is nigh. The secrets are to be told, for in the telling, the legends will be saved. Come.*' You, Hermod, son of Sigurd, are the messenger. On returning to Bassenthwaite, we will meet again. Remember, there are foes amongst us. These you will soon recognise. All is not what is seems.'

He gave Hermod three small rolls of parchment, yellow and damaged with age, tied with hemp. Then Tallis stepped back towards the bushes behind him, raised his right hand and vanished. Hermod looked around the clearing and waited for several moments but he was alone. Then he remembered. 'Not of this world.' Clutching the precious parchment, he leapt upon Kugi's back and turned towards the west. A little later, deep in the forest, a rider sped towards Papcastle. Hermod rode a little pony as white as snow and as nimble as a deer, white ears pricked with anticipation. They darted among the great oaks and crossed the racing waters below the highest crags until Gospatric's fortress lay beneath them.

CHAPTER TWENTY-FOUR
Bassenthwaite, March 1092
Aða

It was late and the village was quiet once again after the commotion in the church. Ivo knelt by the hearth, wiping his wife's brow as she slipped in and out of consciousness. The small brothers perched in a row along the shadowed edges of their home, confused at the sudden upheaval. Radal lay quietly beside little Rikarth, watching. The dog knew the old man by the fire, his voice and his smell. But now he had a new master, a tall young boy with a strong face and soft voice. He nestled close to the sleepy child and looked up as Anketil and Lokin emerged from the darkness with armfuls of wood. Radal wagged his tail and barked once. Lokin laid the wood beside the hearth and stood by his hound. Ivo covered Lucy with a blanket of coarse sheep's wool, muttering quietly in his own language. Lokin watched his father. There was a new energy in his shoulders as he piled the wood upon the fire. Lokin, one hand around Radal's neck, saw everything with his quiet eyes as he watched both men tending the sleeping lady.

A sudden shout from the far end of the village broke his thoughts. Rikarth sleepily pulled Lokin's sleeve.

'Who is that, Lokin? Want to sleep.'

'Don't worry, Rikarth, go back to sleep. Look, Bueth is asleep and by the time he wakes up it will be breakfast. Sleep now and Radal will watch over you.'

Anketil left the hut for a few moments to see what the commotion was. He returned a few moments later and knelt at the Norman's side, talking in whispers. His father glanced around the hut. All was quiet. 'Nothing to worry about, Lokin,' he said, seeing his eldest son still awake in the shadows. 'Get some sleep. It will soon be morning.' The boy lay back on his warm covers and finally slept. Anketil saw the Norman lord and his young wife lying by the hissing fire as night gradually merged into dawn. Lucy slept, watched by her husband and, from the shadows, by the tall Norse farmer.

The early morning came with the familiar quiet, grey light of late winter. One by one, the occupants returned from their dream travels of the night. Ivo shook himself awake, realising in a moment where he was. He glanced at Lucy, still asleep, and then at Anketil sitting by the door. He had not slept. Ivo spoke quickly. 'Call Turgis. I must return to Appleby to fetch my Flemish physician. We will return here tomorrow.'

'As you wish. Your wife will be safe here. You have my word.'

'I have never seen my wife ill before and do not understand her malady,' said Ivo, looking down at the lovely face. 'She was standing by the font, carved by your son, and spoke a language I have never heard before, of a message, of speaking stones, of someone who has returned. I do not know what she meant. I cannot explain this.'

The anguished look in the Norman's ageing eyes touched Anketil. This man loved the small, fair-skinned lady lying on the deerskin covers by his fire. Despite his power, his wealth and his conquests, the Norman's heart was held firm by this young wife. Anketil recognised in his face a gentle expression that surprised him. Standing in the doorway, he hesitated before calling Turgis. Looking again at the sleeping woman, another feeling was creeping into his soul, one that had found life and could not now be destroyed. In that moment, he remembered the last days with Helewisa as she lay by the embers and closed her lovely dark eyes in death's doorway. In this hut by the fire, her spirit was back. He felt her presence and a surge of joy went through his body. He wanted to laugh. Helewisa was home once again, from the forests and the hillsides. In Lucy, wife of the Norman, Ivo de Taillebois, her spirit had returned. Anketil looked away and walked swiftly to the hut where Turgis and the other knights had slept. The tall knight was already standing by the dark entrance and he looked sharply at the farmer as he told him of Ivo's intentions.

'We will be ready to depart in a few moments. Tell my lord.'

Lokin awoke and saw Ivo sitting by the fire, which, unusually for this time of day, blazed brightly. Still the lady Lucy slept. He sat up and looked at the strange morning scene. Anketil appeared in the doorway and spoke to Ivo but Lokin could not hear his words.

Suddenly, and without looking back, the Norman left the hut. Anketil turned to the sleeping lady by the fire, wrapped in woollen covers. Young Ada, Lucy's maid, sat in the shadows and Lokin tried to examine her small face but she turned away. The boy was curious.

'Father, what is happening?' he whispered. 'Why is the lady still asleep? Why the burning fire?' His father knelt down next to his son. He spoke quietly, not wishing to awaken the other boys.

'I am certain Ivo's wife will make a full recovery. He is leaving for Appleby to fetch his own physician and returns tomorrow. Until then, I will watch over her. You fetch more firewood and tend the animals. I will call you when a meal is prepared. I have oats and herbs to make a stew. The lady must eat when she wakes.'

His father looked towards the doorway where the world was moving from night into day.

'A storm gathers in the air and there will be snow from the east. Be sure you wrap up warm. If you need anything, you will find me here.'

Lokin rose and crossed the hut, glancing at the sleeping figure and the small girl in the corner. Anketil seemed different on this cold morning. His eyes were alert and purpose sat on his shoulders. Lokin remembered then his mother and her energy and her joy which supported them all. That was it. Helewisa's energy was back, back in this hut and within his father, in his hands and in his heart. He looked at Lucy by the fireside and then at his father kneeling beside her. Yes, something was different on this cold winter's morning.

Lokin braced himself against the chill of a bitter east wind and stepped out into the yard. He whistled to Radal and the hound reluctantly followed him. Lokin threw a short stick into the thicket. The dog bounded over the fence to retrieve it. This was his favourite game but a sharp whistle suddenly caught the dog's attention. He stopped his chase and turned, head raised, eyes alert. Beyond the picket fence his Norman master sat motionless on his great, white horse. Neither the dog nor the man moved a muscle. They simply stared at one another. Lokin muttered under his breath.

'Stay, Radal, stay with me. Here, you are loved. Stay.'

Seconds passed, then a minute. Ivo whistled again and stared at the dog and then at the boy. Radal lay down in the grey grass and dropped his head. Lokin could not breathe. Then Ivo turned his horse and, followed by Turgis, rode up the slope into the icy eastern wind. In the shadow of the little white church, Lokin hugged the furry neck.

'Thank you', he whispered, 'Thank you for staying with me.' Radal's eyes looked directly at him and Lokin felt himself drawn into another world, of deep pools, of black water and dark shadows, where night was king and where sadness lay on each living heart.

'Don't worry, Radal,' he said in a quiet, determined voice, 'I will look after you, always. We will be together until the end, whenever that is.'

A sudden movement from behind made his spin round. It was Rainaldo, breathless and eager for news.

'Where has the lord Ivo gone? What has happened to his lady? Is she ill? Where is your father? What is happening now?'

'The lord Ivo has returned to Appleby to collect his physician. Lucy is sleeping, not ill, I think, but just asleep. My father is watching over her with her maid, Ada. As for Radal, he is to stay with us. It was his choice.'

'What happened in the church? My father just nods whenever I ask him about it. He keeps muttering about the carvings.'

'Rainaldo, we must speak with him. The language of the stones is the key. Roberto has told me of this. I will explain.'

They ran through the village. It was beginning to snow and the sky was darkening in the east. Chickens argued noisily and goats stood haughtily, eyeing disdainfully the bounding dog who they knew had no licence to chase them. Piero lay by his hearth, propped up on bundles of hay, looking gaunt and pale in the half-light of the snowy morning. He smiled at the boys in the doorway.

'The time has come. The time has come. You will shortly begin a great adventure. Radal will be with you, always. Only trust those who the hound trusts. You will see this in his eyes. Wait for the signal from him. He is now your key and your lock. You will see what I mean....' His voice tailed off in the musty cold. As he spoke, a small timid figure appeared in the doorway behind the boys. It was Lucy's maid, Ada, looking cold and frightened. Lokin put out his hand and took hers. He smiled. 'I am Lokin. What is your name?'

A soft voice replied. 'Ada. My name is Ada.'

Piero looked up at her and smiled also.

'Welcome to Bassenthwaite. I hope your lady will soon recover. There is snow in the wind from the east. My old bones are telling me this. Snow, and lots of it. She may have to rest here for a few days before the lord Ivo returns.'

A sudden cough took hold of Piero's chest. The girl, Ada, knelt unexpectedly and covered him gently. She seemed to feel welcome and at home here, as if she knew the old man.

'Father, are you alright?' asked Rainaldo, stooping to take his arm and smiling at the girl.

'Yes, yes, fine. I just need a new chest, that's all. A new body, come to that.'

'Nonsense, father. Let me fetch you some broth.'

His father spoke again.

'I have been waiting for you. It is time.'

'I don't understand, father, what do you mean?'

The old man pulled himself up to a sitting position and reached for the cup Ada held before him. Piero smiled at her and she returned his gaze with steady eyes. Lokin realised for the first time her small face was beautiful, quiet and serious but beautiful all the same. Piero continued.

'Everything is a matter of time. It is just a matter of knowing the right time. That is the secret of life in this world. Tell me, Lokin. What happened in the church yesterday? You were by the font, I believe?'

Lokin replied. 'The lady Lucy walked towards the font at the steps into the priest's chancel and just collapsed. I was standing just behind her. She said something about a message but then spoke in words I have never heard before. That is all I know.'

'Mmm, interesting, interesting. Lokin, I must tell you many things. Firstly, it was not chance that brought Rainaldo and me to this place. The story is now unfolding. I have waited to tell you of this and of many other things. We will meet with Roberto this evening here and

89

continue. Then, you will begin to understand what lies ahead, for all of us. And, by the way, Lokin, I know of your strange encounter at the edge of the woods.' Piero chuckled and as his whole face wrinkled his eyes disappeared in mirth.

'It feels so good to laugh again. Indeed, I have waited long for this moment.' The old man, straightening his shoulders and taking another peaty sip of brown cider looked many years younger.'

'Piero, please tell us what all this means. What is this message? What is the language of the font? What has happened to the lady Lucy? Who is the mysterious Hermod?'

'So many questions, Lokin, so many questions. Be patient until tonight.'

'Now I am tired and must rest. My journey is almost done.' Rainaldo spoke quietly as he knelt at his father's side. He hesitated as a tear crossed his eye.

'Father, I am full of fear when you say such things as I cannot imagine a day without you. But I understand the truth you speak. I too have been blessed.'

He held Piero's hand for several minutes. In this moment, he left boyhood behind and became a man, carrying the inevitable burden. Lokin watched him with sadness in his heart and he and Ada silently left the hut. Rainaldo sat with his father and stroked his damp brow. The old man sipped some water. Rainaldo spoke quietly.

'I am going out to collect some sticks for the fire.' But no answer came from the huddle of blankets.

Outside, Lokin and Ada walked slowly across the yard to the hut where Lucy still slept, tended by Anketil. Ada stepped away and stood in the shadows, watching him. Something in her soul was touched by this tall young boy and by his sincerity. She did not know the feeling that alighted upon her but she felt a certainty that was unfamiliar, yet comforting. Lokin looked at her small face and smiled.

'Have no fear, Ada.' All will be well.' And they walked together across the moonlit ground, their shadows almost touching.

CHAPTER TWENTY-FIVE
Carlisle, March 1092
The Messenger

Dolfin read again the short message which Gerluff delivered with his customary breakfast of brewed ale and lightly-cooked roach. The identity of the messenger remained a mystery and Gerluff had looked away when Dolfin asked the question, 'Who delivered this?' Gerluff simply shrugged and left the room. Dolfin pondered as he ate, reading the scrawled runic writing over and over again, then decisively rose to his feet and opened the heavy oak door of his room.

'Gerluff', he called into the darkness of the stone stairs leading away into the depths of the castle beneath, 'Gerluff, bring my riding clothes and prepare Tula. And your pony, also, for that matter. We are going to Bassenthwaite. Oh, and find Patric.'

Dolfin heard the heavy tread of Gerluff's step in the courtyard. He soon reappeared, carrying strong breeches, a heavy, grey tunic and a grey cloak of thick, soft wool. Dolfin glanced beyond the window and saw the feathery shadows hanging like cobwebs across the rooftops of his city. Grey smoke rose into the dull air, meeting grey clouds as they reached down and touched the countless chimneys with long, curling fingers. He loved the enticing, magical charm that rose from the city but sadness spoke to him as he looked over his familiar skyline. What if the Normans should take his city from him? Where should he, Patric and Gerluff go? How would the impassive Norman and the greedy Flemish care for the magic of this northern outpost? Would they protect or destroy? Dolfin pulled on his boots. He descended the dark, stone stairway to the courtyard and found Gerluff holding three bridled ponies with coloured cloths across their broad strong backs, bedecked with coloured beads. Patric appeared from the kitchen, munching a large hot crust of bread. Hastily, he pulled his heavy cloak about his shoulders and adjusted his sword about his ample middle. They turned south-east towards the mountains of Allerdale. The ponies were small but sturdy, coated with thick fur and with hooves of stone. The three riders disappeared into the early mists and turned south on the mountain road towards the village of Bassenthwaite.

An hour earlier, Hermod had ridden away from Carlisle through the grey March day, skies heavy with moisture. He headed south towards Greystoke castle, to deliver Sigulf's message. Following the river valley for some miles, he then climbed the slopes above the valley where grey clouds reached down to touch the grey grass of late winter. It was cold. Kugi cantered easily over the rough ground like a white hare of the mountain and soon reached the craggy heights. The mists swirled around the fortress of Greystoke in the valley below. Hermod was pondering his recent meeting with Gerluff, the silent manservant of the Lord of Carlisle. There was something familiar about him and he was puzzled. Many hours later, without passing anyone upon the lonely tracks, he descended to the great fortress of Greystoke. Sigulf greeted Hermod with warmth and read the message. He was silent for a long time and Hermod watched with interest his son, Forne, standing by the fireplace of the great hall, his face hidden in shadow. Hermod wondered what he was thinking as he gave no sign of surprise at the message. Sigulf's words interrupted his thoughts.

'Forne, we must travel to Bassenthwaite, there to meet with Gospatric and Dolfin. Please go ahead to the village and advise them of our plans.' He paused, looking directly at his son. 'Go, quickly.'

Hermod left the hall, relieved his identity had not been questioned. He had no wish to lie to Sigulf but still was uncertain of those he could trust. He found Kugi by the gate, moving restlessly and keen to get going once again. The final journey would bring them home to Bassenthwaite.

'Come, my beauty', urged Hermod into the long mane, 'we are nearly home now.' The pony flew away across the flat meadows west of the castle as the mountains ahead sank into the gloom. The sun was already dipping beyond the skyline and long shadows glided purposefully across the land. Hermod looked neither right nor left and the pony barely touched the ground with his small feet. The shadowed eyes of the forest watched with interest.

To the north-west, Gospatric of Allerdale and his son, Waltheof, rode into the deepening afternoon. The message had arrived earlier that day and none of the guards knew who had delivered it. Gospatric read the words on the faded manuscript and called his son. Waltheof spoke.

'What is so urgent? We have known for some time of the Norman advance. What has changed?'

Gospatric looked intently at his son and spoke slowly. 'Waltheof, you are soon to become Allerdale's ruler and there will be many challenges ahead to protect these lands. For certain, this invasion will happen, and soon.'

Waltheof spoke slowly. 'How can we possibly overcome the Red King's army? We have neither men nor weapons.'

His father replied.

'It will not depend on armies and weapons, but on the victory of trust and honour over treachery. There are good men among the Normans, for example, Ivo de Taillebois. He knows that to conquer these mountainous lands of lake and forest is impossible, even for an army such as theirs. He has assured me that their aim is merely to establish secure bases against King Malcolm the Scot. If this is true then Allerdale will survive, at least for now. There will be much change in your lifetime but you will, I am certain, achieve great things before you follow me to the world beyond.' He smiled unexpectedly, the sudden mirth taking Waltheof by surprise.

'Let us rest for a time. The ponies are tired. Light a fire and we can heat some broth.'

Waltheof laid a small fire and watched the dark orange and purple flames gathering strength in the damp evening air. After a simple meal, father and son lay on the ferny floor while the ponies grazed nearby. Gospatric spoke again.

'Your mother and I talk often of departing this earthly life. This will happen in its own time. All is as it should be. All is as it is.'

The ponies lifted their small heads, watching the shadows. He continued.

'It is difficult to know what really matters. Sometimes little things, sometimes great things change destinies. The secret it seems to me is to know when to act and when to lie still. In our souls, we have an ancient, earth-given knowledge but how do we access this knowledge in our daily lives?'

Waltheof replied quietly, almost under his breath.

'I wish only to fulfil my destiny and bring honour to my family.'

He was thinking of his beloved Sigritha, a beautiful and courageous girl who he had met a year ago, by chance, on the road above Carlisle. She was travelling with her father, a poor Galwegian farmer and, within weeks they were married in the chapel at Papcastle. Gospatric had watched these two young people through the summer days laughing together among the leafy apple and pear trees and he envied their youthful joy. He remembered well the intensity of his own love for Ellesse, Waltheof's mother, when they first touched with trembling hands, a long time ago. Suddenly, a gust of cold wind from the north cut his memories and mist swirled like a cloak across the clearing. They peered into the indistinct night world. Waltheof felt a cold shiver touch his spine and caught a glimpse of a silvery grey spectre gliding silently through the night air. He touched his father's arm but, as Gospatric turned, it was gone, slipping away into the darkness.

'What did you see?' whispered Gospatric.

'It looked like a wolf, but not of this world, a spectre.' The night air touched their cheeks as the mist rose among the black shadows and they did not sleep again. Early the next dawn they left the clearing, the ponies treading carefully through the darkness cloaking the mountain world. They rode towards the black lake and the small village beside its shores.

CHAPTER TWENTY-SIX
Bassenthwaite, March 1092
Piero's Tale

A rider and a small white pony sped along the western skyline until
they reached a small hill above the black lake. In the morning valley
far below, the village lazed in the early light and folk moved among
the huts; young, old, large and small, some very small, going about
their daily tasks. There were tethered ponies, pig shelters, clucking
fowl scratching for scraps, stacks of firewood. The church lay in the
morning shadows, its dark shape silhouetted against the smoky air,
rising like a sleepy monster. Hermod knew every stone and every piece
of carving. He had watched Lokin for many hours and knew the secrets
within its walls and upon the font lying in the altar's shadows. He
descended the stony track. The pony knew the path well, every twist
and turn, every lump and stone and he carefully picked his way, eyes
bright with excitement.

Concealed in the forest glades, another figure remained hidden to
the eyes of day. As Hermod approached the village, this dark-eyed
figure emerged silently from the shadowed mists and stood where they
had been only a few moments earlier. Then he turned and uttered a
soft whistle. From the grey bushes a glint of silver answered his call.
The figure smiled and looked down to the village, staring for several
minutes. Then, stepping towards the black shadows, he vanished into
the forest. In the distance, for a moment, the sound of a horse's hooves
touched the winter trees. Hermod stopped and listened to the
mountain air but heard nothing. Deep in thought he turned back
towards the village.

Lokin and Rainaldo were feeding the impatient and noisy chickens
when they heard a familiar shrill whinny. They ran to the edge of the
village, shouting and waving.

'It's Hermod. And Kugi. Come, everyone. Hermod and Kugi are
back.' Roused from sleep, Radal emerged from the hut and Anketil,
axe in hand, from the wood-shed. Ketel took Rikarth's hand and ran,

scattering the fowl. Others stepped out of their doorways to welcome Hermod. Gathering around the pony Lokin clutched the long white mane. The tall man in the saddle lifted the woollen cloth about his head, his dark eyes sparkling like embers. He smiled at Lokin and the boy's heart leapt in its traces. Hermod and Kugi had returned.

Some hours later, as the day travelled to its close, a shout came from the other end of the village. Rainaldo stood in the doorway. A second shout.

'Riders, from the north, at least three.'

Lokin, too, heard the commotion and raced to join his friend. Reaching the village fence, three figures astride small, shaggy ponies rode into the village. Leading the group was a large, gaunt man with white hair and a black patch over one eye. His other eye stared coldly. Next, rode a small and quite fat man, with a red face and beaming smile, bending forward in his cloth saddle. He looked a little uncomfortable but, to Lokin's surprise, laughed loudly.

'Greetings to you all', he spoke, waving his hand in welcome. 'I am Patric, servant to Lord Dolfin of Carlisle. Well, I must say, I am glad to be out of the forest tonight. The shadows looked even darker than usual.'

He jumped with unexpected energy from his little pony, handing the rein to Rainaldo. The white-haired man also dismounted, staring about him with his single eye. It was then that Lokin realised just how tall this silent man was. He towered above them all but his face was glum and he looked at the villagers with suspicion. Patric spoke again. 'This is Gerluff. Don't mind him.' He chuckled. The third rider was also small and fat and very red-faced. He remained on his pony and spoke in a clear voice which rang across the yard.

'Let me introduce myself and my companions. I am Lord Dolfin of Luguvallum. This is Patric, my poet, excellent story-teller and guide. This is Gerluff, my faithful servant. He does not speak and, I must tell you, never smiles. I apologise for him. But he is a very good cook.' Dolfin chuckled and surveyed the villagers before him. He then turned his pony towards the church rising white against the trees. Lokin could not fathom the expression on the red face but knew for certain the arrival of Dolfin, Lord of Carlisle, Gerluff, his tall silent, one-eyed servant and Patric, the fat Irish poet was part of an unfolding mystery. Suddenly, a little tug at his tunic caught his attention. It was Rikarth.

'I'm hungry,' he said, determinedly. 'Hungry.'

'We'll have some food soon, I promise. We must go back to the hut. Come on.' He picked up the small child and turned away.

A little later, when all was quiet and the visitors resting, Lokin and Rainaldo returned to Piero's hut. The old man was leaning against some hay-filled cushions. He gestured to them to sit down opposite him.

'Well, boys, listen now to a story, a long story. In its telling you will learn of many mysteries. Your lives and the destiny of Allerdale are now inextricably linked.'

The two boys watched his face intently. The old man, pale with age and winter light, unexpectedly sat straight and took a deep breath. His face took on a youthful glow as he told his tale.

'You will be amazed by what I have to say, but have no fear. All is as it should be.' He paused a long while and then began.

'A long time before the sun touched the eastern slopes, before the pines had fully stretched towards the pale dawn sky, many strangers came to this Cumbric lands. They came in hordes across the sea, astride long wooden galleys, bearing carved weapons and bedecked with ornate jewels. These warlike men intended to conquer and subdue, to carry booty and slaves away to the eastern lands over the frozen black sea to the north. Many left on finding reward, whether treasure, wives or cattle. But a few remained in these ancient lands of Rheged, now called Allerdale. They settled along the coastal marshlands and inland on the mountainous slopes above the black lakes. They founded little hamlets in the wide river valleys, green and lush with fowl and fish.

'One young warrior who remained was as tall as a great pine with piercing blue eyes. When he stepped ashore, he felt a little confused. Strangely, he remembered nothing of the journey or indeed from where he had come. Standing alone by the sandy shallows, he watched the departing boats, waiting until the last sail dipped beyond the black

97

edge of the sea. Then, he turned from the sandy shallows and headed for the wooded ridge above the beach. He wondered why he had stayed and what had called him to this strange, green land with its grey skies and black water. What song had touched his soul as he heard the birds call in the evening light? He knew he would not be welcome as his band of companions had left a legacy of fear and hatred. Running swiftly up the bare, rush-strewn slope from the beach and into the trees, the young man watched the dark landscape with sharp eyes. He ran with his head bowed low, his shoulders forward in his haste to reach shelter before night overtook these strange lands. He could not really remember the moment he decided to stay behind. Some strange force had overtaken him and he felt compelled to obey. To stay was certain to bring danger and adventure.

'He ran fast, into the gathering dusk and almost fell into the half-hidden wooden fence surrounding a small hut. He looked around but there was no sign of its occupants, just a small, rotting fence and a little ramshackle hut. In front of the small door, a yellow fire blazed red and very hot and a large pot lay nearby. He knelt on the forest floor and remained absolutely still for several seconds, wondering whether the dwelling was inhabited. Except for the sharp crackles of the fire, silence carpeted the forest. Late autumn trees, hung heavy with leafy cloaks, gold, yellow and black, were carved against the night sky. He peered into the darkness. Suddenly, a little voice spoke in a language unfamiliar to him but the strange thing was he immediately understood the words spoken.

"You have come. We knew you would. Thank you. Thank you, indeed."

'The young man stood up, stretching to his full height. The sight meeting his tired eyes surprised but did not alarm him. Two small figures stood like shadows silhouetted against the red light of the dancing flames. He could not distinguish them clearly but knew from their kind voices that the welcome was genuine.

"Come in to the shelter," said one. "The wind blows cold from the north-east and snow will come. Please, enter. It is warm and we have food. My name is Tallis, Tallis of Tandrallion. This is my father,

Dedrulf, Lord of Dehallion." The young man felt a warm glow on his hands.

"We have been awaiting you for many days now," continued Tallis.

"There are things we must tell you before my father travels to the next world, into the next life, if you see what I mean. We live in many worlds and help when needed. He is off on another task, if you see what I mean. We are young and old at the same time." He chuckled. "I say 'young', well, actually, about a thousand years old which is young for us. You and your children and your children's children are the ones to carry this story forward into the mists of time, to be recited by firesides, across meadows, through woodland depths and across mountain slopes. I, Tallis, am your servant in this task ahead."

'The traveller perched on his heels and listened intently. He understood their language without difficulty and spoke to them in their own words, without hesitation.

"Tell me all I must know as I feel compelled to stay here, in these ancient lands of Rheged, when all my comrades left for the homeland. What you say comes as no surprise. Tell me my task and my journey and I will do as you ask."

The voice moved into the light revealing Tallis's small face, wizened and crinkled with age but his voice was young and fresh. He spoke the following words.

"Hermod, you are the son of Sigurd, the great hero of the northern lands. You have been chosen to retrace his steps in this kingdom and to save the secrets of this ancient land of Allerdale. In a small village by a black lake, a stone font will be carved by a young hand. This carving, and others that follow, will reveal to your heirs their true heritage. North men will come from the north, but, also, from the south. Beware these men from the south, as there is treachery within their bands. Beware, also, the sons of Greystoke. Beware also the sons of Cardew. All is not what it seems. You, Hermod must learn this language of the stones and pass it on to those who will carve the story in these ancient stones. You must find Fafnir, find those who harbour him in their souls, interpret the message from your father, Sigurd, and carve it across the stones. Only then can Sigurd and the people of the lands of Allerdale be free from tyranny and love can be eternal. Be warned.

The dragon, Fafnir, is well disguised."

'Hermod was silent. He knew Tallis had more to say.

"From this rocky slope, take the path through the woods to the crest of the hill. There, turn to the south and you will see the black mountain set against the white sky of winter light. Cross the flat plain of the great river, heading for the summit. Beyond the river, follow the slopes where the forest paths are green with moss and wet with endless dews, where stags and wolves live as one, where night and morning doves live in mysterious song. Follow the path to the heights above the forest, above the slopes of the blackest crags. The rocks cut the sky with their jagged edges and you cannot mistake them. The dark grey surfaces, damp with dew and green mist carve a message against the sky, telling the tale of what is to come. You will understand the words. You will also understand the language of the birds. Trust me.

Follow your heart. The great hound of the north will find you and the black horse in the forest. The swan and the silver wolf are the signs. Sigurd, hero of the lands of Ice, has returned to the lands of Allerdale. Follow him.

You will be assisted on this quest by many creatures which will become known to you as you travel. Do not look for them for they will find you. You must carry this message to others, to free Sigurd, to free Hermod and Siyulph and the men of the ancient northern lands."

Tallis paused and then turned to his father, the ancient Dedrulf, who spoke slowly in a deep voice.

"You, young man, you are Hermod, son of Sigurd. Your father sent you. You will meet again, and soon." A long silence fell upon the hut.'

Piero paused for several minutes and silence lay across the hut. The two boys sat motionless. He went on.

'Hermod sat for a long while, staring at the fire. He had not seen his little companions depart but he knew he was now alone. Hermod, son of Sigurd, of course. A faint memory began to stir in his heart, his father, his mother and his brother, Siyulph. At last, he rose and slipped into the dark trees below the skyline. He felt renewed strength in his legs and ran up the slope away from the coast and into the night hills which opened up to receive him, the forest glades welcoming his steps across the uneven ground. The darkness swallowed him as he ran, searching for the blackest crags beneath the sky. There, he would find the message through the ancient rock, there he would learn the language of the birds and of all creatures.

'Many hours later, Hermod arrived above the forest and saw a rocky slope stretching out before him. He crossed this carefully, his feet sliding amongst the harsh stones. Beyond, the trees thickened once again and he saw a path stretch away into the shadows surrounded by alders and ash trees. Their branches touched him as he ran, their spiky fingers grasping at his coat from their secret darkness. Hermod ran as fast as he could and quickly covered the ground, arriving before long on the crest of a small hill. He stood for a few moments looking towards the southern hills, blue and distant in the evening sky. Beyond these gentle giants rose the angry black mountain, jutting into the white winter sky and jabbing the soft clouds with fierce edges. It was an awesome sight and Hermod was drawn immediately to its magic and its promise. 'This is where I must go,' he spoke quietly to himself and the breeze from the forest replied with its gentle rhythm. The mountain rested uneasily against the sky and Hermod wondered what lay in store for him as he approached its hidden caverns. He ran easily down the slope and through the trees once more and reached the open plain which stretched before him in an endless array of green, brown and winter yellow. In the midst of this flatness wound the great river which flowed to the western sea, carrying the last of the winter snows on its journey to the endless ocean. He kept the black summit in his sight and in his mind as he raced across the plain and crossed the river as it raced in angry torrents beneath him. He found the path he sought and followed its twisting scent as it climbed into the hills once more. Hermod lifted heart and head and knew he was close to the end of his journey. Before him lay the black crags, rutted and sharp against the light sky, writing their own runic letters across the night sky. Hermod knelt on the stony ground and breathed a long deep sigh, speaking these words softly to the night world.

'*Follow your heart. The great hound of the north will find you. And the black horse in the forest. The swan and the silver wolf are the signs. Sigurd, hero of the Land of Ice, has returned to the lands of Allerdale. The carved stones will bear the message to those who must carry it.*'

'Hermod knew now his purpose, to find his father and brother to preserve the lands of Allerdale. Sigurd was his father, and they would fight the evil threatening all in its path. This was why he had remained on the shores of Allerdale. This quest was his life's purpose. Sigurd had told him and now all was clear.'

Piero sat back and paused. Lokin stared at him and then at his friend. But Rainaldo's face wore a strange expression and his eyes were full of a mystery that Lokin had not seen before. Hermod, son of Sigurd, Hermod, their friend and mysterious companion. He wanted to say something but could find no words. Piero continued.

'Sigurd, Hermod's father, returned to these lands many lifetimes ago and killed the dragon, Fafnir. The dragon, however, lives on in many hearts. Evil comes in many guises and you must learn to recognise it. The dragon Fafnir must be banished from this land. Lokin, you were chosen to carve the message in the ancient stone of the font, telling of Sigurd's return to these lands.'

Piero looked intently at Lokin. 'Hermod is, indeed, the son of Sigurd, who still lives in this world and in another. Roberto also knows of his identity.'

Lokin spoke softly, in a small voice which sounded rather strange to him.

'Piero, how did you know of this? Who are you? And who is Rainaldo?' He turned to is friend who said nothing. 'I thought you came from far beyond the white mountains of the south. How do you know of Sigurd and these strange events across our lands.' The old man spoke again.

'I have known of these things for a long time. Evil destroyed my life in Lombardy. My family were murdered including my young son. You ask who Rainaldo is?' The old man paused, then continued in a quiet voice, looking directly at Lokin.

'Rainaldo is not my own son. I found him, very young and alone, among the great white mountains. He had fallen into a stream and would surely have drowned but I caught sight of him from a bridge and pulled him from the water.' Piero paused again.

'Rainaldo is not my son. Rainaldo is not his name. His real name is

Siyulph and he is Hermod's lost brother. He did not drown in the icy depths of the black sea beneath the rocks but was rescued by the silkies who took him into their care until he was old enough to leave on his journey, a journey that would bring him to Allerdale, to you, Lokin, a journey to reunite him with his brother and with his father. Yes, with his father, too.'

The little hut was silent. Lokin felt as if he had been hit by a block of stone. He stared at Piero and then slowly turned his head towards his friend who sat cross-legged in the corner. He wanted to say something but the words stuck in his mouth. Rainaldo looked at him without smiling, his face calm and composed. Piero spoke again.

'Rainaldo has known of his true identity from the start. Indeed, it was he who told me his story. We did, of course, not meet through accident. I knew the boy was not an ordinary mortal and was alarmed at first but was compelled to save him. I was given no choice. It was as if my own destiny was taken over by another power. Sigurd placed his son in my path so that my journey would lead to Bassenthwaite. And, here we are. My journey is almost over and my purpose, too. Yours, Lokin, is only just beginning. Hermod knows the true identity of this boy, his lost brother who will soon return home to the Land of Ice. Hermod's identity was clear but I had to await the right moment to reveal it to you. Now, you know. Take this friendship and treasure it, in your hands and in your heart. Listen, watch and follow the signs that will be given to you. Look at the eyes of all you meet. Eyes reveal all.'

Piero smiled and looked across at Siyulph who took Lokin's hand in his.

'Welcome to my world, Lokin. I am sorry I had to deceive you so long but it was necessary. Trust me now. I am real for now, in this world, but I have also come from another where my mother lives. You have much to do in these lands to save them from Fafnir, the dragon of evil.' Lokin took his hand and smiled, realising that, from this moment, childhood had vanished. Looking into Siyulph's eyes, he spoke to Piero.

'Piero, who was Rainaldo?'

'He was my only son, Lokin. Rainaldo was my only son who died at the hands of wickedness in the arms of his mother.'

Piero lay back on his cushions and closed his eyes. Lokin and Siyulph left the hut and crossed the yard to the church. They said nothing to each other. It was almost dark and there was nobody about. Even the animals had retreated into their roosting places. Pulling the heavy oak door of the church open, a heavy silence greeted them and Lokin was struck by the smell of stone and rushes. He breathed deeply, aware of the calm he felt on entering this holy place. The building slept in darkness except for a single taper light hung upon the wall at the back of the nave. The shadows cast by this single light stretched along the nave into the chancel, a long thread of light leading the boys towards the shadowed font. Light danced in tiny flickers on the beams and touched the tall slender columns beside the chancel. Lokin watched this midnight elvish ceremony and pulled a second candle from his coat. He held it close to the taper, waiting a few seconds for the small piece of hemp to ignite. The cold of the March night crept into the church. Lokin held the candle to Siyulph's face and laughed. 'You look like a ghost in this light. Well, you are a ghost, sort of. I wish I could say I had guessed you were not really you, but I can't because I didn't. You fooled me, completely. What am I to think? One minute, you are my faithful friend, Rainaldo, son of Piero, from the depths of Lombardy, here purely by chance. Then you are the son of Sigurd, brother of Hermod.' He felt quite confused. Siyulph said nothing. It was easy for him as he had known all along. Poor Lokin. What a shock. Siyulph spoke.

'How do you know what a ghost looks like?'

Lokin replied, 'We have heard them described in our stories. Remember Uncle Chetel speaking about a nun's ghost from St Bethoc? That was scary as he described such a figure on the road between Isel and the sea. I believe him, don't you?'

Siyulph did not reply. Lokin held up his candle and the tiny flickering light cast by the small flame interrupted the darkness. They stepped towards the front of the church where the font lay in the secret evening. Lokin's heart thumped as held the candle to light their way.

The church opened before them, sharing its secrets and welcoming them into its world.

As they reached the chancel step, the sight before them forced them to their knees. The font was aglow with a soft light, not the light from Lokin's candle but from deep within its stony surface. The carving tingled with its own essence and the figures acted out their story. The boys knelt beside this stone, no longer tossed aside, faded grey and worn, no longer part of a lost time beyond memory. Upon its surface the young boy had carved a tale unknown to him, in a language which he had yet to understand, for strangers he had yet to meet. 'The time is right. The time is now', Piero had said. And now, Lokin understood what he meant.

'You are right in what you think', said a quiet voice just a few yards behind them, a voice hidden in the shadows. Lokin and Siyulph turned but did not rise to their feet. Unafraid, they knew this voice.

'The time has come. Now, you know who I am and I know, my brother, who you are. I have come to welcome you back into this world, if only for a short while. Sigurd, our father, promised we would meet again and there were many times when I doubted this. I should not have. He knew and I know now, for certain, that things are as they should be, here, now, in this place and for this reason.'

Hermod took a hand of each boy and together they looked for a long while at the font. Hermod spoke.

'It is beautiful, is it not?' The three of them sat in silence in the dark church lit by a single candle, watching the font glowing with its light and its message of hope until, at last, its song faded and the figures rested once more within the ancient stone.

CHAPTER TWENTY-SEVEN
Bridekirk, March 1092
Eltred, Forne and Thorfinn

The church of stone lay amongst the wind-blown ash trees on the mound of a small hill. Dedicated to Saint Brigit who had also given the village its name, the building was some years old now but had a look of an ancient edifice. Ivy grew from its steep roof and moss covered the arches above the dark doorway. The two narrow windows, one high on each side, were almost enclosed with ferns and grasses sprouting their determined way from the ground beneath. The village of St Brigit was small and few people lived here but it was an ancient place and close to the main thoroughfare established long ago by Roman soldiers. Several huts lay to the south of the church and a hall stood nearby where folk from the village gathered for discussion and for celebration. Graves dotted the edge of the clearing where the church stood and ancient stones lay scattered in the surrounding woodland. The long winter storms roared in from the sea and battered this small community. But the church stood firm and the trees bent in submission until the spring warmth touched them once again and people and animals could breathe freely the warm breezes from the south.

Now it was March and the grey pastures were about to reawaken from their winter slumber. Eltred knelt at the small stone altar within the church. Although the sun was shining across the marshes and dipping into the forest, the interior of the building was dark and dampness clung to the air like heavy dewdrops. He touched the cold earth floor. He wished he could pray but the words would not come and his anger with himself and with his God mounted in his heart. He looked up at the tall elegant cross of wood above him. Some said it had been carved by a farmer from the east, others that it was magic and was left by the church door one night when all were asleep. The dying figure of Jesus looked down at Eltred with half-closed eyes. The man shivered.

'This place gives me a strange feeling', he said to himself, looking around the shadowed nave. Two great tapestries hung to either side of him on the walls, lit only by a single candle. The figures spoke to each other with gesture and with expression within their woollen world. The scene to Eltred's left was familiar, representing the Sacrifice by Abraham of Isaac, his son, to the Lord. He had read this story many times in the Latin Bible in the monastery at Bec where his father had taken him as a young boy to be raised. He recalled the horror he felt as he waited for Abraham to kill his son. Here, in this small and remote church, he felt the same fear as he saw the raised sword of the father. He saw the angel grasping its sharp end to prevent the murder and the ram lying in submission in the knowledge of its fate. Isaac was seated on a raised rock and stared at his father, ready to be sacrificed. Eltred felt the angel's gaze directly upon him.

He looked across at the northern wall where the second tapestry hung. At first he could not make out the figures, some of which were a little frayed and torn. The eastern cloth had travelled far to reach this place. Then, as he studied the picture before him, he recognised the death of the traitor Judas, hanging from a tree, surrounded by devils and creatures of the night. Eltred's breath was caught by the horror of the scene and also by its beauty. Judas's body hung in a graceful curve, the trees swaying on either side. The devils' wings wove into a pattern of flowers and vegetation. Eltred saw Judas's face in the agony of death. The devil turned to Judas and reached out a bony hand to touch him, dragging him into the wall that dripped with winter damp behind them. Eltred watched in horror as the figure seemed to writhe and twist in death.

'Oh God, I must get out of here', cried the young man. The heavy wooden door was firmly shut and he pulled with all his might until at last it moved. He was certain he had left it wide open on entering the church but now the oaken beams were reluctact to allow his escape. The sun poured down on him as he ran from the shadows and away towards the forest. Some of the villagers, busy with their daily toil, looked up in surprise at his flight. The door of the church slowly closed behind him, as if pushed gently by a breath of wind from the sea. The eyes of Christ on his tall cross closed once more and the characters in the tapestry theatre retreated into their silent world. The angel of the Lord stood back and smiled an unknown and unseen smile in the darkness.

Eltred ran for some way. He reached a clearing among the alders and stopped. He could hear the sound of horses approaching and the murmur of voices. Two riders rode towards him, walking slowly through the winter light. Forne and Thorfinn. Eltred was relieved.

'I am glad to see you. This place gives me the shivers.'

'What do you mean?' asked Forne, pulling his black horse to a halt. 'Oh, nothing, really. It is just all these stories going around.'

Thorfinn laughed.

'Come on, Eltred, son of the great Ivo de Taillebois. Surely, you are not frightened by a few stories and the odd ghost?'

Eltred bristled. He had disliked Thorfinn since they were small boys. 'I am not afraid of ghosts', he insisted and turned away from the horsemen. Forne dismounted.

'Now, let's discuss plans, not ghosts. We need to send a message to Herluin. He came north to Kentdale with his brother, Hugh, and is, I understand, at Kirkby Lonsdale. He will come north to Carlisle if we request this and meet us there. Do you agree?'

Eltred turned back and looked Forne straight in the eye.

'Yes, I agree. We must meet this Herluin as soon as possible. I believe he has much to tell.'

CHAPTER TWENTY-EIGHT
Appleby, March 1092
Lucy

The sounds of early spring sang across the fells of Allerdale and Greystoke and over the coastal marches of Copeland to the sea. The last snows had crawled back to the highest crags, clinging with their melting sticky fingers of winter. Lucy sat with Morcar by the thick woollen drapes of the north window, occasionally picking up her embroidered cloth. She watched the constant movement of men and horses in the courtyard below. From time to time, she looked beyond the giant walls to the distant western hills. She was restless. Indeed, she was bored. Having a baby was rather tedious. She wanted to be out riding across the hills and along the river banks on her beloved Chanterelle. She thought again of Ivo's words spoken the previous night, of the impending invasion of these lands by his fellow Normans. Lucy thought about this. She was English, after all, born in this native land, of English ancestors. She was English, not Norman. Lucy remembered nothing of the invasion from across the water over twenty years ago although her father recited many stories of those events. But the plight of simple English folk and loss of land and title were fresh in everyone's minds. Now, with talk again of the Norman army, led by her husband, advancing into Allerdale, she felt her own soul was being invaded. She loved these mysterious lands and most of all, the village of Bassenthwaite beyond the high passes. But, whenever the thought of the village alighted on her mind or in her heart, she closed her senses. She could not allow herself to think of this place or of the people she had encountered there. She tried not to think at all when talk of Bassenthwaite arose. She dare not.

Since her collapse in the church and her recovery over the following days, days which turned into almost a month, she thought of little else. The snow had indeed arrived and fell like a great white curtain for several days. All contact with the world beyond the mountains to the north and east was lost. Lucy had lain in Anketil's hut surrounded by a warm love beyond her imagination. She had watched the tall man in his daily toil and, in the evenings, listened to the stories by the fire, a fire that, for her, blazed day and night. She came to love the boys and to understand their different characters. The boys, in their turn, saw in this small and beautiful woman an image of their mother, Helewisa. Lokin watched his father's energy return. Eager to start each day, he skipped out into the winter dawn for food and fuel for his family. Lokin, too, spent many hours with Ada, who, with her gentle nature and soft words, provided companionship and a growing friendship. He found himself looking for her in the mornings and ensuring her every need was met. She just smiled shyly and thanked him for his care. Those days were magical. Lucy, and Lokin, wanted them to last for ever.

But the day came when it was deemed safe for her and Ada to cross the high passes, deep with March snow, to return to the Norman fortress of Appleby where Ivo's physician and Morcar would care for her during these long months of waiting. Now even her baby, for which she had longed, was overshadowed by her thoughts of the tall, blond Norseman with his calm, blue eyes. On this grey day these thoughts were disrupted by her sister.

'I think Ivo will return before the middle of the day. I will order some food. You must eat too. You have a child to feed now and you are so thin.' Morcar looked intently at her older sister. Since her mysterious collapse some weeks before, there had been a change in Lucy. She was distant and distracted and questions sat in her soft eyes, questions she wanted to ask but could not. She trusted nobody with her secret self, not even Morcar. It was unfair to expect her to carry the burden of such thoughts. At the sound of horses she glanced up and Morcar saw a brief flash of hope in her eyes, touched with secret joy. It was so unexpected that she quickly looked away. Words, however, were unnecessary. Morcar suspected the source of this joy and feared the enormity of what had happened. Now the unspoken words between the women created a silent bond. Lucy held out her hand and Morcar held it to her heart. Lucy's pleading eyes spoke of love, confusion, of guilt and secret longing. Morcar knew for certain.

Lucy was in love for the first time and it was not with her husband, the powerful Norman Ivo, to whom she was bound by marriage and the law of church and land, but with a humble Norse farmer, father of four sons, a widower, a woodcarver and a stranger to her family and to her way of life. As Morcar looked at Lucy, carrying her husband's child, she knew their story would, from this moment on, become Anketil's story too.

'You are right, Morcar.' Lucy's words cut through her thoughts. Morcar stood up and stepped away. Lucy continued, in a clipped tight voice.

'Ivo will shortly return. Please fetch some food. I feel fine again. In fact, in some ways, I feel stronger that I have before.' Then, without warning, she burst into tears. Morcar knelt down and took her hands and Lucy cried, tears falling in a shower of fear and hopelessness. After a long while, the sobbing ceased and the softness returned to her voice.

'I can't explain any of it, Morcar. I have no words for how I feel. It is as if something has entered my soul, giving me meaning and purpose I have not felt before. Forgive my ramblings. It is so hard to explain.' She paused. 'It is as though I have been waiting for something all my life but not really knowing what it was. Now, I know. I have found my destiny and my secret soul. And there is nothing I can do about it. Nothing.'

Lucy looked away, her eyes carrying a desperate sadness. Her thoughts moved from this turreted room, from her unborn baby, across the castle walls, beyond the western hills. The baby would come, the invasion would come, but the secrets of these ancient lands were in her heart now and a message passed to her. The font had spoken. She had heard the words as she stood in the shadows. She could not forget.

You are Lucy, daughter of Thorold, daughter of the forest and the mountain glen. You are not the wife of a Norman, and he is not your husband. You are the true wife of all magic in the hearts of the Celtic people of Allerdale. You are Lucy, earth wife of Anketil, but beyond this world, you are Queen of all that is good and true. Have courage. Your time has come. You must leave your husband and the child you bear in death. Be brave. Death haunts them and will find them. You and Anketil also have little time but time you do have. Listen to your heart and to the strings of the Celtic lutes as they are played across the forest and in the depths of this stone. Listen. Listen to your heart and its singing and to the music of this ancient stone. Have no fear. All will be well, when the song and the stone are one.

Lucy remembered every word as clearly as if they were being spoken to her now, in this great Norman castle, in the room where she and Ivo had loved and laughed and been happy. She could not understand the message but yet she knew it to be true. Anketil was her true husband and it was he to whom she would return. But fear stalked her nights at the thought of death, of Ivo and of her baby. This she found hard to bear. And yet she knew she must, if, indeed, it was true. Morcar watched her now as these thoughts raced through her head, as they had a thousand times in the past days. Her sister looked restless and unhappy. She wanted to help but could only wait and and hope. As for her love for Turgis, what happiness, if any, could this bring?

Lucy moved to the window and her mind fled over the distant blue of the hills. She knew Anketil would be watching the hills, awaiting her return. She knew, as he did, that she would return. She shuddered suddenly as little threads of fear caught her throat. At that moment, a shout from below caught their attention as a lone rider galloped into the main gate of the castle and leapt from his horse. There was immediate commotion as he ran towards the main hall beneath. Lucy stood, clutching her chest.

'Morcar, go and hear the news. Where is Ivo? What has happened?' Morcar sped away into the shadows and Lucy sat alone, her mind racing, her thoughts bursting in her head. How ashamed she felt. Where was her concern for her husband? She had almost forgotten him these past days, thinking only of the blue, blue eyes and sun-bleached hair, far beyond the hills. Until now, Ivo had been the centre of her life. Now, her life had changed and she had grown beyond him into an unknown place where she already felt at home. Morcar reappeared with the news that Ivo had journeyed directly south to Kirkby Lonsdale to meet with two Norman knights, Hugh of St Bec and Herluin of Mue, sent by the King. Turgis had returned to Appleby.

Lucy saw the trace of a warm smile on her sister's face.

'I know all will be well, Morcar,' Lucy spoke. 'I know this. But much lies ahead for us. I think I am quite excited.' For the first time in weeks Lucy laughed. The sound filled the room and Morcar saw the joy in her face. And she understood the reason for it. For a few days, alone and without guilt, Lucy could think only of her beloved, in a village beyond the hills, in a small and simple hut, surrounded by his sons, watching for her return.

CHAPTER TWENTY-NINE
Bassenthwaite, March 1092
The Meeting

Two days later, a messenger had arrived with news of Ivo's impending visit the following day. The air buzzed with conversation and with questions. What news would Ivo bring from the south of the Red King's intentions? Lokin and Siyulph listened to the talk with excited anticipation. They had seen little of Hermod who often stood alone by the lake beyond the church. Piero spoke sternly.

'You must wait for him to speak his tale. He will, when the time is right. Be patient.'

Later that afternoon, as the village prepared for the Normans, Anketil stood alone by the church in the early and rather murky darkness. Suddenly, in the twilight, he saw a lone figure riding swiftly away towards the darkening eastern hills. It was Forne, son of Sigulf. His horse lifted its proud, black head and cantered easily up the steep slope towards the shadows. At the edge of the woods, rider and horse stood for several minutes, looking back towards the village. Then, turning abruptly, they were gone. Anketil walked thoughtfully back towards his hut but something stopped him and he looked back at the church. A sharp glint of light in the shadows caught his eye. He stared into the darkness. 'I think I am beginning to see things that aren't there', he thought to himself. The winter air was absolutely still. No breeze stirred and dead leaves lay motionless on the stony ground. Perhaps he was mistaken. The pale walls stood like ghosts against the black thickets.

As he turned homeward, Lucy returned to his mind. He had thought of little else these past weeks since her departure, carried away through the snow in a rough, wooden cart. She was taken from his sight but not his heart. Anketil could not see her face as the cart rumbled away over the rutted ground but he knew the expression of her eyes concealed beneath the heavy hood, eyes full of questions and unspoken thoughts. Anketil's hours in the church, carving the

114

magnificent crucifix, had given him time to imagine her constantly and to remember every detail of those magical days when she stayed within the confines of his humble home. At first, he had felt guilt at his betrayal of Helewisa but as the days passed he began to understand what was happening. It was she, Helewisa, who had sent Lucy to him, to bring his heart back to life and to fill his soul with love. Anketil needed strength for the task ahead, to fight for his homeland. Helewisa knew, from beyond this world, that Lucy would rekindle his resolve to play his part in Allerdale's survival. Since her gradual recovery in his small hut Anketil had, indeed, changed. He laughed again, picked up his young boys and tossed them in the air, chased the sows across the muddy hollows and told stories in the late evening hours of renewed hope and of ancient wisdom. Lokin watched his father and saw clearly what was happening within the confines of their little home. He thought to himself,

'I hope this doesn't lead to trouble. My father has a new joy in his heart. He is so different. These are dangerous times.'

He confided in Roberto and his answer was quite surprising. The old man, friend of Piero, just smiled and said, 'The time is approaching. Everything is as it should be. Have no fear.'

The next morning, as expected, another messenger arrived from the south announcing the arrival later in the day of Ivo and two Normans, Hugh of Bec and Herluin of Thaon. Lokin listened to the names and wondered who these men were and the reason for their visit. As preparations were completed, the Lords of Allerdale and Greystoke, Dolfin and Waltheof met once again within the church. Forne had not returned and his father Sigulf announced that he had travelled to the castle of Greystoke above Penraddock to gather support from the folk of Ullswater. As they awaited the visitors, Gospatric asked his servant Patric to read aloud to the whole company a letter he had composed during the previous night, a letter to all his subjects across Allerdale, reassuring them of their rights and freedoms, freedoms which would not be sacraficed at any cost. Gerluff, silent one-eyed sentry, stood by the door of the church while Patric read the letter in a loud voice to all those present.

Gospatric sends friendly greetings to all my wassenas and to every man, free and dreng, dwelling in all the lands that were Cumbrian, and to all my kindred. And I inform you that I give my consent and fuller permission that Thorfynn mac Thore be as free in all things that are mine in Allerdale as any may be, either I myself or any of my wassenas, in weald, in scrubland, in enclosures, and in respect of all things that are above the earth and under it, as far as Chalk Beck as the Waver as the Wampool as Wiza Beck and the weald at Caldbeck. And it is my will that the men dwelling with Thorfynn at Cardew and Cumdivock shall be as free as Melmor and Thore and Sigulf were in the days of Eadred. And let no man be so bold that - with what I have given to him - anywhere break the peace which Earl Siward and I have granted him as freely as to any man living under the sky. And let everyone abiding there be free of geld as Waltheof and Wygand and Wibert and Gamell and Kunyth may wish, and all my kindred and dependents. And it is my will that Thorfynn shall have sake and soke, toll and team, over all the lands in Cardew and Cumdivock that were given to Thore in the days of Moryn, free from the obligation of providing messengers and witnesses in the same place.

Have no fear of the coming months. We shall stand together and fight for our lands and our freedoms. This I assure you all. My son will lead the defence of this kingdom and requests that all able bodied and fit men join his ranks in the event of a war against these invaders. There is hope, however, that the Red king will only wish to garrison our Carlisle as a bulwark against the Scottish people and that he will leave us and our way of life and our lands alone. I have the promise of the Lord Ivo de Taillebois that no harm will come to our people and our dwellings. This is the way forward and is best for all, to negotiate and, in the end, to compromise, without giving up our ancient freedoms. Remember at all times we stand together, you, all of you, myself, the Lord Gospatric of Allerdale, my sons, Waltheof of Allerdale and Dolfin, Lord of Carlisle, Sigulf, Earl of Greystoke, Forne, his heir, Thorfynn, son of Thore, of Cardew and Cumdivock, Anketil, son of Aegir, Harvey, son of Moryn of Salkeld and all the others, Wygand, Wibert, Gamell, Kunyth, Ketel, son of Eldred and Eilife of Penrith. We stand united and together, now and always.

I bid you farewell. The Lord Gospatric of Allerdale.

Silence followed for several moments as Patric finished speaking. Gospatric looked intently at Sigulf who nodded slowly. The freedoms and the assurances had been given but Gospatric knew, as did every inhabitant of Allerdale that they must fight for these rights and for their land. The Lord of Allerdale spoke.

'This letter is to be read throughout the realm, in every vill and to every free man, to every man of God and to all who work in the fields. Everyone must know we are free men of Allerdale and will fight for this if, and only if, it becomes necessary. Waltheof, when the scribes have prepared copies, you must leave this village before Ivo de Taillebois arrives and travel the land with this letter.'

Waltheof left the church, deep in thought. He hoped for peace and, having met Ivo, considered this possible but the Norman bullies had yet to show restraint in other areas of the Anglian kingdom. Why would they do so here in the ancient Cumbric lands? He crossed the yard to the makeshift stables, head bowed, thinking of his father, now so old yet still so wise. He hoped he would be as good a ruler in his turn. Waltheof did not notice the dark eyes watching from beyond the wicker fence. A small figure was waiting in the shadows for the young man to leave the village with the letters, to ride along the forest paths, heading west, first of all, to Isel, to Torpenhow, to Kirkbride and on to St Bethoc. Tallis watched all from his secret place.

Later in the day, a great meal was prepared. Rabbits, herbs and nettles were brought to the door of Anketil's hut and Gerluff stirred a huge iron pot. Anketil paced up and down and, from time to time, glanced up at the skyline where Forne had disappeared into the forest the day before. He was puzzled. Lokin, Siyulph and Radal scouted through the thickets just above the village, hoping to catch sight of the approaching Normans. Their journey would bring them across Westmoringeland, past the settlements of Castlerigg, Keswick and Crosthwaite, by Kendal, along the black lake by Troutbeck, past Kentmere, Rydal and on through the deep forests above Threlkeld to Borrowdale. These ancient settlements, south of Borrowdale and Wythburn and west of the Great Long Water, stretched north towards Penrith and Greystoke, the centre of Sigulf's kingdom. It would have been a long journey.

It was Radal's sharp ears that heard the travellers first and alerted the boys who saw three weary horses approaching the black lake. They ran down to the village. By the hut, Bueth grabbed young Rikarth's hand and the two small boys hid behind the old sow lying in the hay. Anketil and Ketel appeared in the doorway and watched the riders emerge from the twilight. Lokin glanced at his father's face but could not fathom his expression. Before the three riders rode into the village square, another rider on a red horse, rode away towards the north. He went unseen, by villager and by Norman, except for one pair of eyes which ran swiftly behind him as he rode away into the forest. Waltheof disappeared quickly into the evening and the horse's galloping hooves were swallowed up by the encroaching night. The messenger had departed.

Ivo rode into the village square on his white horse, Eagle, followed by Herluin of Thaon and Hugh of St Bec. They saw inquisitive faces in every shadowy doorway, some watching with distrust and suspicion. They rode almost as far as the church where Dolfin, Gospatric and Sigulf waited to greet them. Ivo was reminded of Lucy as he studied the white building in its ancient setting and sadness touched his troubled heart. 'It will be here long after we have all gone', he thought to himself. Dolfin stepped forward to greet them.

'Welcome, Lord Ivo, to Bassenthwaite. We have much to discuss, I think.'

'Indeed we have, Dolfin. It is good to see you again and to arrange this meeting here at Bassenthwaite. I have news from the south and wish to discuss our king's plans concerning Allerdale.' There was a rustle in the crowd gathering around the riders. Herluin moved uneasily in his saddle. He distrusted these folk and watched their rough and weathered faces with dislike. Hugh of St Bec sat still and straight on his horse, his long brown robe falling beneath his saddle, his face without expression. Dolfin turned to the villagers.

'We are here to listen and to make plans, to protect the lands of Allerdale and Copeland, of Greystoke, Cardew and Cumdivock and all our ancient lands. We are also here to avoid confrontation. Please offer these men your best hospitality. Gospatric, Sigulf and I know of your concerns and we share these with you. We must all work together.'

Gospatric stepped forward and surveyed the sea of faces, some anxious and confused, many frightened. He now spoke, loudly and with sadness in his ageing eyes.

'Soon, I will leave this life. I am an old man and know my time is approaching. My son, Waltheof, will take over my leadership. But, for now, I remain Lord of Allerdale and lead these discussions with the Lord of Carlisle and Sigulf, Lord of Greystoke. Ivo de Taillebois and his fellow Normans are to be welcomed by all in this village. There will no acrimony towards them. I believe this Norman lord is not here to hinder our cause.'

More murmurs followed and the atmosphere tensed but nobody spoke. Ivo dismounted and handed Eagle to Lokin who was standing nearby. The Norman looked intently at the boy for several moments.

'You are the famous sculptor and your father the famous woodcarver. I owe you both much gratitude. My wife has recovered well and rests in my castle at Appleby. She is carrying a child which, it seems, was the cause of her ailment in the church.' He studied Lokin intently and the boy returned his gaze with steady eyes. He wondered if his father had heard these words. Ivo waited a few moments before turning to Anketil, standing in the doorway behind him. As their eyes met, he spoke.

'I thank you, sir, for protecting my wife and allowing her to recover here. She is well and in good spirits.' He looked directly at the tall Norseman. Anketil merely bowed his head and returned the gaze. Words were unnecessary. There was no animosity. If Anketil had questioned for a moment the strength of Lucy's feelings for him, all doubts were now dispelled as he looked into Ivo's eyes. Lucy would not have spoken to anyone but the honesty within her eyes made deceit impossible. Her eyes revealed her secret, her love for another, and Ivo knew. Now, Anketil knew also that his love was returned. His heart bounded with joy beneath his expressionless, unsmiling face. He merely bowed slightly towards the Norman but said nothing. Ivo turned away and Anketil slipped back into the shadows of his hut. He dare not reveal his joy.

Hugh and Herluin dismounted and stood by their horses, waiting for Ivo and wondering what his interest was in this rough farmer. Dolfin and Gospatric held out their hands in greeting.

'Come, rest after your journey', said Dolfin, in his sort of Norman dialect. 'This evening, after food and wine, we will hear what you have to say about your king's advances to the north. But for now, welcome to Allerdale and to Bassenthwaite. This is our new church, built with Ivo's generosity and we are grateful. I expect you have seen many similar churches across England and Normandy but when you see the interior of this one, I think even you will be surprised at the craftsmanship. We will wait for daylight to show our treasure to you.'

He led the group past the church towards a large hut. Here, they talked for many hours of the Norman encroachment upon Allerdale and its effects. It was now certain that, in the early summer, the Red King would order his troops to advance north from Kentdale to Carlisle and take over the city from Dolfin. As the night settled across Allerdale they talked and ate. Gerluff brought an endless array of steaming dishes from Anketil's hut and stood silently by the doorway with a strange expression on his face. Lokin and Siyulph listened in vain, trying to interpret the unfamiliar Norman language. Dolfin acted as interpreter when required and his face was unexpectedly earnest. He looked much older in the candlelight and Lokin was sad for this man whose home was threatened. Anketil appeared several times in the doorway but he did not stay long. He was restless and preoccupied and barely glanced at his eldest son. Several times, he looked across at the church in the winter moonlight, watching the dark bushes as if waiting for something. Lokin longed to speak with his father but could find no words to reach him.

The following morning, the three Normans mounted their horses and rode from the village towards Appleby. Ivo de Taillebois and Hugh of Bec turned and raised their hands in a gesture of farewell as they rode towards the forest but Herluin stared towards the mountains and looked neither right nor left at the throng of villagers. The old man, Gerluff, watched, single-eyed, from the hut and saw the dark look of this stranger and the angry brow above his eyes. It would not be long before he met this Norman knight again. Of this, he was certain.

CHAPTER THIRTY
St Bethoc, a Long Time Ago
The Bracelet

The ancient settlement of St Bethoc lay on the western coastline of Copeland, a lordship established long before the coming of the Norsemen. Bethoc was an Irish saint who lived many centuries before the time of Gospatric and Sigulf. She came to the coast of the Cumbric lands to evade capture and forced marriage in her own native lands of the Scotii, across the western sea. After drifting for many days in her small craft, she found herself in a village beside the shore where, with the help of the local inhabitants, she built a small, wooden church, later dedicated to her name. The village was thereafter named Kirkby Bethoc (village of the church of the saint Bethoc) in her honour. In time, the church developed into a small monastery where holy men and women would gather to worship God in heaven, to raise sheep and cattle and to sow seeds of corn and maize across the meadows surrounding them. Here, they also learned to make precious manuscripts telling of the Scriptures and of the wondrous lives of God's saints on earth. It was a heavenly place.

From this monastery, chosen men would travel the land of Allerdale, carrying out pastoral duties in the little wooden churches scattered across the fells. They married and buried the local folk and recently had started to baptise all in the name of God and Jesus, his son. In almost every church, fonts were now being placed. One monk from St Bethoc travelled every month to Bassenthwaite to perform these duties among his flock of Christians. His name was Columba and he came originally from the Island of the Kingdom of Man, across the sea. An old man now he was considered wise by all. He had married Anketil to Helewisa and then, eight years later, had buried her in the stony ground outside the village fence. Columba was surprised when he heard of Ivo's wish to build a stone church by the black lake and a little sad as the old wooden chapel was very beautiful. When, however, he had come to Bassenthwaite and had seen the finished building in the spring sunshine and its carvings of wood and stone, he was astonished. Lokin and Ketel showed him round the church with pride and delighted in his amazement when he saw the font for the first time.

'It is the most beautiful carving I have yet to see,' he said slowly, studying the figures of Jesus, St John, St Bethoc and Sigurd.

'Magnificent. Where on earth did you get these ideas from?'

Lokin resisted the temptation to say the ideas had come from another world. He wanted to say something because he liked this quiet man but something held him back. Piero and Anketil had warned him not to speak to anyone about the message on the font. 'Such things can be misconstrued', warned his father. Lokin was silent.

Bethoc wore a golden bracelet given to her as a small child by her grandmother, reputedly a magical witch from the mountainous land of the Scotii. Made of burnished gold, the bracelet shone softly in the light of the summer sun. Upon its surface were carved mysterious letters in an unknown language. Many attempted unsuccessfully to interpret the words and it seemed the language had long since passed into legend. One day, a man came to the village of St Bethoc. He was tall and very thin and had a sad expression. He did not give his name but asked for food and a place to rest. With him was a large, black horse and, while the stranger slept, the animal stood by the door of the hut watching all with large, brown eyes. Several days went by and the man conversed with the elders but never gave his name or told the purpose of his visit. On the evening before the full moon rose in the sky, as Bethoc prepared food for all, this stranger asked to see the bracelet. Bethoc held out her hand and showed him the strange writing which shone clear in the moonlight. He said nothing but smiled a deep smile and his face immediately grew younger. The next day, the day of the round moon, St Bethoc offered the bracelet to the stranger.

'Please take this gift. It is precious to me but must go forth on its journey.'

This stranger thanked her and tucked the bracelet in his pocket. He rode away on his horse and disappeared over the hill above the village. A small boy ran after him, trying to follow him over the rough ground but when he returned he said the man had disappeared above the forest. As if by magic, he and the horse vanished. Nobody believed him and they all laughed. Except Bethoc. She had seen the truth in Sigurd's eyes. She knew this man's identity and his purpose and that he carried with him the bracelet of gold.

CHAPTER THIRTY-ONE
The Forest, March 1092
Forne and Thorfinn of Cardew

Hermod ran swiftly through the tall pine trees, following the path made by the deer through the winter. He had followed Forne, son of Sigulf, from the village and ran up the slopes to the north-west with feathered wings on his feet, unseen from all seeing eyes. A forlorn neigh had broken the silence of the night but Hermod whistled a quiet reply which was carried on the wind to the little white ears in the darkness. 'I shall return before the full moon. Trust me.' Kugi understood.

Now, two days later, it was dawn in the forest above St Bethoc and Forne, son of Sigulf, sat motionless on his black horse. Tendrils of daylight spread through the trees, touching the gaunt branches and caressing the damp ground beneath. Winter still held the reins of this secret world. Behind him, in the thickets, dark eyes watched. Hermod had followed the son of Sigulf to this place, anxious to discover his plans and the reason for his departure. He knew now who this man was and needed to ascertain his intentions. Forne had told his father his journey was to Greystoke but Sigulf had watched his son with quiet eyes and knew a secret not shared lay in his young heart. Hermod also knew this was a falsehood and, once away from the village, Forne had turned his great horse and headed northwards up the valley before turning west towards the sea. Just as the white dawn emptied its soft light over the mountains, Hermod stopped beside a dark glade, still heavy with night in this forest world. Hermod's senses were as sharp as a deer and as quick as a salmon and he knew, just ahead of him, out of sight but very near, stood a horse. He had found Forne.

Minutes passed slowly and even the birds of early spring hesitated their daily chattering. Then, quite unexpectedly, another rider emerged from the forest gloom. Hermod recognised the figure approaching Forne. It was Thorfinn, son of Thorne of Cardew, friend and compatriot of Gospatric and Sigulf. What was this secret meeting? Forne had lied to his father and here was another man who could not be trusted. Hermod watched with narrowed eyes, angry at the deceit. From the outset, he had known Forne was false. The two young men talked earnestly and Hermod edged closer to listen. The black horse moved restlessly. He heard the silent step of Hermod and turned his head, watching the shadows. Hermod froze and his eyes met those of the horse. They stared for what seemed an eternity. Within those black eyes there was an otherworldliness that caught Hermod by surprise. He knew this creature, he was certain. One or two words floated across the glade, 'Greystoke .... saved ... for you .... Descendents .... Normans ....'

Then, 'Sigulf, father .... St Bethoc .... lost .... Taillebois .... Eltred .... secret ....'

A little later, the riders rode away down the slope towards the coast and St Bethoc. Hermod knew the treacherous path ahead for its devilish marshes and rough fenland ways. He followed, some way behind, running with long strides that swallowed the uneven ground, through knarled hillside thickets and down towards the great oaks. He glimpsed briefly two figures ahead and then lost sight once more as they galloped away across the flat, marshy lands of Copeland. Suddenly, Hermod heard the sounds of a horse close behind him and his heart jumped. He spun round and was astonished to see Waltheof, son of Gospatric.

'Hermod. It is me, Waltheof. I thought it was you a while back but was not certain. What are you doing on the road to St Bethoc?'

'I could ask you the same question. I thought you were at Bassenthwaite to await the Normans.'

'My father has written a letter to all his subjects which I must take across the land, assuring his people of their freedom. Please read it.'

As Waltheof stretched his hand into his leather pouch, a cry cut the winter morning like a knife. It was an unearthly sound and he spun round in surprise. Hermod looked towards the shadows.

'Have no fear, Waltheof', he said quietly. 'Have no fear.' They moved slowly towards the forest and Waltheof's horse danced nervously. Hermod took his long mane in his hand and whispered to the creature.

'All is well'. A few minutes later, they came upon a clearing where the sun reached through the tall pine branches, casting an eerie spell over the late winter forest. Before them, upon the soft ground, a figure lay. It was Thorfinn, son of Thore, and he was fast asleep. On his face was a look of great fear and his hand was held before his eyes. His horse stood grazing close by and seemed unconcerned at the events that had taken place here. Waltheof knelt down but could not wake the fallen man.

'He is not dead', he spoke.

'More's the pity', murmured Hermod.

'I wonder what that noise was that we heard and where is Forne?'

'He will have ridden away to save his own skin, no doubt.' Hermod glanced around the clearing and saw no sign of horse or rider. But, then, of course, he realised, the great black horse of Forn, of course. He smiled to himself and knew all was well.

The sun was setting into a sky of angry red when Thorfinn awoke. He rubbed his eyes and stood up. He was alone but yet felt another presence also. Where was Forne? He remembered nothing, except ....
.... except .... no, he must have been dreaming. A silver wolf, that was it, standing in the glade before them. Bright silver, faded silver, he could not remember but he was sure it was a wolf. His horse had shied and he remembered nothing more. Where was Forne? He mounted his horse and headed towards the coast. Behind him, hidden in the grey forest, a silver creature watched with its dark eyes. Then it slipped away and disappeared into the approaching night.

CHAPTER THIRTY-TWO
Carlisle, March 1092
Ivo's Message

Dolfin lifted his tired eyes from the heavy leather-bound book, a scientific study of Arabic geometry. He had lost track of time and sat back watching the snow falling heavily through the narrow window. Only yesterday, he had felt the touch of the bitter north-east wind on his cheek but this was late winter snow and would not lie long. The spring air was hiding just over the southern mountains, awaiting its orders to bubble across the land. Dolfin thought about the message he had received the previous day from Ivo who was returning north from Winchester. It had arrived late in the afternoon with a tall messenger, riding a small wiry white pony. They must have travelled fast and far but neither seemed tired and, when offered rest, the young man merely bowed politely and pointed towards the south-west. The gates were reopened and he and his little steed sped away into the approaching night.

Dolfin called Gerluff and sat by the fire in the hall, attended only by this silent giant. He read the message written in Norman French and gazed into the flames, turning the parchment over and over in his ageing hands. It was inevitable now. The Normans intended to cross the mountains from Appleby and he must leave his beloved city. Despite Ivo's assurances, surely the Norman king, amid his ignorance and greed, would not allow him to remain.

'Well, Gerluff,' he said slowly, staring at the orange flames, 'this is it. The time has come and we must prepare for the worst. Sigulf has offered us refuge at Greystoke and I have accepted this kindness. My cousin Malcolm, king of the northern mountains, has also offered his assistance but, as you well know, my trust in him goes not even as far as the doorway!' He stopped and looked up at the silent man, wishing he could give his opinion on the matter. Gerluff's single eye looked at the window and watched the late snow covering their city. It was almost April and the message had read of Norman plans to move north early the following month. Carlisle would be established as a base to protect their northern border.

'Gerluff, please pack my things, and yours, too. Pack the books also, at least as many as you think we can carry with us. Prepare two carts for these. Leave everything else. We must travel light. Tell Patric to be ready to leave as soon as the snows melt on the southern hills. Announce this to all the servants. Those who wish to stay and take their Norman chance are free to do so. Those who wish to come must be prepared for a long journey and an unknown destination. We will head for Greystoke, but, beyond that, I do not know.'

Gerluff's wizened face gave no signal that he had heard these words. His eye remained black and his mouth never moved. He merely nodded. The time was approaching when he must reveal his true identity. For now, he remained the silent, one-eyed servant, Gerluff, unable to speak. For now.

CHAPTER THIRTY-THREE
April 1092, Bassenthwaite
Rikarth

Rikarth had just woken up. He rubbed his eyes. His brothers lay asleep, curled up beneath warm covers. A faint light came through the doorway and he knew his father was already outside, collecting wood and feeding the chickens. It was April now and, although the days were longer, the late snowfall of the previous days had melted and the sun glowed warm on the land once more. Rikarth was surprised that his eldest brother, Lokin, was still asleep. He was usually up long before his brothers. The little boy crept out into the half light of early morning. Ketel stirred but did not wake. The chickens and ducks were already pecking at crumbs, chattering amongst themselves, busy with their own importance. He knew every bird and dreaded the moment when the time came, as it inevitably did, for a quick death at the hands of his father, Lokin or Ketel. The little boy saw with sadness the loss amongst the flock as they searched among the rafters and beneath the floorboards for their fallen friend. Sometimes they searched for several days, before giving up hope.

On this early spring morning Rikarth knelt and talked to Wela, his favourite duck, a small, scruffy brown bird, uncertain of her place in life and cautious in her approach. The young boy saw in her the uncertainty of life and loved her for the nervousness she carried with her through the short winter and longer early spring days. Surely, Wela would not be killed for their supper because she was so small and would hardly feed one of them. She followed him as he strayed away from the warm hut in search of his father. Anketil was nowhere to be seen. The light of the sun reached up from behind the hills casting a watery glow across the spring ground. The trees were still quite bare but early buds were pushing through and a light green glow lay on the forest beyond the staked fence of the village bounds. The morning shadows danced with the shafts of light of the new day in a constant waltz through the thorns. A breeze touched the tree-tops, heralding a change in the weather and Rikarth felt its soft warm touch on his cheek and saw the yellow light stretching from the mountain beyond the forest. Suddenly, Wela fluttered clumsily across the clearing. A voice called out.

'Rikarth, what are you doing out here, so early?' Bueth took his hand.

'Father, father, I look father', replied Rikarth, a little grumpily, clutching his brother's shoulder.

'Father will return. He told me last night he would go early into the forest to hunt a boar for our feast.'

'Go and look', insisted Rikarth. 'Go and look father.'

'Well, just a short way. You know we are not to wander from the village.'

The two boys crossed the clearing into the thicket. Like giant cobwebs the branches spread across the path and the two small figures and the little duck quickly disappeared from view.

Meanwhile, Anketil moved stealthily across the forest floor in search of a boar to celebrate the birth of St Bethoc and the arrival of spring. Anketil was a Christian and after Helewisa's death found comfort in the stories of Jesus Christ and in the stories of the saint. Although her miracles confirmed his belief in the Bible, his Nordic beliefs lived deep in his soul. As she lay dying he saw her spirit flying in a graceful curve from the smoky confines of their home into the blue, blue night. He saw the moonbeams descend to guide her to the heavens, leaving a touch of stardust on the hearth beside her cooling body. She was gone from this world but her presence remained with the boys as they chased butterflies and picked the tall summer grasses. She was within the deep blue shadows of the winter forest as they collected firewood behind the dark grey shadows of their hut as they curled in sleep. Helewisa flew with the angels but also with the woodland spirits and she touched each one of them daily with a wisp of her new found world.

On this early spring morning, Anketil stood and listened to the forest sounds. He felt, just for a moment, a soft breeze touch his cheek. He knew it was she, smiling, guarding and waiting for him to come to her, to a place as yet beyond his sight. Anketil looked north and the breeze turned a little cold as he gazed at the black summits. He breathed deeply, watching the forest ahead of him, waiting for any sign of movement. But he was uneasy and his hands were cold. He tried not to think of Helewisa for now in his heart another love was growing. Here, among the ancient trees of the forest where honesty cost nothing, the memory of Lucy's face engulfed him, her soft smile and quiet voice, her bright eyes, inquiring and without pain, and her small, slight body that lay beneath her long cloak. He closed his eyes and she was there. Now, sensing Helewisa's presence, he wanted to ask for her forgiveness and suddenly, as if in answer, from nowhere a young boar raced from the shadows across the clearing. Anketil lifted his short spear and ran in pursuit. The tall pines above him swayed in unison, their backs turned towards the distant north to welcome the southern breezes.

Some hours later, he descended the steep path to the village and watched for the familiar sight of his youngest son playing in the April sun outside the hut. He looked for Bueth, never far away and often busy with his own small world of make believe. The door of the hut was open but there was no sign of the boys. He knew Lokin would be working on the final carvings of the church and the painting of the walls. Ketel was fishing with Uncle Chetel on the black lake, in the small craft made by Hermod from rushes and hemp. But where were the little boys? He adjusted the boar across his back. It was a heavy beast and would feed the whole village. The feast and the dedication of the church would go ahead despite the uncertainties across the land. He walked through the trees into the open area beyond the picket fence but still there was no sign of his sons. He dropped the boar by the hut and called. No answer. As he called again, a fear gripped his stomach. Rikarth had been asking many questions recently about the forest and magical creatures and what happened when he was asleep. Surely, Bueth would not take him beyond the village bounds, into the forest, not alone? Quickly, he crossed the yard to the church and found Lokin painting one of the piers in the nave. He was surprised at the choice of colour.

'Where did that idea come from?' he asked his son. The pier was white, but, top to bottom, and around its width, Lokin was painting red diamonds. It was beautiful but Anketil was uneasy.

'The Lord Ivo ordered this', said Lokin, not looking up, 'like those, I am told, at Kirkby Lonsdale and in the great church at Durham.'

Anketil's mind returned to his young sons.

'Lokin, have you seen your brothers? Would Rainaldo take them to the lake to find frogspawn? He wouldn't take them into the forest, would he?'

Lokin's heart lurched at the mention of Rainaldo's name. His father clearly had no idea yet of his true identity. Should he tell him now? No, he realised this was not the time as he looked up at his father's anxious face.

'I haven't seen them, father. When I left the hut, they were playing outside, chasing some chickens and that old duck, Wela. I am sure they won't be far away. I'll come and help you look.'

They left the church and walked around the perimeter of the village, asking all if they had seen the boys. Nobody had. There was no sign. They began to run across the rough ground by the burial mounds and into the stunted woodland. As they climbed the slope a heavy silence hung above the oaks. The April birds, clothed in their spring attire, were silent. Anketil ran forward, uncertain which direction to follow. He was being led by an unknown force towards the part of the forest where the oak trunks grew like great brown statues and where branches reached the sky, touching the clouds with tiny fingers. Lokin followed him, running across the waking green and yellow spring ground splashed with red as the lichens and mosses emerged from their winter sleep. Father and son barely glanced at the trees as they ran but, if they had, they would have seen a small figure, dressed in red with a pointed hat of green, seated on an ancient fallen trunk. Tallis had watched the little boys since the moment they left the village bounds and followed them into the forest. He knew their father and brother would soon be on the path to find them. Then, from the far side of the great oaks he heard an eagle call from far above the craggy heights. There was danger near. He stepped from his oaken seat and bounced away through the trees, unseen except by the eyes of the great oak trees. He passed Anketil and his son, running with all their speed and, invisible, flew among the great trunks towards the crags. Landing in a clearing he saw the two boys just ahead playing in the shafting sunlight. The tiny duck pecked the April earth and appeared quite unconcerned at her new life in the depths of the forest. Suddenly, Rikarth looked up and pointed directly at the trees where Tallis stood.

'Look, Bueth, look at the silver wolf. Big wolf. Look. Magic wolf. Wolf in story.'

Bueth spun round in alarm but saw only the ancient trees and the mossy green of the clearing.

'Don't be silly, Rikarth', he said, feeling a little afraid. They were a long way from the village. 'Anyway, it is time to go home. We have been away too long.'

Anketil ran into the clearing and, seeing his young sons, scooped them up in his arms, unsure whether to be angry or relieved, relieved beyond measure. The heavy fear lifted like a veil in the breeze and was gone. Lokin grinned.

'Father, you can't be angry. They're safe. That is all that matters. Let's get home. There is a strange presence in the forest today.'

Anketil looked around and directly at Tallis but did not see him. In fact, he looked straight through him. Tallis smiled to himself. He had no wish to deceive but must preserve his powers for when really needed. Every time he revealed his true identity he lost a little of his magic strength. He watched the man and his three boys leave the clearing. Rikarth clutched his little feathered friend who quacked loudly with indignation at being hastily removed from her new world. Lokin stopped as he passed the little man and looked intently into the trees, sensing a presence he could not explain. Tallis saw his calm, quiet eyes and knew of the courage of this young man. He had been well chosen for this dangerous journey. Lokin dropped his gaze, shrugging his shoulders.

'I must be mistaken', he said to himself, turning to follow his father away from the unwritten language of the forest. But, descending towards the lake, he was sure he glimpsed a grey shadow, like a wolf, on the crag above the forest. For a second it stood, its glittering coat caught by the sun, then it was gone. Only the grey crag and the grey clouds remained.

CHAPTER THIRTY-FOUR
Carlisle, May 1092
Herluin

The rain poured down in torrents, soaking the city and its inhabitants. Horses shivered in the heavy shower of spring and people ran quickly to find shelter. The winter was moving north beyond the black mountain and southern breezes nudged across the plains. Herluin walked quickly along the narrow street that led from the castle towards the river. He ignored the inevitable stench and pushed his way through the crowds, not wishing to dally in this place. The mud quickly deepened and folk slipped and slid in this treacherous world. Soon, he arrived at the edge of the river, the great river Eden that flowed from the sparkling valleys of the east below Appleby. Here, it broadened out into a vast white estuary and disappeared west beyond the horizon. The water, however, had lost its silver sparkle beneath the heavy dank walls of the harbour. It was dull and brown, swaying lethargically between the boats. Pieces of driftwood floated with the tide and seaweed choked the little stream flowing helplessly to join the river. No silver salmon or orange trout swam in these waters.

Herluin saw at last what he was seeking. A small and brightly painted wooden craft lay beyond a tall ship which was busily unloading its cargo from the Spanish south. Tied to a mooring and almost hidden by this great vessel, the small boat bobbed enthusiastically on the brown water beneath its gaily coloured hull. Two men sat upon its deck, one small and very dark-skinned, the second a tall man with a mop of black hair. These were not men from Carlisle. This was clear to any casual observer and certainly Herluin knew this. The dark-skinned sailors had travelled from the island of Sicily in the distant blue of the Mediterranean. Their journey to this northern outpost was not for trade but for quite another purpose, unknown to all but for Herluin, the Norman. The tall man raised a hand in greeting and Herluin recognised his familiar face. The small man he did not know and wondered who he might be. Carefully, he stepped aboard and greeted the two southerners.

'Welcome to Carlisle, Beco. I hope your voyage was not too rough. Where are your sailors? At least, I assume you did not sail this boat yourselves?'

'No, of course not,' replied the foreigner in broken Norman French. 'The other lads are away enjoying the delights of the city of which there are many I hear. Umberto and I always stay with our ship. This is more precious than anything the city can offer.' He laughed and Herluin noticed his companion did not. He merely looked suspiciously at the Norman and said nothing. Reading Herluin's thoughts, Beco chuckled loudly.

'Don't mind Umberto. He never smiles. Ignore him.'

Herluin looked away but remained uncomfortable. Something was bothering him. Beco continued.

'So, we are here, my friend, Herluin. We journeyed from the Isle of Sicily and only stopped in a port in the very south of Spain, by the great rock, to collect supplies and to stretch our legs. The journey has been uneventful. Now, tell me, what news do you have for me? I have plenty for you, I can assure you.' He laughed again, a deep, throaty sound which Herluin disliked intensely. He had no wish to linger here with these sly foreigners but needed their services and they knew it. He sat on a broad slab of wood covering the galley below.

'Carlisle is shortly to be taken over by my Norman compatriots. Dolfin, I have heard, is planning to leave the city shortly and travel to Greystoke. He could still be useful in the days ahead so nothing is to happen to him. There is, however, one problem and this is where you come in. Ivo de Taillebois must be disposed of, and soon. Once this is achieved, you are to load your vessel with salt as we planned and leave as quickly as possible. Nobody is to know of you presence here and when the two lads return, I suggest, for their own safety, they remain aboard until you carry out this task. These are dangerous times and many things are happening which folk cannot explain, across Allerdale and here in Carlisle. The forests and the streets are full of shadows and strange sights. You must be on your guard. As for Ivo, I have personal reasons for wishing him gone, as you know, Beco.' The weather-beaten sailor looked directly at Herluin and this time did not smile.

'Oh, yes, my friend, Herluin, you are much in my debt. Remember this.'

His friend and fellow sailor, Umberto, stared at the Norman and said nothing.

CHAPTER THIRTY-FIVE
Allerðale, May 1092
The Death of Ivo

Several days later Lokin returned alone to the forest. Early summer was his favourite time of year and life had returned in full measure to the leafy heights above the village. On this morning, he perched on a log in the shadow of a pine tree. It was not a particularly large tree but as ancient as the hills and as wizened as the rocky crags above the valley. Lokin loved this tree whose spindly needles clung to the knarled branches throughout the long winter despite every attempt by the north wind to tear them to shreds. The tree bent with the winds, leaning right over and almost touching the ground when the icy gales blew. But, resolutely, it stood firm. The creatures that lived in its tunnelled root world knew they were safe. It sheltered all from the winter storm and the bright sun of the summer noon from the westerly winds blown in from the distant silvery sea and from the bitter east wind of the winter months. The spring had once again brought the inevitable new growth, tiny green shoots emerging with determination. Radal was with Lokin, of course, his constant companion. There had been no mention by his father or by Ivo de Taillebois of removing him from the boy's care. The dog lay down in the warm sunshine and watched the dark shadows beside the glade, pretending to be asleep but, in fact, watching with one eye for the slightest movement in the bushes.

Lokin used to spend hours in this place with his mother during the early summer days when winter was chased from these lands of Allerdale. They came to collect fir cones beneath the ancient pine for the fire and herbs for the pot and his mother would wander among the trees, singing and calling to the birds as they, too, awoke from their winter numbness. She had often sung a song for this great pine tree in her gentle voice, the lonely sound of which stayed in Lokin's heart every night and stirred him awake in the mornings. It was a sort of lullaby, a sort of ode, sung with love and gratitude for the tree's constant attendance on the creatures of the forest.

On this May morning, as the tall pine, the great oak, the imperious beech, the delicate birch, the stooping ash and alder, spread their green, green wings, Lokin heard the song in the breeze above the forest.

Gentle pine tree, tall and strong
Aged like the stones beneath
Old like the rocks of the mountains above
Young like the fallow fawn grazing the new grass
Young like the new dawn as the summer sun pushes her way into
the ready sky
Gentle pine tree, tall and strong
Brown like the grass in winter
Brown like the rabbit's fur in the burrow
Grey like the water on the lake in a storm
Grey like the heron by the deepest pool
Golden like the sun's finger touching the soft earth
Golden like the yellow moon hanging above the mountain
Gentle pine tree, tall and strong
Watch over me, one more year, watch over me
Watch over my children as they grow like you
Tall and strong
Gentle pine tree

Lokin was alone with his dog. As the breeze sang his mother's melody, he felt a sadness crawl over his young body. Where had she gone? Why had she left? The pine tree listened from its timeless place. Here, with Radal, with the song and the tree, Lokin moved in a world where only peace dwells, where beauty swells with untouched pride and where creatures step without fear across the forest floor. But in Allerdale, now, there was no peace. Evil hung in the air and mistrust sang its enchanting song, creeping across valley and fell. The Red King was preparing to take Carlisle and to establish a Norman presence across these lands. Lokin had come alone to this place on this morning to get away from all these whisperings. He only wished they could live in peace. In fact, hearing his mother's song, seated beneath the tall, grey trunk, he wished he could be somewhere far away, with her and her songs and her untarnished beauty. A tear sat in his eye. He was thirteen years old, growing into a man and yet he missed his mother this morning more than ever.

Have no fear
Do not look
Follow the path, one step, one step only
Do not look back
Only forward
What lies behind does not belong to you
What is before is yours
Walk straight, follow the path, do not look back
The path is your friend
The path leads you forward
Do not look back
One step
One step
You will find me
I am waiting

The words lay on the gentle summer breeze touching the forest green. Lokin listened. He heard the words clearly. The leaves danced gaily to and fro, holding hands and bowing to each other. He wondered if he had enough courage to take each step, without looking back. Today, on this day in May, in the year 1092, what plans for his lands were being crafted by the Norman king? What would happen to Allerdale, to his village and to his family? How could Hermod help and what was the meaning of the message on the font? What was Siyulph's role in the story? Why had he come to Bassenthwaite? Was Sigurd real? There was so much he did not understand. Lokin rose and walked slowly back to the village. The grass was lush with the green thrust of early summer. He had not meant to be away so long from his duties but needed time to be alone. He walked with head bowed, Radal close by, and was unaware he was being followed. A small figure ran hastily from bush to bush a little way behind. He was dressed in red and on his back he carried a small pack which bumped and bounced upon his small frame as he leapt his way down the path to the village. A sudden shout came from the group of huts below and Lokin was shaken from his reveries. It was Siyulph and he was calling urgently. He ran towards Lokin and his face bore a strange expression.

'Lokin, Lokin, have you heard the news? The Red King's troops have entered Carlisle. Dolfin has taken refuge at Greystoke, for now. But what is more, it is rumoured that the Lord Ivo has been killed on the road from Carlisle south to Appleby. Nobody seems to know anything for certain but it appears he was attacked in the forest by two foreigners. His sergeant, Turgis, survived and managed to ride for help but it was too late to save the lord.' Siyulph said all this so quickly that Lokin found it hard to take it all in at once. Dolfin exiled, Carlisle in Norman hands, Ivo de Taillebois dead. He could not believe it and, yet, at the same time, it all seemed horribly real.

'Will Dolfin be safe? And his servants, the silent one and the jolly, fat poet?'

'Your father was discussing this with Piero earlier and it seems Dolfin and Patric are already at Greystoke. As for Gerluff, it is said he vanished like a puff of smoke. He simply disappeared. Gospatric and Waltheof are at Papcastle but there has been no threat to his castle, only to Carlisle and the surrounding forest.'

'I wish we could go to Carlisle to see for ourselves everything that is happening', said Lokin, for, despite the horror of this news, there was also excitement in the air. 'Now, it won't be possible.'

'You will see Carlisle but you must be patient.' The boys turned in astonishment. Behind them a small man in a red cloak emerged from the bushes and stood as tall as he was able. 'I am Tallis, by the way, son of Dedrulf, and I know who you are, of course. Hermod and I know each other well. As for you, Siyulph, I have seen you often but this is the first time you have seen me, I think?' He chuckled merrily.

Lokin stared at the little figure and felt like laughing although nothing was particularly funny but he looked so comical in his red suit and pointed green hat curling down over his shoulders. He knew he was telling the truth, not just because of his demeanour, but because he knew Hermod and Siyulph.

'Why have you come, Tallis?' asked Lokin.

'You know I speak the truth but you are right to question me. You must question everyone from now on. Come, follow me back to the village. Hermod awaits us and your father also. Have no fear for Dolfin and his two companions. They are safe. It is, however, true what is said of Ivo de Taillebois. He is dead and others with him. The forces of evil are at large and we must fight to preserve the secrets of Allerdale. There is much to do. Come, let's find Hermod.'

Tallis led the two boys beyond the church and towards the black lake. He ran with great speed and looked neither right nor left. Lokin and Siyulph followed and, as they ran, Lokin saw, for the first time, an unearthly glow above his dear friend, a gentle light that seemed to enclose his head with its soft caress. Siyulph's feet barely touched the soft earth and his stride was effortless. They reached the dark water's edge where the rocky shallows licked the brown rocks and Tallis stopped. Ahead, on the black water lay a small craft. A man sat motionless, watching the shore. He raised a hand in welcome. Lokin and Siyulph waved back. Hermod smiled but said nothing. As he rose, the boat gently turned and drifted back towards the shore.

CHAPTER THIRTY-SIX
The Forest, May 1092
Sigurð

A soft tap on Lokin's shoulder awakened him. He was at first a little confused as this was not his father's touch. He rubbed his eyes and saw Hermod standing above him. Putting his finger to his unsmiling lips he beckoned Lokin to follow. Radal rose also from his sleep and they ran quickly from the village without stirring even the cockerel. Lokin followed Hermod through the lightening forest and his legs felt stronger than ever before. His eyes were as sharp as flintstones, watching every shadowy place beside the path waking in the hazy summer dawn. They climbed easily beneath the unfriendly crags to where small wiry alders clung determinedly to the hillsides. The ash trees were pushed aside by the relentless wind of successive winters that tore the hills and trees with its wild and unforgiving force. Hermod knew every path and every tree and led the way across the slopes, westward towards the sea and St Bethoc.

After many hours, man and boy stopped. Radal was just ahead and he hesitated at the top of a steep gully, sniffing the warm air with his long nose. He looked back.

'Radal knows this land. He lived here many lifetimes before his journey with the Norman. He knows exactly where we are going, and why. We must listen to him and watch.'

On hearing this, Lokin was not surprised. He knew Radal was a creature from another place and time with a secret knowledge. Hermod continued.

'Radal ran with my father in the forgotten wilderness of the northern wastes. He saved him on many occasions from savage creatures of the hidden worlds. He watched over him during many long northern nights when the earth never rose from its sleep of darkness.' He paused and the wind whistled sharply in the trees above. Suddenly, a long cry cut the dawn, a haunting sound that Hermod knew. Radal raced into the shadows beyond the clearing. 'The silver wolf', called

Hermod to Lokin. 'The silver wolf. He has many answers for us and we must find him. Quickly. Follow Radal.'

The earth sped away beneath them and the wind called its urgent song.

Run, Hermod. Run, young Lokin.
Find the wolf. Follow him to the heights above Allerdale.
Find him and listen to his story.
Follow the wind and hear its song.
Now is the time to take up arms against the dragon.
Run, young Lokin. Follow Radal.
The ancient stones have spoken and you must listen.
Hear their story and listen to the words of those who have gone before you.
Follow Radal. Listen to the song of the wind.
Listen.

Lokin followed Hermod through the trees as the wind urged him forward. There was no sign of the hound and soon he lost sight of his companion. Far below roared the sound of rushing water and, emerging from the trees, he stopped. He found himself in a small glade, bedded with the greenest grass he had ever seen, surrounded by a circle of small and bent trees. The river below burst with song as the last touches of melting snow poured from the craggy hills above. Lokin realised his legs were aching now and he looked around a little anxiously. There was no sign of Hermod or Radal. Apart from the joyful water, the ancient trees of the glade and the grass in its astonishing greenness, he was alone. He sat down on a small stump that lay at the edge of the clearing and wondered what he should do. Hermod must be in pursuit of the silver wolf. Then, at first in the distance and then quite near, he heard footsteps, soft on the forest floor yet quite distinct. It was a man's tread and with no inclination to conceal his approach. Lokin looked expectantly behind him and was amazed to see a tall gaunt figure with a patch over one eye approaching through the trees. He felt no fear and stood to greet him. The man stared at Lokin, his one eye unblinking.

145

'Gerluff, it is you. What are you doing here, in the forest? What do you know of this place? Where is your master?'

The tall man replied in a deep clear voice, 'It is not Gerluff you see before you. I am not Gerluff. I come from another world, far from here. You are one of the chosen. You know my sons, Hermod and Siyulph and my hound, Radal. I am Sigurd, hero of the sagas, Lord of the Land of Ice. Sigurd himself now stands before you and not carved in stone.'

And the tall man lifted the eye patch from his left eye and smiled. Behind him, from the forest shadows, appeared Hermod and Radal. Hermod spoke with a wry grin on his face.

'Ah, I see you have met the silver wolf.'

CHAPTER THIRTY-SEVEN
Appleby, May 1092
Lucy

The news of Ivo de Taillebois's death in the forest above Salkeld came to the castle at Appleby. There was little explanation and Turgis had ridden away in haste to report the news to the King. Lucy and Morcar were silent for many hours. Lucy tried to cry but could not. Nothing moved in her soul and she sat like a stone, feeling nothing. Dead, Ivo, her husband. Soon, however, fears began to emerge from hidden places and creep across her body. Of course, she had known all along something must happen to punish her wickedness. And now the baby, due any day, what would become of her child without a father in this dangerous land? Ivo had been her rock. He loved her and she had betrayed him. She stared from the window and felt utterly alone. Fear was a cold, cold companion and she shivered in its presence. Morcar watched her with alarm, knowing full well the emotions that were beginning to tear her apart, guilt, regret, and, of course, the love within her soul for a man who was not her husband. Morcar's thoughts, also, followed the wind south with Turgis, comforting his sadness and his horror at such terrible events. She loved him and without him would inevitably die. But, strangely, she was not afraid. She had no reason to be as her conscience stood clear and calm in the middle of this terrible storm. She clung to the mast of certainty that he, Turgis, would return and all would be well. As for Lucy, she did not know what the outcome would be but saw on her small face such fear that could send her mad. Ivo. She had betrayed him. As she stared at her sister, beseeching her to forgive, Morcar realised the baby was moving in her body. The time had come and all her strength must be put to this test.

Many, many hours later, Lucy lay grey and asleep on the floor of the great hall where her daughter, Maud, had entered the world. Morcar and Ada had delivered the baby safely but it had taken a terrible toll on both mother and child. The little girl was tiny and very white and, for a long time, cried no cry of life and joy at her arrival. She lay silently in Ada's small arms and the tears blinded the girl's face as she tried to find a flicker of life. Morcar cared for Lucy and covered her with clean linen, wiping away the inevitable stains of childbirth. She washed her unconscious brow and carefully laid her long, fair hair around her head, as if to protect her mind from fear and pain. She then took the baby and heard the first, very tiny, cry. The little girl was alive and Morcar thanked every God she could think of, in heaven and in the forests.

'Welcome, Beatrice, welcome. You are safe now.'

In the days that followed, Lucy lay listlessly in her bed, unaware of her newborn child and with no interest in feeding her. A wet nurse from the Appleby below the castle walls came and fed the tiny child but the infant showed little sign of flourishing. Sadness filled the castle and the shock of Ivo's death nibbled at everyone's souls. Eventually, Turgis returned from the south. He looked broken with guilt at his inability to save his lord from the dangerous forests of Allerdale. He was relieved that Lucy and the baby had survived but, when he saw the condition of both mother and child, he was deeply concerned. He watched with admiration as Morcar went about the constant business of caring for mother and baby. She was grey and exhausted and yet there was strength in her that Turgis had not seen before. He loved her now in a way that he had not thought possible and he must tell her this.

It was late in the evening and summer sun was still quite high in the western sky when Turgis took Morcar's hand and and looked into her tired eyes. He asked her to marry him and to face the uncertain future together. She lent against him as a soft tear wandered down her cheek.

'Thankyou, Turgis, I promise to love you always, no matter what happens.'

They married a few days later, in the chapel constructed within the castle walls. The Norman monk, Hugh of St Bec, took the ceremony and Ada was the witness. Morcar looked into Turgis' eyes and knew she loved him deeply and that they would face the future and its troubles together. A few nights later they were dealt their first challenge. Morcar was woken to find Ada crying hysterically for her to come quickly. The new bride fled down the dark corridor behind her to find the little baby in the cot, lifeless and still. The tiny baby was dead.

'I just found her like this', stammered Ada, terrified. 'I just found her, not breathing.'

Morcar took the tiny body and held her close. The tiny face was at peace. She had just been too frail to survive. She must tell Lucy but not tonight. She must leave her in peaceful sleep. She would wait until her sister was strong again. Turgis comforted her.

'She was too early, barely seven months. Ivo said they expected the baby around harvest time.'

Morcar was unable to tell Turgis of Lucy's terrible guilt at her betrayal of Ivo. Indeed, she thought, it was better for him never to know. The days passed and blurred into weeks. Turgis gradually came to accept that he could not have saved his lord. Morcar and Ada tended Lucy who never asked for her baby. It was as if the child had never existed. She grew slowly in strength and spent her days staring across the plain from the narrow windows of the castle. She prayed daily in the chapel and asked for God's forgiveness but, as her strength returned, she could not forget the tall farmer in the distant hills.

One day, an old man came to the castle gate, asking to see the lady Lucy. He was dressed in ragged clothes and appeared to have an old injury as he hobbled with a long, bent piece of birchwood. His face was half covered in a long hood and his cloak hung low over his misshapen limbs. He stood at the gate but the guards just laughed and pushed him away. Turgis, however, happened to be crossing the courtyard on his daily round of inspecting the stables. He heard the laughter at the gate and immediately chided the guards for their ignorance. He was, however, curious about this strange figure and, inviting him into the courtyard, asked his business. The man merely replied again that he wished to speak with the lady. Turgis pressed him but he looked away and repeated his request. Eventually, Turgis instructed the man to remain where he was and returned to the tower room. Lucy looked up and he realised her eyes were regaining her colour and her cheeks beginning to blossom once more but she still lacked her former beauty. He had yet to talk with her about the loss of her husband and Beatrice was never mentioned.

'My lady, there is a man here in the yard who wishes to speak with you. He refuses to leave until he does. He is ragged and dirty but I believe him to be a good man. Do you know such a person? Oh, and he is lame, with a bent leg and a long stick.'

'I have seen many beggars. I will come down to speak to him. I need some air and today, for the first time, feel like getting out of this room.' She paused. 'I feel as though I have been in here all my life.' She stopped and Morcar saw a look of such desperate sadness she was compelled to look away. It was almost too much to bear.

'Come, follow me and I will take you to him,' said Turgis, softly.

They descended the stone stairs which spiralled down into the great hall and crossed to the heavy oak door. Lucy looked at the door wondering what a beautiful tree it must have been in the forest, a great oak standing tall and proud, a home for many creatures. Why was it here in this Norman castle, hidden away from the sun of noon and the winds of the night? Turgis pulled it open and she saw the old beggar standing in the middle of the courtyard, watching for her arrival. He did not move as she approached but lifted his hood with a filthy hand and broken finger nails. Lucy stopped and dared not breathe. She immediately knew the eyes, blue as the night hills, blue as the sky of the summer evening, blue as the river under the bright moonlight of autumn. Her silence spoke to him and she smiled a tiny thread of a smile and bowed her head. She then took out her purse and held it out to him.

'Take this, old man. I have no further need of this gold. I wish you to have it all. Go now, return to your forest home. It was by the painted cross of stone that I saw you, was it not? The cross that lies by the road to Bassenthwaite? I am sure we will meet again. Return to your cross, with its patterns, stories and painted glory in the evening light of the full moon. Go home.'

Lucy looked directly at him for a few seconds and, as she dragged her eyes away, knew he had understood the message of her words. In three nights the moon would once again fill the black sky with its roundness. Three nights. Anketil watched her disappear into the black doorway. She did not look back. Then, without a glance at Turgis or the guards standing at the gate, he limped slowly away from this Norman world, across the fields beyond the village of Appleby, into the forest by the great river. He left his love a prisoner within the white walls set awkwardly upon this green world of Allerdale but he knew that, in three days, in the forest above the Eden, by the cross carved by his forbears, when the moon was round in the heavens, she would return to him.

CHAPTER THIRTY-EIGHT
The Forest, May 1092
Sigurd and Lokin

Sigurd led Lokin deep into the forest where he had not dared wander before. Even with his father, he had only taken familiar paths within well known glades. Now, he followed this tall figure who stepped out with energy and purpose. Lokin wondered if this was all a dream. Here he was in the forest with the greatest hero of all the sagas. Where were they going?

After many hours, as the sun dipped down to the west, they reached a steep ravine where the oaks gave up struggling to cling to the rocky crags and the ash and the pine took their mountainous seats. The trees were dotted along the steep slope beneath the sheer rock face above. Sigurd did not look back and Lokin had to scramble painfully over the rocky outcrops to keep up with him. Eventually, they came to a small cave, its entrance hidden in the dark, narrow crevices of ancient rock and knarled trees. Sigurd tapped the stone three times with his stick. Then he turned to look at Lokin with eyes of an indescribable blue that reached into his heart. For several moments, neither moved. Suddenly, Sigurd unexpectedly smiled.

'Come', he said, softly, 'Follow me, this time beneath the earth. There I will tell you the purpose of our meeting and this journey through the forest. You must be tired now. You see, I have no memory of tiredness thus my body needs no rest. It is only our memories, of fear and regret, of sadness and guilt that hold us back. Once the memory has gone, then they cease to exist. You will see.'

Lokin wanted to say something but felt rather foolish. He was not really sure what Sigurd meant but felt he ought to understand.

'Do not worry. You will soon feel these things in your own soul. Give it time. Time is the most important ingredient in wisdom. Nobody, not even a Norse hero becomes wise in an instant. Time is required for all beings.'

Shoulders stooping, they moved into the shadows, passing by the flat stones. Sigurd listened, edging forward slowly in the darkness. A passageway gradually opened up before them and soon they were able to stand straight. A large space, although dark, in fact black, stretched out around them. Gradually, however, Lokin's eyes became accustomed to the lack of light and he could make out certain details of this cavern. Then, to his astonishment, rows of candles emerged from the night earth, throwing their tiny lights across the cave. The shimmering lights danced like genies let joyfully from a bottle. Lokin looked at Sigurd. His face, its features caught up in this dance of light, looked like that of a noble god.

'No, I am not a god, Lokin, believe me, just a soul from another world, a world very close to this one but a world few can see and even fewer can enter. Welcome to this middle world, between the land of Allerdale and the land of the ice-gods. This land, deep within many mountains, only allows the chosen few to enter. Others pass by the caves and do not see them. They have, as yet, no need of them.'

A polite cough interrupted him.

Sigurd turned to the shadows and chuckled.

'Ah, there you are, Tallis. Tell me your news.' The little man, dressed in red, shimmering in the candlelight, stepped forward and greeted the two visitors.

'Welcome, young Lokin, I knew we would meet again before long. Sigurd has kept an eye on you these past few months, from a distance of course.' He danced a little jig on the spot. Then he spun round and jumped upon a large stone beside the row of candles.

'I expect you are wondering lots of things. Why you are here? Why was Sigurd dressed up as Gerluff? Why was he with Dolfin in Carlisle? Why was Rainaldo in fact Siyulph? What is going to happen now, to your family and to your village? Who on earth are we, so to speak, because we are not really on earth, if you see what I mean?

'So many questions, so many questions,' went on Sigurd. 'I, for one, and I am sure Lokin, too, would just like to sit down for a while and have some of your delicious brew and, of course, some of that bread, the chunky kind you make so well.'

Lokin suddenly felt his legs give way and he realised how sleepy he was. He wanted to stay awake and to hear more of Sigurd's story and have some of the questions answered. He leaned his head against the rock and was surprised to feel the grey stone as soft as a cushion beneath him. He sank back into the soft warmth of this pillow-stone and fell fast asleep.

CHAPTER THIRTY-NINE
The Forest, May 1092
The Cross

It was almost the middle of the night and the sky was a deep purple. Anketil had left Bassenthwaite at dusk and followed the track to the east, up the slopes, over the mountain top and down into the forest. He knew the path and, although darkness overtook him as he reached the summit, the moon rose round and replete, filling the black sky with its warm yellow glow. Several times, he stopped and stared at the heavens stretching away into eternity. His father had taught him about the stars, where they lived, their names and why they stayed in the sky without falling. He remembered the first time that Lokin had asked the same question 'why do the stars not fall to earth?' and Anketil had told the same stories of his father and his grandfather.

There was a land long ago, a land of fire and ice and hidden pools of hot water that came to the surface when the gods were angered. This land was white as snow and blue as ice and black as the deepest ocean. Few people lived there as it was dark and cold and nothing except lichen and seaweed on the stormy shores could grow. One day, a small boy, whose family managed to survive on a rocky cliff overlooking the icy wastes, left his hut and its warm fire, stoked with the mosses of the shore, and found himself alone on a path which led towards the great black mountain. Few ventured towards this place as those who had never came back. It was told in the sagas that a wicked God lived on the mountain and spurted fire and huge clouds of burning ash whenever he was threatened by outsiders. This evil God reached up and caught the stars in the heavens and threw them into the black sea where they lost their glow and faded away. Many stars in the heavens died this way and the people of the land were very sad. They were afraid and did not know how to attack and kill this evil presence. But, on this cold night, the little boy walked quickly from the safety of his home and did not look back. He was soon out of sight of home, crossing the empty wastes with purpose and without fear. A long time later, he reached the edge of the great plain and the darkness fell around him and covered the land but, at that moment, a strange light started to glow above the black mountain and to encircle its tops in a ribbon of green and red and deep orange. The little boy wondered if this was the wicked God about to descend to the plain and chase him away or worse but then he realised the lights were dancing up to the stars, touching their lights and dancing with them far above the icy wastes. He watched in wonder as the stars danced and raced each other in the night sky. Then, a great roar came from the mountain and the boy knew the wicked giant was angry with the stars and their freedom. He wanted to tie them to the earth so he could use their light and their power to set off his giant fireworks in the mountain. He needed the stars to terrorise the people of these lands.

The little boy watched the mountain open up and the great fire of ash and rock poured forth, in a great roaring which shook the earth. The ice under the boy's feet cracked and moved. He saw the giant's hand reach up and try to catch a fleeing star as it raced away on the ribbon of colour far above the earth. He saw the angry face appear as he stood within the burning flames to control his heavens and to subdue the earth. Then, suddenly, the mountain rose up and roared like a great bear of the polar lands. It exploded like a huge wind in the autumn, over the forest, when the leaves are sent in all directions. The mountain was fighting back, no longer wanting to be controlled by this hateful God, who brought no joy or peace to this frozen land. The mountain opened its great jaws, brimming with fire and bursting with huge chunks of rock. The boy watched in amazement as he saw the evil giant rise up in agony and fall away into the darkness beneath as the flames took over his wicked world and destroyed his cavernous home. The noise was tremendous and the fire raged for a long time. The little boy suddenly realised he was cold and looked around him. He was so far from home but then he saw the stars, free at last, singing and dancing in the heavens, touching the darkness with joy once again, leaping away from each other in their steps of light. He saw the green ribbon of light swirling above the mountain and saw it close its summits to the sky once more, trapping the giant in an eternal tomb, defeated and concealed for ever. Then the ribbon of green and red and deep orange touched the boy's cheek and warmed his small hands, taking him gently in its arms and lifting him high above the snowy night. He felt his small body flying, not far above the ice, and heading for home. He saw his village across the snowy plain and his hut, with its bright fire and warm covers. He realised how sleepy he was and how much he missed his mother and father. The green ribbon let him down gently on the snow and then flew like a snowstorm back up into the sky, far away from the land and into the black night. He watched as it flew back towards the mountain and, as it did so, saw it touch the stars, the little lights shimmering in the sky. They were free, free from this world at last, to fly and to light up the world, to lighten the path of the heavens. The little boy turned once more as he entered his door, just to make sure, and, yes, there were the stars. For evermore.

Anketil loved this story and had told it many times to his young family. Now, on this night of the round moon, he saw the stars in all their joy and freedom. But his attention was suddenly brought back to earth. He had reached the stone cross by the lonely track through the forest, the stone cross that Lucy had so loved when first she saw it with her husband, Ivo. Within this forest world, lit by the moon and the stars, where long shadows fell away from the path into unknown glades, Anketil once again saw the coloured beauty of this carving, with its stories of his ancestors and his homeland. He stood quite near the cross, near enough to see it but not too close. Somehow, although carved of stone, this tall ornate object occupied its own space, commanding respect from those who viewed its decorative surface. He looked again at the figures, Sigurd, Loki, Brynhild and Regin and wondered what hand had carved this. Nobody seemed to know. It just appeared one autumn day many years before beside the track, set against the dark shadows of the forest. Lucy had mentioned this cross to him often during her stay in Bassenthwaite. She wanted to know about the stories behind the figures and she had listened with wide eyes in the darkness of the hut by the embers of the fire.

He thought now of Lucy in this magical place, in the late summer evening, the moon already high in the sky. News of Ivo's death had hit him like an arrow from his bow and he felt sadness at his passing as he had respected the man and believed his love for Lucy was profound. But he was gone, at the hands of dark-skinned foreigners, so it was said, and no barrier stood between him and his beloved now. And he had gone to find her. Now, on this evening of the round moon, there

157

remained a glimmer of the passing day in the western sky but night was almost upon the forest. Suddenly, one of the stone figures on the silent cross began to glow. It was Sigurd, hero and dragon-slayer. Anketil fell to the ground, staring at the figure touching his soul with unspoken words. He felt a deep sadness within him but also joy which touched his face and cradled him in its arms. Sorrow and joy, together. He remembered hearing these words spoken by Piero. Joy and sorrow, the two dancing through life, hand in hand. Anketil realised then that Sigurd was speaking to his heart. He must find Lucy and love her for time was short and life tenuous. He must love her now in this moment. Then, the figure receded into the darkness and Sigurd's wisdom returned to the grey stone of the night. The cross and the forest lay still. The message had been passed to Anketil and he had understood.

He looked around the night world and knew she would come to him, to this place. He knew she had understood his message and would find him, to live their short moment of eternity, as precious as the forest, the streams and the mountains lying beneath the stars of freedom. He closed his eyes, immersed in the dream of the night and turned to see a small figure dressed in a simple brown cape. Behind her walked a small white horse, Chanterelle. Lucy had come to this cross as he knew she would. She stepped forward and held out her hand, a small hand without ring or adornment, and Anketil took it in his. Their eyes, touched with little fronds of moonlight, held each other and made their silent promise. Joy in this moment and also sadness. A tiny shiver sat for a moment on Anketil's spine as he moved forward and took his beloved in his arms. For a long time, the two figures stood by the cross in the depths of the moonlit forest. The little horse stood still and waited for her mistress. Then, without a word, they turned and walked together towards the village of Bassenthwaite. Sigurd, back in his stony world, smiled.

CHAPTER FORTY
Greystoke, May 1092
Forne

Forne watched his ageing father, Sigulf, from the window high up in the turretted tops of Greystoke castle, an ancient and formidable structure that had witnessed many lifetimes in Allerdale. He knew the old man had little time to live. Sigulf had been deeply saddened by the Norman invasion of Carlisle and Forne had witnessed a change in him. But he felt no guilt. He, Eltred, son of Ivo de Taillebois and Thorfinn, son of Thore had betrayed Allerdale but he felt no guilt. It was their choice to be on the winning side and any fool could see that the taking of Carlisle by the Normans was just the beginning. Soon, their fingers of power would stretch across the northern fells and valleys of the south. All resistance would be quashed by the conquering machine of arms, men and government. The young man turned from the window and crossed the great hall of stone, his footsteps echoing to the rafters far above. Soon, Sigulf would be dead and finally he, Forne, would acquire Greystoke and all its wealth and prestige. He would make quite a name for himself, he was sure, and become a powerful ally to the Normans. With Eltred and Thorfinn, he would succeed in his master plan, to control all of Allerdale, Copeland, Greystoke and the small kingdoms of Wigton, Cardew and Cumdivock.

Now, he must leave and ride north to meet the new player in the unfolding story, Roger de Romara. An ambitious and cunning Norman who, it was said, had designs on Ivo de Taillebois' widow. Roger was certainly a man they would need. Forne had heard he was already at Appleby with the Norman, Herluin, and, once the newly strengthened castle of Carlisle was complete, would take control of this city and its surrounds. He must leave this very day and speak with Roger and Herluin as soon as possible. First, he would send a message to Thorfinn and Eltred who had returned to the village of Saint Brigit to await instructions. Forne, however, spoke his thoughts.

'Perhaps it would be better to deal with this myself. Yes, I think so.

I will keep this meeting a secret from all until the time is right.' He moved again towards the door and called his servant to prepare his horse. He would ride alone, through the forest, to the north and meet with this Norman incomer whose part in his rise to power seemed inevitable.

Some time later, the sound of a horse crossing the harsh cobbles of the yard caught the attention of an old man as he rested from the heat of the summer day. Sigulf heard the horse leave the castle and knew its rider to be his son. He knew also that the eyes of the forest would be upon him as he rode on his treacherous mission.

CHAPTER FORTY-ONE
The Forest, June 1092
St Bethoc's bracelet

Lokin and Radal were far above the village. The huts were scattered like ants in the valley and above them the stony heights rose beyond the forest, where sparse trees squatted below the craggy summits. He looked west, to the silver sea and across to the northern hills. He loved this place and needed time to find a peace that the village with its buzzing rumours for the time being had lost. The future of Alleidale and its people was uncertain and the arrival of the Normans had shifted the natural balance of life. Disquiet lay on the summer breezes. Lokin sat on a lichen-cloaked log in the midday sun, tipping his head back to catch its molten rays from the blue world above. Radal dozed on the soft ground, his long legs pushed out across the dusty earth. One eye was shut, the other open just a fraction, watching every movement in the laden world of summer. The slope, although spared of foliage for much of the winter year, was now a concert of green and yellow and gold. Immersed in the song of this ancient forest, the breeze hummed through the trees and birdsong bubbled across the glades. A lonely crow croaked it way across the blue sky, a distant speck of black that tossed and turned with the gentle winds blowing from the south. Lokin watched the bird until his eyes gave up searching the heavens and wondered where it was going in this lonely place. It, too, must have a home, a family and other crows. 'Do birds love each other?' he thought looking down across the green velvet below. He had never considered this before. 'What about all the other animals in the forest? What about Kugi?' He was sure Kugi loved him, at least, he hoped so. Perhaps this was the answer. In order to be able to love, animals needed to know people. It was people they loved, not each other. He patted Radal's head. The dog rose and walked slowly towards the edge of the slope and peered down towards the village. He stood for several moments, as if waiting for something. Then, without warning, the dog turned, looked back and barked, one short bark and then lay down again, watching the village far below. Lokin waited for him to move again but for a long while the dog lay still.

The sun grew in strength as the afternoon wore on and the air became heavy with summer heat. Radal stared at the rocky slopes beneath. Lokin fingered the rotten bark on the old trunk and pulled away some old pieces of dead wood. He was amazed at the life in this knarled remnant of former glory, coated with lichen, grasses and moss. Ants and small beetles with grey backs scurried away into the crevices, alarmed at the sudden shaft of sunlight delving into their hidden world. Lokin's hand was drawn into the mossy layers beside him and, to his surprise, touched something hard. Pulling back the lichen robes he saw, lying on a bed of soft brown earth, a golden bracelet, glinting in the sunlight as if awakening from a long sleep. Carefully, he pulled the tiny object from its earthy home and held it up to the sun. The dull gold gathered strength in the summer light and began to glow with a new brightness that sparkled and glittered. Lokin was astonished. This was no ordinary bracelet and he wondered a little anxiously what powers might have been unleashed in its finding. He sat for a long time, holding the shining gold in his hand. Radal touched Lokin's arm with his soft head, his eyes speaking of a sorrow that Lokin had not seen before. What had he seen in the gold?

The quiet scene in this late summer afternoon was interrupted very suddenly. Lokin's attention was caught by a fleeting movement in the trees below him. He saw a momentary glint of silver shining in the darkness of this wooden world. He stared. Nothing. No, there it was again. This time he was sure. Without warning, Radal leapt to his feet, ran across the clearing and disappeared into the shadows. Lokin sprang to his feet. Clutching the bracelet tightly in his hand, the gold glowed with warmth caressing his fingers. He waited for a few moments, then followed the hound into the trees. On reaching the shadows, cast by the lavish furnishings of the great oaks, Lokin stopped and listened. He heard a distant cry far away across the craggy world above. The bracelet glowed warm in his hand. With a deep breath, he straightened his shoulders and stepped into the shadows. The branches closed behind him, shutting out the world of sunlight and summer, closing the door on his world.

He ran for what seemed a long way, occasionally catching a glimpse of the dog ahead. At last, reaching a steep incline which dropped sharply to the river below, he stopped, the golden treasure deep in his pocket. Radal sat perfectly still on the edge of the bank. Across the clearing stood another hound which stared at Radal and Lokin with enormous eyes. It was bigger than Radal and a light grey which appeared in the summer light as silver. This great hound stood like a statue of stone amidst this wilderness of Allerdale. Lokin held his breath and waited. For a long time, the hounds remained still and it seemed the creatures of the forest had fallen into a summer sleep. The trees held their leafy breath and the clouds hung in an empty sky. Life was suspended in this ancient world and Lokin felt on the edge of eternity. Finally, the silver wolf raised its great head and called to the sky, a timeless call that echoed through the shadows of the forest. Then, turning, he walked slowly away into the darkness of his secret world and vanished.

CHAPTER FORTY-TWO
Bassenthwaite, June 1092
The Death of Piero

The day of the wedding arrived. Anketil and Lucy were married in the church by the priest called Columba from St Bethoc. They chanted songs as incense flowed into every stone crevice and the congregation swayed rhythmically as Anketil and Lucy said their vows before God. Morcar and Ada had arrived the day before, escorted on the journey through the forest by a knight from the castle. Turgis had refused to acknowledge this deceitful act, as he called it, but Lucy's sister knew she must attend whatever the cost. Ada came with her, perhaps for other reasons, to meet once again the young boy who had touched her hand with such gentleness and whose shadow had walked with his. The night after the wedding, however, a very different celebration took place in the moonlit glades of the forest. Anketil took Lucy's small hand as they crossed the leafy floor, following the magical notes of flutes and lyres leading them away into the night. High above the village, amongst oaks and ancient beeches, they sang and danced, touching the stars and the smiling moon with their joy. Lucy's radiance shone among the night shadows and elves touched her long gown with mischievous fingers. Anketil touched her soft cheek and saw, as he did so, a bright star racing across the heavens. Helewisa. She was with them now in this magical place and all was well. He did not see, however, a brief shadow cross the moon as a small cloud touched the night sky. A black swan, flying and unseen among the stars, watched the forest and saw everything.

Piero may have been an old man but since his arrival in Bassenthwaite, unexplained as it was, his stories and quiet wisdom had become known and loved by all. Now Lokin knew Rainaldo's true identity, Piero's job was finished. His task was to bring Siyulph to this place and now his part in the unfolding story of Allerdale had come to its end. For many weeks, he remained quietly in his hut, propped on cushions of hemp and hay, eating little, listening to events across

Allerdale. When he heard of Ivo de Taillebois's death, he just smiled and spoke quietly.

'Ivo was a good man but evil followed his steps also. He has paid the price for his part in the loss of my family and in the death of my only son, Rainaldo. He has lived his life and now he will face the powers of the next world. All is as it should be.'

Piero's cough worsened as the warm weather unrolled its clammy covers across the mountains. It was difficult to breathe but he never complained. He knew his departure was close and he confided in Siyulph.

'I feel quite excited. After all, what is death but a new journey? An adventure? You know already what to expect but don't tell me. I want to be surprised. Anyway, young man, if you are a product of the next world, it must be good place.'

They sat together and Piero smiled, thinking of his beloved Firenze, the winding river, the boats, the bridges of red stone and brick and the ancient churches. Siyulph adjusted his cushions and offered him some cold herbal waters to ease the cough. Piero looked at this boy from another world and then, as the evening drew its curtains across Allerdale, he sat up and said just two words, 'Firenze, Rainaldo'. He closed his eyes and lay back against the soft cushions. Siyulph had seen death many times and knew its stillness. Now, Piero was at peace. Much later, the boy left the hut to announce the news that Piero was dead.

The burial took place the following day and, once again, the church bell sounded in Bassenthwaite. The church filled with the inhabitants of not only Bassenthwaite but also Isel and the surrounding villages, Bridekirk, Brigham, Kirkbride and St Bethoc. They came from across Allerdale, Greystoke and beyond to honour this man from the dusty southern lands. It was unusually hot and the land steamed with a blanket of sultry air. The people of the valleys sought shade in the villages and in the forest the woodland creatures moved high in to the hills to catch the breath of wind flowing from the sea. The land was quiet as if the shock of the Norman invasion had paused life for the people of this ancient land of Allerdale. Piero had left this place and

165

as Roberto, Anketil, Lokin and Siyulph carried his small white shrouded body to the burial place, it seemed Allerdale had lost a dear friend.

'He is returning home,' said Anketil, quietly, to himself. 'He is returning to his forefathers. Of this I am now sure.' Behind him walked Lucy, no longer a carefree girl, who had come to know the pain of birth and the pain of losing a beloved. She looked at Anketil. She was, like Piero, home.

CHAPTER FORTY-THREE
The Road to Carlisle, June 1092
Waltheof and Hermod

Waltheof, son of Gospatric, rode along the ancient road built a long time before by the Roman invaders that stretched from the sea at Mary Port north-east to Carlisle. He was almost at the village of Saint Brigit when his horse suddenly shied and he fell to the ground. It was so unexpected that he sat in the dust thinking what on earth could have frightened his pony. Nothing moved in the shadows and Waltheof watched the bushes anxiously, rubbing his badly bruised leg. He was travelling to Carlisle to meet the Norman priest, Hugh of St Bec, who had been instructed by the Red King to plan the building of a great new church with a monastery. It was said the new buildings would ressemble the great cathedral and monastery of Old Sarum far away in the southern lands. Waltheof was taking a message from his father asking for his presence at Papcastle. Gospatric had met Hugh at Bassenthwaite some weeks earlier. He spoke little of his life in the monastery but had known Ivo de Taillebois and his brothers, William and Ralph, from their childhood in the Mue valley of Normandy. The Lord of Allerdale wanted to discuss with Hugh the Norman plans for these ancient Cumbric lands. Now Ivo de Taillebois was dead who would become Lord of Carlisle and what place did Gospatric of Allerdale and Sigulf of Greystoke have within this new regime? But old age was creeping upon Gospatric's shoulders and as the summer progressed he became confined to his castle at Papcastle set deep in the hills to the south of Carlisle.

Now, sitting in the dust, Waltheof realised he was not alone. From the bushes appeared a tall figure. Waltheof was relieved. He recognised this man from Bassenthwaite but did not know his name.

'So, it was you that frightened my horse. I know you from our time in Bassenthwaite, don't I?' Waltheof pulled himself up. 'What is your name?'

'My name does not matter for now', replied the tall man. 'I know the reason for your journey and this is why I have stopped you.'

Waltheof looked at him in surprise.

'A short way up this road there are those who wish to harm you. We must travel a different route to find the Norman monk, Hugh of Bec. Trust me in this. It is important that your father's message reaches him and nobody else. There is evil now in this land. Even the bushes have ears and berries and fruit eyes. You must not travel alone.'

Waltheof remounted and was astonished when, with one short whistle, a small white pony emerged from the trees.

'I recognise that pony', said Waltheof.

'He is called Kugi, but he is not what you think him to be.'

Hermod leaped on the white back and disappeared into the oaken glades. Waltheof urged his old brown pony as fast as he could go. Later they reached the top of a steep ridge and looked northwards down over the city of Carlisle, glistening in the evening sunshine. It looked peaceful enough but evil now lurked in its ancient streets and taverns.

'At dusk we will go down to the edge of the city to find Hugh. We will be guided so do not be afraid.'

They sat amongst the shaded rocks and the two ponies grazed quietly behind them. Waltheof asked his companion.

'Who are you? Why have you come to help us?'

'These things you will come to know. For now, be patient, Waltheof. The secrets of Allerdale are threatened. We must watch and be ready. At all times.'

When they arrived at the edge of the city, they remained hidden beneath the great stone walls. Waltheof watched the shadows with anxious eyes. Soon, a small figure approached through a narrow gate and beckoned them to follow but Waltheof could not see his face. They followed him as he bounded away into the dark streets ahead.

'Kugi will look after your pony. We will return soon. Trust me and trust our guide.'

With these words, they ran through the dark lanes of Carlisle, hidden from the eyes of the night and protected by Tallis, son of Dedrulf.

Hugh of Bec stood in the shadows of the old church. It was an ancient building, built of stone long before the conquest of the Normans. Some said that the stones had been taken by these ancient builders from the great wall of Hadrian, the Emperor, who ruled these lands in the distant past. He looked up at the great height above him and felt sadness in his heart. This tall and silent building was to be destroyed, except for the crypt beneath its cavernous nave, and rebuilt in the new Norman fashion. Hugh had seen many such new churches in his native land and throughout the southern lands. They were magnificent buildings, there was no doubt, and no expense had been spared in their making. Yet, he also honoured the ancient stone edifices and wondered what God in his heaven was thinking as so many were torn down to make way for the crisp, white stones of the Norman masons. Deep in his reverie, he did not notice a little figure standing near the great west doorway, hidden in the shadows. Tallis waited and then whistled sharply. Just once. Hermod and his young companion, Waltheof, emerged from a narrow street beyond the great church and stepped into the light of the lantern above the doorway. Hugh turned and saw them. He raised his hand in greeting and beckoned to them to follow. As they climbed the steps to the entrance, Hermod glanced back at the shadows of the city. He saw Tallis and watched him dance his little jig, his green hat bouncing across his shoulders. He waved his hand just once and disappeared into the church. All was well.

CHAPTER FORTY-FOUR
Bassenthwaite, June 1092
Roberto's departure

Roberto, Lokin's kind master and friend, announced one morning early that he was to leave Bassenthwaite. They were sitting by the church. It was early and, after a cold night for June, mist gently rose and fell in graceful layers above the damp earth. The black lake beneath the village stretched into the distance, touched by fingers of grey and silver. The wind had moved away across the hills of Allerdale to the sea and all was still.

'Lokin', Roberto said slowly, turning to look directly at his young companion.

'I have come to a decision. I must leave this place. My work here is done and I have travelled far from my home. You must carry on with my work and there is much to do, churches to build and stones to be carved. The secrets of this ancient land must be preserved above doorways and across the fonts within.'

He smiled, taking Lokin's hand.

'Fear not. You are well protected and Allerdale is in good hands, despite the evil that threatens this land.'

'Who are you? Tell me, please. Who are you, really?' asked Lokin suddenly, watching the familiar face of his master.

Roberto paused.

'You will know soon enough. I promise.'

The old man stood up and stretched and Lokin thought he seemed younger as if a weight had been lifted from his shoulders. He looked down at the boy.

'Come to my hut at noon when the sun hangs high above the forest. There, we will say our farewells.'

Roberto strode away purposefully across the yard, leaving Lokin to ponder his words. He must tell his father this news.

Lucy and Ketel were following the path back to the village when Lokin appeared ahead of them, quite out of breath.

'Ketel, Anketil wants you and Lucy to return quickly. Roberto is leaving us and we are all to gather. Come, quickly.'

'What does this mean? Why is Roberto leaving so suddenly?' Lucy asked.

They reached the village to find several folk gathered by the church. Anketil stepped forward.

'We wish to say farewell to Roberto. He will be much missed.' Lokin stood apart from the crowd and touched the golden object nestling in the folds of his pocket. He had yet to tell anyone about his find, not even Siyulph. But then, thinking about it, of course he already knew. Anketil faced the crowd and raised his hand.

'Roberto, master-mason, creator of this church, teacher of Lokin and others and our friend has announced his departure from this place. He wishes to return home.' A mumble of surprise went up from the gathering.

'Let us meet at his hut as he prepares for his journey and give him our thanks, our grateful thanks for his friendship and for our church.'

He led the villagers to Roberto's small hut, set a little way from the rest. Lokin realised he had never entered this place before. Roberto had never asked him to. The door was open. Anketil waited a few moments and then stepped from the white heat into the shadows. Everyone waited. When he reappeared his face was pale and his eyes a little dazed.

He spoke slowly, looking up at the forest and the distant hills.

'He has gone. The hut is empty as if he has vanished.'

Just then, there was a shout from behind them and the crowd spun round to see a stranger walking down through the thickets, a tall man, slightly bent, carrying a long stick. Beside him walked a great black horse. Lokin ran forward, then stopped. The man waved his hand in greeting and stopped. Murmurs went through the villagers but nobody moved. He then turned to Anketil, drawing him and Lokin away from the crowd. He spoke in a quiet voice.

'Anketil, father of the famous Lokin, we meet at last.' Lokin stared at his father. The stranger went on.

'I am Sigurd. This is my horse. And, of course, you know the hound,

Radal.'

Anketil and Lokin just stared in disbelief.

'Come', said Sigurd, 'come and sit with me. I am weary, hungry, too. Yes, even the great Sigurd needs his food.' He laughed and, with his faithful horse, followed Anketil across the village square to their humble home. Lokin was sure he knew those eyes, eyes of the deepest blue. Sigurd's eyes. Yet, they reminded him of someone else. Across the village, unseen by anyone, the door of Roberto's hut gently closed.

CHAPTER FORTY-FIVE
Kirkby Lonsdale, July 1092
Forne and Roger de Romara

Roger still considered himself a young man. He was small in stature and very fat which gave him the nickname to his rivals of Rodge the Podge. He was also greedy, not just for food but for wealth and power. His father was a key player in the great battle all those years ago when the King of England was killed by the Norman invaders. He had fought at the side of King William of Normandy and, it was said, once saved him from certain death at the hands of a wild Scotsman. Roger's father had been well rewarded with lands in Normandy and his children were brought up in splendid surroundings. His mother was from Lombardy and spoke only in the Italian tongue. Roger never heard her say a word in the language of the Normans. He was one of many brothers but lost his eldest and favourite brother in a sqirmish up in the northern lands which led to his hatred for all things English. Now, Roger was one of the Red Kings' favourites, hunting and dining together at castles across the kingdom.

He had arrived in the castle at Kirkby Lonsdale some days earlier after a message arrived at his castle, delivered by a small man on a fat pony. The identity of this messenger was not revealed and when challenged to give a name he galloped away at great speed into the night. Roger was intrigued by the message which told him of developments in Allerdale and suggesting he might find fame and fortune and, indeed, much more among these lands. He was summoned to Kirkby Lonsdale, there to meet with a tall young man who would only give his name on his arrival. Now, several days later, he awaited the arrival of this mysterious stranger and all would be revealed. He heard shouts from below in the courtyard and watched as a single rider walked in from the forest to the north. His horse was huge and black and Roger immediately felt a surge of jealousy. 'Now that is a horse I would like', he thought to himself. The rider approached the great door below and Roger saw his face for the first time. They greeted each other warily but both Roger and his young visitor recognised the need for each other. They ate and drank and talked as the night blackened and Roger was intrigued by the stories that Forne had to tell, of fortune, of land, of wealth, of silver and gold. He also spoke of a widow, of course, the widow of Ivo de Taillebois who most unfortunately died. Roger, for one, was not sorry about this loss. He realised as he listened to Forne, son of Sigulf, much was to be gained.

Many hours later, Forne rode from the castle and headed north. His horse cantered easily along the track that climbed steeply into the forest towards the hills rising above Allerdale. He wanted to return to Greystoke by dusk and knew he must not stop to linger. He was thinking of his conversation with Roger and the power and wealth he would attain once the Norman's plans were put in place. Things were working out just fine, especially since Thorfinn had decided to stay loyal to his father. Ever since their journey to St Bethoc, Thorfinn had been different, nervous and on edge. He kept talking about a silver wolf or some such thing. Ridiculous. He just fell off his horse, nothing more. Of course, Forne would have stayed to help him but his own horse, the great black beast, just took off across the marshes, flying above the rushes and Forne had been quite unable to change his course. He must have been spooked also, he thought. But now, with Thorfinn out of the way and Eltred and, of course, Herluin, on side, prospects were good. Deep in his greedy thoughts, the lone rider was unaware of the eyes that watched from the shadows beside the darkening path. He was unaware too that his black horse saw the eyes and nodded in recognition. Forne thought the forest empty but he was mistaken.

CHAPTER FORTY-SIX
Bassenthwaite, August 1092
Siyulph

Siyulph was sitting alone in the hut he had shared with Piero. He had grown swiftly into a man and his boyish smile had become serious. Sigurd, his father, had come to Bassenthwaite. Now he, Siyulph, could return home. He had come from a land of dragons, the land of ice and fire and blue-ribboned skies, streaked with golden-edged clouds and impossibly orange suns dipping to the north. This was his home and now he could return. Lokin had told his friend about the bracelet late the previous evening as the dying summer haze unfolded across the mountains. At first, Siyulph sat and said nothing. Then, staring at the distant mountains, he spoke in a deep voice, a voice that Lokin had not heard before.

'I know now that I must leave this place. The bracelet had lain there for many lifetimes. My father, Sigurd placed it in the busy care of beetles and ants until you found it. It was given to him by the saint herself, Bethoc, our saint. Now, you must carry it with you until it is time to conceal it once again within the secret places of the forest. Keep it safe and you will know your path.'

Siyulph's face glowed mysteriously with a shade of deep red ochre and his eyes shone blue as deep as the star-laden sky of summer. He smiled at his friend and took his hand.

'Yes, I must leave you. This is our destiny, to greet and then to say farewell, with sadness in our hearts but also with pride and knowledge. You are part of my destiny, I, of yours. We will not meet again in this world but I will stay close to you. The message you carved on the font and must carve again on other ancient stones is the key to preserve the mysteries of these lands.'

Siyulph looked away to the hills.

'The outcome of your journey will not be what you expect but, and this I know, the secrets of the heart of Allerdale are now safe. Follow your heart, trust your instinct, love your father as you did your mother,

175

care for your brothers and protect the creatures that have come to assist you. Your path will open before you, I promise.'

Lokin felt deep sadness at the approaching farewell. The two friends sat together as the the balmy night rolled across the land. It had been a hot, hot summer and even now, with the harvest time at hand, the nights were gripped by the southern winds, as if the earth was storing up its heat for the inevitable months of winter. Finally, Lokin slept and dreamed of a deep lake set in tall mountains rearing to the heavens. From this lake arose a tall man dressed in black and bearing a sword of burnished gold with a shield of bright silver. He walked steadily through the shallows towards the shore. Before him, standing on the shallow sands, appeared an old woman, dressed in a long gown of white, her hair as white as mountain ice and her face as cragged as the rocks above the forest. She raised her crinkled hand in greeting and held it out towards him. As she did so, a little glint of light sparkled in her ancient palm and shimmered in the moonlight. There lay the bracelet, speckled with a golden hue. The old woman spoke to the tall figure.

'This I give to you. Take it to your heart and carry it with you to the distant land where you must go. I have already chosen the place and you will know where to place it. Have no fear. The person who uncovers its dark secret place will carry it safely with him until the time comes once again for its secret to lie hidden.'

The tall figure took the bracelet which glowed brightly in his hand and placed it within the deep pocket on his breast. He bowed low and Lokin heard her words clearly.

'Thank you, Sigurd, Lord of the Isles and all the Seas that flow between. Thank you.'

On waking, he rubbed his eyes and wondered where he was. It had been so real that he imagined cold water around his ankles. He looked around the familiar hut and realised that Siyulph's cushions were empty. Lokin knew he would not see him again in this world. He rose and through the open door saw the village world had yet to waken. It was still early and even the fowl slept. But far above in the sky, with its first hint of autumn cloud, Lokin saw a swan, as black as the lake, flying in slow circles above the village. For a long time, he watched it circling and gliding in the gentle currents of this new day. The bird gracefully twisted this way and that, rising and falling with delight at his freedom. Then, with a final steep dive towards the forest, the swan turned to the north, towards the land of his own kind, to fly with the winds taking him home. Lokin watched the bird grow small and faint in the new blue of the rising day until he could no longer see it. But he knew the swan was there, high in the blue mists, flying north to the mountains of the moon far above the ice-cold seas. He knew that Siyulph, his friend, was going home.

CHAPTER FORTY-SEVEN
Carlisle, August 1092
Forne, Eltred and Herluin

The day was hot and the stench from the streets of Carlisle almost unbearable. Herluin walked quickly through the throng of folk going about their daily business and had no wish to dally in this place. He had received a message some days earlier from the son of Sigulf and hastened to the city as requested, from the cool retreat of Egremont, near the coast at St Bethoc. There, in the ancient castle built from the stones the Romans had hewn from the hills to the east, he had been for some days, thinking on his own future now the invasion of Carlisle was complete. Herluin was a clever man but also greedy and he had no scruples in sweeping aside those who might stop his ambitions. As he walked through the motley Carlisle crowd on this hot August day he thought about the events of the past months. Certainly, Ivo had opposed the move into Carlisle and still Herluin wondered why this should be so. He had much to gain and little to lose from such an invasion. Perhaps his conscience had caught up with him. The responsibility for the murders all those years ago sat squarely on his shoulders. Now, he was dead and at least one of the de Taillebois brothers had paid their due. And Carlisle was in Norman hands. Herluin knew the wealth and power to be gained from these events. But, when he received word from Forne, he knew which way his path must now go. Eltred, son of Ivo and Forne, son of Sigulf, were young, ambitious and greedy men like himself. At least he knew how to deal with such men.

He reached a small tavern close to the harbour and entered the narrow doorway. Inside, the heat of the summer city was compounded by the noise and clamour of men, eating and drinking and discussing all manner of things. A tall man came up to him and ushered him through a door into a small room at the back of the building. Here, an open window allowed a little air into this hellish place. Herluin stood by the window and was almost immediately joined by Forne and Eltred.

178

They must have been awaiting his arrival.

'Welcome, Herluin', said Eltred, looking directly into the eyes of the foreigner.

'I came when I received your message. What do you want? I have done my bit already if you know what I mean. What more do you want?'

Forne looked at him sharply.

'We must all now benefit from the change of power in this city. My father is about to die, Gospatric, your father, also. Allerdale is changing and I, for one, intend to hang on to my power, my wealth and my lands. My question is how and what do you want out of all this?'

Herluin was silent for a few moments. At last, he spoke.

'Forne and Eltred, my decision will surprise you. I came to these lands with one purpose and this is now fulfilled. I had intended to stay and to reap the rewards of this rich conquest. But, and this is final, I have decided to return to Normandy, to my own lands and to find some sort of peace in my heart and with my God. You have your opinion of me, I am sure, and I have earned my reputation without doubt. But, and my brother Hugh would agree, there is still time to find redemption. You have now all you need and I know Odard, the newly appointed Sheriff of Carlisle, wishes only for peace with his neighbours, for now, at least.'

Forne looked across at Eltred but said nothing in reply.

'I am leaving now, leaving this city and the lands of Allerdale. I do not expect to return.'

With these words, he left the room, pushed his way through the throng of the tavern and walked back into the heat of summer. As he walked, he smiled. He felt lighter, his step quickened. Yes, at last, he sensed that peace could still come. Perhaps, yes, perhaps his sins might be forgiven and his heart restored. Herluin lifted his head and hurried forwards. He was returning home. A little way behind him, hidden in the shadowy doorways and beneath the eaves, walked a tall and aged figure, an eye patch across his wizened face. He saw Herluin and his recognised the peace that lay upon his shoulders. At last, this man was free of hate and anger. As the Norman passed the great doorway of the great hurch, the tall figure behind him stopped and, looking up at the tower rising above him in the late afternoon sky, he smiled. Then, Sigurd turned away and vanished into the alleyways of Carlisle, heading south once more towards the fells and hills of Allerdale.

CHAPTER FORTY-EIGHT
St Bethoc, August 1092
Hermod and Lokin

The grey sea stretched out for ever before them. Hermod and Lokin walked side by side, seldom speaking, along the path from Bassenthwaite. Some way ahead, Radal trod the path uneasily, looking sharply into the forest at the slightest sound touching his pointed ears. Lokin was a little tired now and wondered how far they still had to travel but did not wish to disturb his companion's silent reverie. Hermod had been distracted for many days and had yet to confide in his young companion. He stared ahead at the grey mantle of water covering the earth with its cloak. The sky was grey too, with only a hint of yellow where the sun pushed its way through. The summer was still hot and the sky had been a deep blue for many weeks but now, with the harvest safely stored, the weather had turned a little colder and the autumn mists were gathering across the mountains to settle in the valleys below. Grey mist dripped from grey clouds and gentle rain fell on to grey ground. It was remarkable how quickly the summer world had moved on and seemed a distant memory to Lokin as he trod this grey path.

Hermod had decided to travel to St Bethoc as soon as Lokin told him of the bracelet's discovery.

'We must travel to the sea,' was all he had said. He had said little since Siyulph's departure and Lokin now wondered if his friend had yet arrived home. Hermod suddenly halted and turned to him. He knew the boy's thoughts, but of course he did. Lokin was no longer surprised.

'Yes, Siyulph is safely across the black sea. I can tell you no more at this moment and, yes, you will meet again. When, I do not know. Tallis will tell us more. You see, not even I know everything.' He smiled. 'Not even my father, Sigurd, knows everything.'

They walked along the path enclosed by the misty morning and Radal ran ahead.

'Where is your father? Tell me. And was Roberto also Sigurd?'

'I cannot answer these things yet. My father's work is not finished in Allerdale. But I tell you now why we are travelling to St Bethoc. Let us rest for a while. You see, very few things are actually as they appear to be. By the way, the same goes for people.'

They sat on a low, grey rock that provided a dry seat amid the damp morning. Hermod brought out a hunk of bread and cold meat from his sack. Lokin chewed hungrily, grateful for the rest.

'We are seeking a carving which was made in this place many lifetimes ago in honour of my father's defeat of the dragon, Fafnir. We must find this stone. Upon it there is a message. Tallis will meet us in St Bethoc as he knows of its whereabouts. He knew this carving when once a splendid and magnificent stone. It was damaged by those who wished Sigurd's story to be forgotten.'

'Who would want to destroy his story and his secret language?'

'Who do you think? The Normans, of course. They may have been men from the north a long time ago but they have lost the magic of these lands and their souls have been corrupted. They are evil and their intentions are only to plunder these lands.'

He paused and called Radal from the bushes beside the path. They sat for a long time and the dog watched the forest world with sharp eyes and even sharper ears.

'We must continue', said Hermod, suddenly, taking Lokin by surprise. They rose from their rocky seat and turned to the west. It was not cold but the night was drawing in and Hermod was keen to get across the marshes before dark. It was a dangerous road over bog and fen and many travellers had foundered. Bandits also waited for the unwary and Lokin had heard many stories of foul play. He shivered and thought of home, his brothers and his father and Lucy stoking the early autumn fire and stirring the broth. As they left the forest and ventured across the marshes, the world was haunted by mist and shadowy shapes that constantly shifted in the hazy sunlight. Lokin was mesmerised by the spectres and was glad not to be alone in this strange and unforgiving place. Radal growled menacingly once or twice at the swirling fog beside the rough track. To Lokin's relief, they reached the

182

small village of St Bethoc as the final glimpses of sunlight touched the damp earth. The small huts nestled in a circle around a large wooden hall and a little way off lay the small church of stone. The rough ground was surrounded by a picket fence beyond which lay many gravestones. Sheep and a few cows grazed peacefully and chickens clucked contentedly in the evening air. Beyond the little settlement lay an expanse of sand stretching far to the south. The sea moved restlessly beyond the glistening shadows, once again gathering her strength to cover the shore with her determined waves. It was the first time that Lokin had ever seen the ocean and its spell immediately captured him in its watery web.

St Bethoc was a monastery, founded by the saint who gave her name to the village. Here, holy men and women prayed to the God in heaven, sang together, worshipped the saints and welcomed travellers. They also tilled the land, producing corn and vegetables, enough to live through the long winters. They fished the shallow waters below the steep cliffs and foraged for herbs and other plants in the rough woodlands inland from their holy place. The monks travelled across Copeland and Allerdale, to marry, bury and baptise the inhabitants. At the gate of the monastery Hermod asked where they might find Columba. They were immediately escorted to a small hut by a short brown-robed man with a red and smiling face. Here they found fresh water, pieces of bread and hunks of cheese. Lokin realised how hungry he was but Hermod did not eat.

'Stay here. I will return shortly. Sleep if you need to. We are safe.'

He disappeared into the gloomy night. Lokin tried to stay awake but eventually sleep engulfed him in its arms. Early the next day he awoke to find Hermod seated on the floor of the hut.

'Ah, you wake at last.' Lokin sat up, rubbing his eyes. The day dawning beyond the door was quite different to the previous one, clear and blue. The mist had rolled away and he could see the sea stretching to the horizon with waves that tossed and danced upon the blue water. 'I never imagined the sea was so huge. Where does it end? How far does it go? Can we cross it one day?' He spoke as if to himself but Hermod answered him 'One day, you will.'

Lokin walked a little way from hut and stared at the miracle that was the sea. Then, turning to look across the meadows to the monastery, a busy scene met his eyes. There were brown-robed monks working in the gardens and in the surrounding fields. There were goats and chickens, ducks and geese. There were three or four small cows and a few sheep grazing under the shady oak trees by the small river that ran to the sea. Two women were busy washing clothes and scrubbing pots. There was a small hut a little apart from the rest and there, drying in the sunshine, stretched across wooden frames, was the skin of an animal, perhaps a sheep, a goat or even a young cow. A monk brushed busily with stiff bristles, cleaning and polishing the surface.

Hermod appeared beside him.

'What are they doing, Hermod?' Lokin asked.

'He is preparing the skin of a calf to make vellum. This is very valuable and very expensive.' He paused. 'Do you know what these are used for?'

Lokin shook his head. 'Perhaps for drawing on,' he said, uncertain of this.

'In a way. These are to make manuscripts and precious books. It is a complex and skilled process and later we will ask Columba to show us books made here in St Bethoc. Dolfin, Gospatric and Sigulf all have these in their possession. They take many months and sometimes years to make. Some have writing and also beautiful paintings. You will see.'

'What do they write in them?' asked Lokin, again feeling rather silly.

'They write and illustrate stories from the Bible and the lives of the saints. There are books on philosophy, magic and mathematics, books on astrology and astronomy and history. Some illustrate the fables of our world. The story of St Bethoc that you carved on the font, telling of her miracle with the bracelet, is also written in such a precious book on the skin of a sacred animal. Dolfin, I know, has this in his possession. Come, we must find Columba by the church. He would tell us all we need to know.'

'I remember him well at Bassenthwaite. I have seen him often. He reminds me of a wizard.'

Hermod did not reply.

They crossed the yard and found Columba by the oak door of the small, stone church. He smiled an aged smile above his long pointed beard and Lokin noticed that his teeth had withered away. He led them into the dark interior with its damp and mossy walls. The floor was bare earth and two narrow windows flanked the narrow building which smelled of the sea. The chancel was raised by a single stone step here a table with a white cloth was lit by a single candle which cast an eerie light. Lokin's eyes were drawn to the object that lay upon the table and he gasped.

'Oh, it is beautiful. It is a book, quite the most wonderful thing I have ever seen.'

Columba gently lifted the book from its resting place.

'Come, we will take this precious thing to my hut and there I will read you some stories. Then you will understand why you are here. Come. No questions now.' Lokin's mouth opened to speak.

'Come. We have much to discuss.'

They left the church to its candle, its dark stone walls and its silent secrets. Pulling the heavy door behind them, Lokin jumped with surprise as a small figure darted from the shadows, laughing at Lokin's surprised expression. Hermod and Columba seemed unsurprised.

'Welcome, Tallis, we have been expecting you', said Hermod.

'And good evening to you, my dear friends. I have much to tell you. The forest was very busy this last day or so and I have been somewhat occupied. Let us sit by the shore.' He leapt away towards the waves lapping incessantly upon the sand. Hermod, Columba and Lokin followed. The sound of the water licking the shore mesmerised the boy. He saw the sea and the waves and watched as the moon sprinkled lights across the bay. It was like a magic story. Tallis sat on a rock and looked at the water, swaying slightly with the rhythm of its dance.

'I have come from Greystoke and encountered many in the forest.' His broad smile stretched across his wrinkled face like sunbeams across the forest floor at dawn.

'Allerdale is changing and needs our help, all of us. Listen.' Hermod and Lokin sat silently awaiting his words while Columba stood in the shadows clutching the precious book in his ancient knarled hands.

'The sea was as black as the darkest night of winter and the boat was tossed on a great wave. The night was endless and the rain beat heavily on the rocks that jutted from the craggy shores. It was cold and the cold dug deep into the waves and into the shivering sky above, sending the creatures of the deep back to their sacred places far below.

'Siyulph travelled home across the sea in a boat they found by the shore. It had been left there long ago by you, Hermod, when you arrived on these shores. You thought it had been broken up by the waves but it was sheltered from harm in a small cave and protected. I must admit I had a small part to play in keeping it safe.'

He smiled but then his face took on a serious cloak.

'He is returning home to another land and also to another time of which I cannot speak now but rest assured he is safe. Lokin, you cannot go yet to this place. Hermod, you must follow him for now. I have come to urge you to hasten north. Follow your brother and listen to the stories of the sea. Lokin, your task is just beginning and Grani, Radal, Kugi and, of course, myself, Tallis (who bowed) will help you. Sigurd is never far away. Have faith in yourself and in those you can trust. Above all, remember this world is but one of many and you will, I promise, meet again those you have loved in Allerdale. Do not be afraid.'

They were silent for a long while. Lokin at last fell into a deep sleep rocked by the lullaby of the waves which healed his tired body. He woke and was startled to see bright sunlight already stroking the dusty ground above the bay. The birds of the shore dabbled amidst the dappled golden rays on the sand. He looked around for his companions but the bay was empty. There was nobody except the fowl and one large dog sleeping on the warming sand. Radal lifted his head and stared at the sea for a moment, then at the boy, but closed his eyes once more as if to say, 'No, I am not getting up yet. Let me sleep.' Lokin looked back at the monastery and the small stone church lying in the morning sun. He wandered along a path that led from the wall by the church to the small patch of ground where lay several graves, marked by a random collection of stones. He stopped and looked around and wondered about the lives of those who now lay beneath the cold, rough ground. Who were these people and where were they now? Some stones were engraved with rough carvings and letters. Others lay unnoticed and unkempt, bare and barren. Suddenly Lokin stumbled upon a stone lying half hidden in the grass, covered in moss and worn by the winter winds that had knawed at its bones. There was no writing but, as he pulled back the green mossy cloak, there emerged a helmeted figure in armour, standing over a dragon. He held a spear which pierced the beast with great strength and the dragon's mouth gaped open and gasped a dying breath. Lokin scraped the surface with his fingers and reached the edge of the stone. There, above the dragon was a bird that sat and watched from its eerie, perhaps an eagle, perhaps a swan. Of course, Sigurd learned the language of the birds as he killed the dragon and ate its heart. The language of the birds, the swan, the eagle far above the village and this was the stone that they sought, this was the story of Sigurd, carved in front of his eyes. He had found it.

He sat for a long while and stared at the fallen stone. Who had made this story in stone and why? And Sigurd? Was he real? Was he here? Lokin stood up and looked around. There was nobody about. He walked slowly away from the carving and crossed the meadow towards the sea. Behind him, stood a familiar figure, dressed in red, hidden in the shadows. Tallis had watched all from his secret place. Lokin had seen the story of Sigurd and would carry this knowledge with him.

CHAPTER FORTY-NINE
Carlisle, September 1092
Turgis and Odard

Turgis rode like the wind from the castle at Appleby where he had left Morcar, his betrothed, very ill. She had succumbed to a disease that the Norman incomers had brought with them, a sort of cholera, which had never been known in Allerdale before.

'All those wretched foreigners,' he muttered as his horse leapt across the wide ditches of the plain. In Carlisle there was a man of magical powers who could help Morcar recover. He had come, so he was said, from the island called Sicily that lay in the blue ocean of the southern lands. It was a magical land of Arab, Moor and Christian and the Norman king, Roger, was well regarded and ruled this strange kingdom with a fair hand. Turgis had heard Ivo speak of this place and hoped one day to see this land for himself. At last, he saw four church spires and the city's myriad of chimneys. A new castle was being built for the Red King and the sound of hammers and shouting men echoed across the plain towards him. A man named Odard had been placed in charge of the city and it was he that Turgis sought.

Turgis rode into the central square where two great churches stood, one dedicated to Saint Mary and the other to the ancient saint, Cuthbert. The town was a bustle of activity and men of all races thronged the streets. As he walked quickly through the crowds, Turgis heard many languages. It was just as Ivo had described it to him, a city of magic and mystery. His horse jogged uneasily at his side and he was aware of unfamiliar smells, scents from Spain, spices from the seas of the Mediterranean and perfumes from the far eastern lands of the infidel. Suddenly, a small boy tugged at his long coat. He spoke in a language Turgis did not understand. Pointing towards the church of St Mary, standing tall and elegant amid the chaos of the crowded alleyways, he appeared to know of Turgis's quest. Arriving at a large doorway on the west side of the church, the boy pointed into the shadows. Turgis gave his horse's reins to him.

'Wait here,' he said and the boy seemed to understand.

Turgis entered the great portal and stood for several moments as his eyes became accustomed to the darkness. It was the middle of the day but the windows were high above him. The tall, dark church reminded Turgis of his native Normandy. Normandy. It seemed a life time ago. He longed to return with Morcar but she was determined to remain in Allerdale to be close to her sister. Lucy's departure to Bassenthwaite and the reasons for it had affected Morcar deeply. After the wedding, she and Ada returned to Appleby and life settled into a routine once again. She missed her sister more than she thought possible but knew there was nothing that could be done. This was where she must wait for Lucy to return. One day, he knew she would.

A voice startled Turgis. A small man came forward, with a pointed face and narrow eyes.

'I am Odard, Sheriff of Carlisle. I know you are here to see me. Follow me.'

They walked briskly up the nave and through a narrow door behind the chancel wall. Odard then led Turgis down steep steps into the candlelit crypt that stretched the width of the church. Broad columns were topped with round circles of carved leaves, flowers, strange creatures and faces, peering from the vegetation. Turgis was reminded of the monastery at Caen where he had spent much of his youth.

'The carvings were done by a team of sculptors from Bishop Roger's castle at Old Sarum. Before that, they worked in the crypt of the great church at Canterbury. They came from the Norman lands and one man from as far as Spain, beyond the great white mountains.'

'They are beautiful,' said Turgis, thinking of the little church at Bassenthwaite and of Roberto, the mason. Turgis had thought him rather a mysterious man.

'I know why you have come and hope we can come to an agreement. You wish to leave Appleby, is this right?'

Turgis was taken aback by the directness of the question. He had no wish to dally in this place and was anxious to return to Appleby.

'Yes, this is right. I wish to return to Normandy, to my home in the Mue valley. Appleby Castle is finished now. My work is done.'

'Mmm,' Odard narrowed his eyes, rubbed his pointed chin with his small hand and considered this.

'I realise you wish to return home but I have another proposition. You would be wise to consider it. We need a strong frontier against the Scots to the north-east and the area called Liddesdale needs guarding. I have talked with the King and he will offer you vast lands in this lawless part of the land. There is already a castle of sorts and one or two other keeps but you will need to erect a stone castle which shall, of course, be paid for. Would you consider this? I know you of your loyalty to Ivo and we need men like you to stand firm in this part of the kingdom.'

The two men were quiet for a few moments. Turgis saw in his mind his home, his lands, his mother and father but he knew his destiny was to remain here and to protect the new Norman kingdom. He would become a wealthy man and perhaps he and Morcar would at last find happiness. Anyway, she would never leave this northern world without Lucy. After a long while, he spoke.

'I accept the offer. I am honoured.'

'Good', said Odard. 'You are a sensible man. I know you will establish a strong border to the north. Now, return to Appleby and in a few days you will meet the Norman who is to succeed you there. You know him already, Roger de Romara, whose father fought valiantly in Normandy. He is close to the King.'

Turgis's mind jolted for a moment. Yes, of course, he remembered Roger de Romara. How could he forget? His face must have shown sudden concern as Odard went on.

'Have no fear about him. I will keep an eye on his antics and know him to be a ruthless individual. But he knows his job and is the only available candidate. Trust me in this and we will work together. You had better guard your lass, however, or he will scoop her from under your nose.'

Turgis bristled at the thought.

Odard went on.

'Talking of her, I have been informed she is unwell. Have no fear. I have arranged for a physician to accompany you back to Appleby. She will recover in a few days. I think her sister's disgraceful antics must have upset her deeply. Come, let us find this man and then you can be on your way.'

They rose and left the dark crypt with its staring faces and strange creatures. The small boy still held his horse. Turgis tossed him a coin and pulled himself into the saddle. Odard appeared from a small side door followed by another man, a tall and rather bent individual. He stepped from the shadows and glanced briefly up at the mounted knight. Then he dropped his head again and Turgis could not read his expression. A small white pony stood by the western gate and the tall man stepped easily across its back and headed out to the eastern gate of the city. They rode from Carlisle and followed the familiar track through the forest and down the banks of the Eden. Roger de Romara. Well, after all, they were to meet again and this time it was on Turgis's ground. He would have the advantage. The tall man on the white pony followed him through the evening, watching the shadows and reading their secrets. Turgis rode ahead and saw nothing.

CHAPTER FIFTY
Isel, SeptembeR 1092
GRani

Lokin and Anketil left Bassenthwaite early in the day and headed for the village of Isel where Aunt Gretil and Uncle Thorro lived. Anketil had told him that all was not well and his uncle had become ill. The reason for this was not clear but he had met a strange man on the road from the village of Kirkbride, a man who said he was of Flemish origin and had come here to seek his fortune. He said that many of his countrymen were being encouraged to settle in these parts and to start a new life here. Thorro had returned to tell of these things to Gretil and the other villagers. The following day, he felt unwell and Gretil had sent a messenger to Anketil. They set out immediately, leaving Lucy to care for the other boys, saying they would return early the following day. The path they knew well and they made good progress on this autumn day and the sun felt strong in their faces. The recent rains had swelled the streams and rivers and the sound of rushing water sang across the forest as they walked north and then westwards towards Isel, a small village and an ancient one, lying beside the great river. Reaching their destination late in the afternoon, Anketil was immediately concerned at the sight of Thorro, hot and swollen and speaking incoherently. Gille, his cousin, spoke anxiously to Lokin.

'I have never seen my father like this before and, for the first time, think what life would be like without him. Death is so final. I know we are all supposed to believe that there is more but I mean have you ever seen a ghost, or a spectre?'

Lokin looked quickly away, unwilling to share any thoughts on the subject and unable to conceal his surprise at the question.

'Well, have you?' asked Gille again.

'Well, it depends on what you mean by spectre', said Lokin slowly.

'There are spectres and spectres, aren't there?' Just at that moment, a call from within caught Gille's attention and the boys rushed to the door to be greeted by Gretil.

'Boys, you must go to find old Gault. Anketil thinks he has a touch of scarlet fever, perhaps passed from the stranger he met recently in the forest. Apparently in Carlisle many people are dying. Wretched foreigners and their diseases. You know where to find him, Gille? You went there with your father, do you remember?'

'Yes, into the high valley above Broughton Moor. It is not far but a steep climb. From the valley, follow the stream up to the waterfall and you will come to a narrow cave entrance which looks to the south. There are two large willow trees at the entrance. Do not pass these trees until you are given the message to do so. We don't want Old Gault turning you into stone, or worse.'

Gretil managed a sort of smile on her anxious face. She had known Thorro all her life and his illness had come as a shock.

'Don't worry, Gault will find a remedy to heal him,' Anketil reassured her. She managed a smile and turned to the boys.

'Tell Gault of the symptoms, swelling, red face, strange speech and also his left hand which is speckled with dark spots which I have not seen before. Go now and do not stop for any reason. Go.' She watched the boys climb quickly from the flat ground beside the river. Back in the hut, Anketil was bending down beside Thorro. Wiping his brow, he tried to comprehend the strange words he was speaking but could not. Anketil and Gretil knelt together and waited for the boys to return.

Lokin and Gille ran through the forested slopes above Isel. Daylight was fading but the sky was clear and a moon would soon climb from behind the mountain to provide light as night descended. The forest was eerily quiet. They stopped to catch their breath as the path rose above the great Moor of Broughton. Reaching the clearing where the cliffs rose steeply, they found the entrance to the cave just as Gretil had described. Two ancient willows stood at the entrance, their summer leaves tinged with autumn gold. They swayed gracefully in the night breeze and Gille shivered, whispering to his friend. The boys looked into the dark hole but saw nothing.

'Quite a spooky place', said Gille. 'How long shall we wait, do you

193

think?' He looked round anxiously.

'I think Gault will appear when he is ready. He will know we are here by now, for certain', answered Lokin.

'How do you know? You are being so mysterious.'

Lokin put his finger to his lips, gesturing silence and Gille shrugged his shoulders. The moon rose and the boys grew sleepy. Suddenly, a small round figure emerged from behind one of the willows. He had a green cap and red cloak and Lokin recognised him immediately but stayed silent. The little man danced in front of the entrance and Gille looked as if he might faint with fright.

'Do not be afraid. I am Gault. I am many things. I am of this world and not of this world. Have no fear. I know why you have come. I know Thorro and your mother Gretil and, of course, all the family. I know everything but this need be no concern of yours. Come, follow me into the cave which is not a cave. You will think it is. So, let's leave it as a cave, just to clarify matters, if you see what I mean.'

Poor Gille looked very confused and said, 'Well, no, I don't see what you mean at all.'

'Well, well, it does not matter, not at all. Not at all.' He did a little dance. 'Not at all', he repeated.

They followed him into the cave which opened into a small room, bright with little candles along the edge of the stone walls. It was almost as bright as daylight and Lokin shielded his eyes. The little man called Gault reached into a cupboard, half hidden by the wall, an ancient cupboard of ancient oak. Gille's eyes nearly popped from his head. A magic cupboard. What on earth was happening?

'Well, you may not be on this earth any more, young man', said Gault, chuckling quite loudly. 'But don't worry. Fortunately, I know where we are.' He stretched inside the cupboard and pulled out a little jar made of glass. This he handed to Lokin.

'Take this to your father. You must not, under any circumstances, open it and allow anyone to hold it, not even Gille. Anketil will know how much to give your uncle. When he has finished the medicine, you must leave the jar by the roadside leading from the village. Do this on the night before the moon rises. There is a small rock with an ancient cross carved upon it and by this rock leave the jar.' He led them beyond the cavern and pointed to the village.

'Now, go. Stop for nobody and nothing. There are those who wish you harm and you must be prepared to defend yourselves. But, rest assured, if trouble befalls you, then rescue is at hand. Trust me. Farewell.'

And, with a sudden whirl of his cloak, he was gone. The boys looked around but there was no sign of him.

'Well, you wanted to see a spectre. I think you just did', said Lokin to his friend who was too stunned to speak. They turned and ran down the hill, Lokin clutching the small treasure in his hand, and disappeared into the thickets below. The clouds crossed the moon and darkness covered the land of Allerdale.

They ran for a long time, unaware of strength ebbing from their legs. Lokin knew the importance of this journey and that Thorro's life depended on it. Suddenly, he heard a shout and stopped, turning to see his friend lying on the stony ground, rubbing his knee and groaning loudly.

'I think I have broken my bones,' he sobbed as the pain spread across his leg. 'I can't run, I can't. Lokin, you must go on and deliver the medicine. I will wait here for you to return. Please. Go. My father must be helped.' He broke into sobs and Lokin realised the danger they were in. He could not leave him here in the dark and dangerous forest and yet the magic jar of medicine must be delivered. What could he do? He stared up at the trees above, swaying in the night air and wished for help. 'Where is Hermod?' he muttered. Lokin heard a sharp snap of a twig in the undergrowth and looked around anxiously. Standing tall in the night forest was a black horse, the same black horse that had carried the wicked Forne across these lands. He realised now why this creature had stayed close to Forne, to learn of his misdeeds. Lokin and the horse stared at each other for several minutes while Gille sat, mesmerised, his tongue stuck to his mouth. The horse approached and dropped his head, touching Lokin with his velvet nose. He then stood by a fallen log and waited for the two boys to climb into the soft leather saddle trimmed with gold thread. Lokin lifted his friend from the forest moss and climbed on to the log, pushing Gille over the horse's back. Clutching the precious jar, he jumped up behind his friend. The horse stood still for a few moments, then sped away through the forest, following unknown paths and leaping streams of rushing water. The boys clung on and the horse held them securely in his heart and knew they were safe. For many miles, they floated above the night world until they reached Isel just as the early sun touched the eastern horizon and a glow began to spread across Allerdale. The horse stopped and Lokin helped his wounded friend to the ground. Then the creature wheeled away and vanished into the dawn. Lokin raised his hand but he was gone, Grani, the black horse of Sigurd. Lokin clutched the jar safely in one hand and took Gille's arm in the other. They walked slowly into the village.

CHAPTER FIFTY-ONE
Carlisle, September 1092
Waltheof and Hugh of St Bec

Waltheof stood alone by the castle gate. Hermod had disappeared, assuring the young man he would soon return. Waltheof watched the busy streets of Carlisle and wondered how to find one person in this chaotic city. He had been here many times now and wondered how so many people could live so close to each other. He was accustomed to the open spaces of forest and fell and felt quite uneasy in this strange and threatening place. Hermod had instructed him to remain by the gate. He would return with the Norman monk, Hugh of St Bec, a good man, so it was said, and one that could be trusted. Waltheof wondered about this. The only Norman he had trusted was Ivo de Taillebois until his death at the hands of two foreigners. Nobody knew who the murderers were and from where they had come. Nor was the reason for this atrocious act clear to anybody. It was all shrouded in mystery although there had been a rumour of a murder long ago in the lands of Lombardy that Ivo had been involved in, just a rumour, nothing more.

At last, he saw two men approaching the gate. Both were tall, one dressed in a brown robe of dusty cloth, the second dressed in a dark green coat. They walked slowly together and seemed to be deep in conversation. Waltheof wondered what all this was about and why Hermod had been keen for the young man to meet the Norman monk. Soon, he would discover the reason. At least, he hoped so.

'Waltheof,' called Hermod as they reached the castle wall by the gate. 'This is Hugh of St Bec. He arrived in Bassenthwaite some weeks ago and now resides here in Carlisle, overseeing the construction of the great cathedral and the monastery beside it. There is much work to be done and he needs your assistance.'

'I know your father, Waltheof, a fine man. I know also his death is near and that you will soon become leader of Allerdale. I am a Norman, as you know, and must remain loyal to my countrymen and my king, whatever my personal wishes might be. I need to work with you on this project in Carlisle to create the greatest cathedral of the northern world. I need you to find masons and sculptors for the project and craftsmen of the finest order. Above all, I wish to place a font in the church and this must be carved by Lokin, son of Anketil, whose name is known across the city for his carvings in Bassenthwaite.'

'You are right about Lokin. He has a special gift and one that will be much admired across the land. If you wish, I will take you to Bassenthwaite to meet this young man.'

Hermod smiled quietly to himself and stepped away from Hugh and Waltheof as they chatted about the plans for the building. He heard the words 'Old Sarum ..... Roger ..... Bishop ..... font ..... Soon ..... St Bethoc .....' and knew all was unfolding as it should. The sounds of the city filled his thoughts and he longed for his homeland once more. The time was approaching and before long he would be reunited with his brother and his mother. It was almost time. At that moment, a single bell sounded across the city, a deep bell echoing across the rooftops and along the twisting lanes. It sounded a dozen times, slowly and with resonance, announcing the death of the Lord of Allerdale. Waltheof listened to the bell and heard its solemn message. His father, Gospatric, Lord of Allerdale, was dead.

CHAPTER FIFTY-TWO
September 1092
Dolfin

Dolfin walked slowly around the great hall in Gospatric's castle at Papcastle. He knew his father would have allowed him to stay indefinitely but now he was dead Waltheof was anxious for him to leave. The brothers had never been friends. Although they shared a father, Dolfin's mother had died a long time before Gospatric had married Ellesse. Some said they had never married which made him a bastard, although this had never worried him and his father had treated him with respect and kindness. But not so, Waltheof. He resented Dolfin, despite the difference in age. Dolfin knew, better than anyone, Allerdale's sadness at the loss of Carlisle to the Norman invaders. He had done all he could to prevent this catastrophe but was powerless in the face of the sheer number of soldiers that arrived and also the numbers of incomers that came on the back of the army, English and Flemish and men from the distant south, from the Mediterranean sea and the deserts beyond. Strangers arrived every day and houses were hastily erected on the outskirts of the city. It was rumoured that a new castle and a great cathedral church were to be built, based on other great Norman edifices elsewhere and bands of masons and stonecutters were seen camping outwith the bounds of the city. The cathedral would be a monastery, similar to the great monasteries of the south, Old Sarum, Canterbury, St Albans and Glastonbury. Dolfin knew he could not stem this tide and he must leave or face the consequences.

Now, late in the afternoon on this September day, four months after the invasion, Dolfin decided to cross the sea to the Kingdom of Man where he knew refuge awaited. He was neither a soldier nor a churchman and had no power over his brother's inheritance in Allerdale. A sudden knock at the door interrupted his reverie. It opened slowly and Patric entered, his face grim and determined. He put a large jug on the table and held out a glass to his master.

'Do you want something to drink, something to take the pain

199

away?'

Dolfin did not answer but nodded and took the cup offered to him. They stood for many minutes and said nothing. Dolfin knew his servant wanted his decision.

'Patric, we are going to the Island of Man.' Dolfin straightened his shoulders and looked directly at Patric. 'In fact, we are going to leave tomorrow. Tomorrow. Go and make the arrangements. Decision made. We leave tomorrow.'

Patric smiled at this good news. He loved Dolfin and respected him and knew this decision was the only way. He hastened down the stone steps, to prepare clothes, food and horses for the journey to the coast. He would send a messenger to arrange a small boat to take them across the sea to the island of Man. There, they would wait and watch. As he crossed the dark courtyard, he wondered where Gerluff was. What had happened to him and where had he gone? It was a mystery. Patric missed the old man and his one-eyed silence, his one eye glinting in the shadows. It was, indeed, a mystery.

CHAPTER FIFTY-THREE
Bassenthwaite, October 1092
The Message of the Font

Lucy waited for Anketil to return with the firewood he had promised earlier in the day. The fire was black and cold and the wind had picked up these last few days. The children had run home early, ready for a hot meal and warm clothes. Winter was hovering just beyond the distant mountains to the north and they knew it. Lucy had quickly become accustomed to life in Bassenthwaite and the boys grew to love her gentleness and her smile. Their father was completely transformed and his energy affected everyone around him. There had been no word from the king in the south as to Lucy's marriage to this Norse farmer. Trouble could still arise as she was still the owner of great lands in Lincolnshire and also claims now in the north-west, through Ivo de Taillebois. But they thought little of these things as they moved through the autumn days into the approaching winter, aware only of each other and their family. Anketil fashioned ornaments and jewellery for Lucy and tools for the village. He often sang as he worked and Lucy would come back from picking herbs and mushrooms with Rikarth and Bueth to hear his song from the forest glades. She quickened her step towards the village.

Sometimes, in the early evening when the light was still touching the western sky, they would walk together alone to the church where their love had begun, to sit by the font and read again the unwritten words upon its decorative surface. They touched each other and the brightly coloured stone with love and with gratitude. As the darkness beyond the thick stone walls grew into night, they would light a candle and sit in silence, offering a prayer, perhaps to Jesus, perhaps to one of the gods of the forest, perhaps to the saint Bethoc whose magic bracelet Lokin had mysteriously found in the ancient and fallen tree in the glade above the village. Sometimes they sang quietly together, a hymn of praise for the forest, for the mountain and for the animals which lived in these places and for the love that they had found in each other

201

so unexpectedly. Sometimes they simply sat and looked deep into each other's eyes and touched each other's souls with love and peace. It was as if they knew their time together in this world was short. They knew this golden moment could and would end quite suddenly.

One evening, as darkness gathered once more above the hills, they sat by the shadowy font. The candles were yet to be lit and the church was almost completely black. Anketil held Lucy's hand and silently thanked Helewisa for bringing them together. She was always near and touched his soul daily with her love and with her grace. Suddenly, as complete silence filled the church, the font began to glow, just faintly at first, then with a stronger light as the figures emerged from their stony world. Lucy and Anketil sat absolutely still, amazed at the colours and the light emanating from within the beautiful object. They waited for several moments as the figures moved within their world and the great dragon with its two heads swayed from side to side, watching all with its dark, shining eyes. The figure of Sigurd moved his head and looked directly at Anketil. His eyes glowed in the darkness as he stretched out his hand and held high a sword, pointing out beyond the door of the church behind them. The words he spoke were clear and, although in a language that neither Anketil nor Lucy had heard before, they understood the words.

Leave now, both of you
Leave this place where you have found great love
Leave this place in love and in peace
Neither will return for other worlds beckon
Be not afraid
Be at peace
All will be well when the fire and the night become one
Leave this place
The time has come
All will be well

Anketil held Lucy's hand and stared at the font for several moments, and, as he did so, the soft colour of the figures once more faded. The stone figures stood silent. The dragon breathed no more and Sigurd's sword lay by his side. Anketil lit two of the candles that lay on the altar above them. Their tiny lights flickered, throwing long fingers of shadows across the silent church. He and Lucy said not a word. There was no need to speak as both knew the font message could not be resisted. Anketil rose and took Lucy's hand. They left the church and crossed the yard to the hut where the boys had gathered to eat and to sleep a long autumn sleep. Lucy prepared some broth which they ate with pieces of rough bread. Lokin looked many times at his father but could not read his expression. The silence worried him and he wondered what had taken place in the church earlier that evening. Lucy sat by the fire after the meal and stared into the flames which reached up towards the roof. It was warm, she thought, so warm. She did not wish to think of the cold beyond the walls and the storm hovering above the northern sea, awaiting its signal to move south over Allerdale. Many hours later she fell asleep and dreamed of the sea and a boat and an endless horizon that disappeared into the sky just as she reached it. Anketil was there with her, steering the boat and singing to the wind. Then, as night fell to the earth from a frozen sky, she turned round and he had gone. She was alone.

CHAPTER FIFTY-FOUR
The Forest, October 1092
Anketil's death

The autumn lights were settling on the golden leaves and the coloured carpet of the forest lay like a tapestry across the fells. Everywhere, trees gave up their summer struggle for greenness and became, sometimes overnight, wrinkled images of their youth. The cold air in the morning nipped at every creature and every leaf as the frosts took hold and layers of mist coated the valleys of Allerdale. Anketil loved this time of year and followed the familiar paths through the forest with joy. He ran easily and without fatigue. The message that had arrived the day before would lead him into the depths of the mountains but he was not afraid. He thought of his boys. Lokin was almost grown now. Over these past months, he had become a young man and was as tall as his father and as nimble through the forest also. Anketil was proud of all his sons. But secretly in his heart Lokin was his favourite, perhaps because he was the most like him in mind and body but also had the gentleness and free spirit of his mother. He thought of his eldest son now as he ran and was comforted by the knowledge that he was caring for his brothers and Lucy while he, Anketil, was far away in the forest.

Many hours passed and still he ran, ever northwards, towards the great black mountain. He had never travelled this far from Allerdale without company and was anxious to reach the highest fells before dusk. The autumn day was bright despite the cold wind on his face and the light lengthened kindly for him as he travelled. The message he had received simply read:

Anketil, it is time. Go north. Cross the wide plain and climb high into the black mountain. Climb high and reach the fell where the caves of knowledge lie. You will know this place when you arrive. Your knowledge is already within you. Enter the cave to find the ancient rock within. Read the message upon it and you will know your path. Be not afraid.

Anketil had read it several times, scrawled in scaly runes across a piece of bark. The little man who delivered it was not familiar but the twinkle in his eye told of honesty and truth. He had wanted to ask this messenger many questions but when he turned to speak to him, he was nowhere to be seen. He had told Lokin of his journey but said not a word to Lucy who was caring for Rikarth and preparing a meal for the family.

'Do not worry, Lokin, I will return before very long. Hermod will be close and, of course, you have your own guard, Radal.' He smiled and patted the dog's head affectionately. Within a few minutes, Lokin's father had left the village and disappeared into the forest above the slopes.

Anketil reached the high crag and found the cave in the rocky walls of the black mountain. It was dark now and the moon had yet to rise above Allerdale. He let his eyes become accustomed to the dim shadows and moved quietly into the dark world beneath the mountain. The ceiling above him dripped with black damp and the walls glistened with the aged water of the mountains. He walked carefully, touching the dank world with his hands, feeling his way into the depths of this unknown and extraordinary world. He was not afraid but was unsure of his place in this strange universe. The darkness deepened as he went and any light from the entrance was soon extinguished. Finally, he reached what seemed tobe a wide cavern, lit only by a row of tiny candles on one side. The roof was touched with sparkling moments of light as the candles shimmered in this unearthly place. Anketil looked around for signs of the message which he expected. He examined the flat stone surfaces of ancient rock and ran his fingers along the dark walls. There was nothing. He wondered then if he had come to the right place, if his instinct had led him astray. He walked slowly to the middle of the cave and stretched to his full height, peering into the darkness behind him, into the entrance through which he had come into this night world. There, dimly at first, but then gathering light and form as his eyes became accustomed to the sight before him, a figure slowly emerged from the shadowed passage, a small figure, with long, long hair and a gown of purest white. This unearthly creature stepped forward and her face became clear to Anketil. He stepped back for a moment, unsure of this spectre but yet unafraid. Then, Helewisa smiled. She held out her hand to him and took another step towards the tall farmer of Bassenthwaite. Anketil took her hand, moved towards her and smiled also. They stood for a long time, watching each other with love and peace, their two faces lit by the candles that touched their skin and danced upon their hands. Then, very slowly, the two figures began to dissolve into each other and, as the candles were extinguished one by one by an unknown breath of wind, they disappeared into the darkness of the cavern.

CHAPTER FIFTY-FIVE
Carlisle, October 1092
Eltred, son of Ivo

Eltred crossed the busy square. He had seen the tall man enter the church which lay on the south bank of the River Eden. The church was being rebuilt in the new style and the surrounding lanes and yards were busy with carters, masons and sculptors, with wood-cutters, horses and young lads. Carlisle had changed over the past months since the Normans arrived and occupied Dolfin's castle that was being enlarged and strengthened. The familiar keep with its round tower room and steep stone steps to the kitchens below was hastily demolished and a much large building planned. The rest of the city lived on as usual although the two great churches were also to be enlarged and a monastery begun close to the ancient church dedicated to St Mary. Travellers came and went, poets sang their songs and told their tales, fishermen dragged their carts through the streets, hawking their latest catches, soldiers weary of battle found rest and comfort in the taverns, village folk from the fells came to sell their sheep and wool. It was a restless city and a city that did not sleep.

Eltred watched the dark entrance of the church and waited for several moments. He wondered who this man was. Somehow he seemed familiar. He had not seen his face but thought he saw a patch over his left eye. He was sure he knew this man. He wanted to have answers and, after hesitating, stepped inside the church. It took a while for his eyes to adjust to the gloom of the interior and he stood in the doorway and looked around. There was no sign of anyone and yet he felt he was not alone. He peered into the shadows but saw nothing except the dusty ageing stones of the building, holding their secrets of the ancient rock within. Moving forward, he touched the edge of the chapel wall near the entrance. It was cold, very cold and damp beneath his fingers. November. Damp. Cold. He shivered. Despite the busy world of the city beyond the open door there was only silence within this hidden world. Was he in the presence of God in this place? The silence was quite unearthly. Eltred tried to pray but fear stuck in his throat. He wanted to feel safe in this place, in this presence, but did not. Suddenly, he turned and walked swiftly to the door, towards the daylight of the approaching winter day, towards the comfort of the visible. He reached the doorway and took a long deep breath. Stepping into the busy street, he quickly disappeared amongst the throng, heading for the new castle rising from its midst. What he did not see, however, was the tall figure with the patch over his eye leave the church and follow him along the narrow lanes and through the crooked corners of the city. Eltred did not look back as he hurried on his way.

The Forest

For many days after his father had left to journey through the forest, Lokin searched the woods above Bassenthwaite and scaled the heights of Greystoke and the fells to the north. He went alone with Radal and covered many miles of Allerdale in search of Anketil. Lucy remained in the village with Ketel, Bueth and Rikarth and neighbours came daily to provide comfort and support to her and the boys. She felt alone and very afraid but knew that her task was to care for the boys and to be strong for them and for Lokin when he returned nightly to eat and to fall asleep exhausted in his bed of wool. Hermod had not been seen for some days and Lokin wondered if he, like Siyulph, had left once more for the Land of Ice beyond the black sea. Surely he would not leave without explanation and farewell?

On the fourth day, his prayers were answered. Lokin ran easily through the glades below the high fell and followed a familiar path. He would travel even further today to follow the track towards the black mountain. He had often heard his father speak of this place and felt compelled to journey there to see if he could find any trace of Anketil. The day was cold and the air sharp on his face but he felt fresh this morning as his body adjusted once more to speed across the golden ground of autumn. Far above, Lokin saw a great swathe of geese, flying towards the southern lands. The cries of these enormous birds floated on the restless wind and he wished he understood their language. Could they help him in his search? As if in answer, Lokin saw one of the birds peel away from the busy band of black dots and circle far above the forest. It was bigger and darker than the rest and he watched in amazement as the creature swooped low over the fells above him, almost touching the trees clinging to their precarious crags. Then the bird disappeared beyond the northern mountain and was lost from sight. Lokin watched for a long time, hoping to see it emerge once more into the autumn day but it did not. The sky was empty and the cries of the geese no more.

Lokin sat on a fallen oak lying across the path. There was something in the sight of the swan that had brought sadness and at the same time joy into his heart. He knew it had appeared to tell him something but what he was not certain. As he sat in the fading sun, a figure appeared above him in the trees. At first, Lokin was unaware of another presence. Hermod stood and watched him and waited. He, too, had seen the swan and knew its message. Now, he must tell Lokin that his father, Anketil, had left this earth and gone to another time and another world. He knew Lokin would feel terrible sadness but also knew this was just as it should be. He was once again with Helewisa and was no more to be seen in these green lands of Allerdale. Hermod approached Lokin slowly and, as the boy looked up to greet him, saw the grief in his eyes. Lokin knew already the message of the swan.

'Be brave, Lokin. Your father is now with your mother and they are in another place where you cannot follow. Anketil's task is done in this world and yours is just beginning. You have much to do and a long road to travel.' He looked down at Radal, lying watching him with intense eyes.

'And you have many helpers. You are well protected.' He smiled and sat next to Lokin whose eyes fought the tears that threatened to burst forth. He took his hand and together they sat for many hours, watching the sky as it darkened once more into night and listening to the sounds of the forest creatures as they left their daily tasks to sleep once more. Finally, they turned and walked slowly back towards Bassenthwaite, there to impart the news to all that Anketil would not return.

CHAPTER FIFTY-SEVEN
Appleby, November 1092
Lucy and Roger de Romara

The short and rather fat man strode across the large hall of the castle at Appleby. His face was red and he was puffing with the effort of climbing the long stone stairs that curved their way from the courtyard. He was restless and moved this way and that across the stone floor. Roger de Romara had known of Ivo de Taillebois's wife for many years but this was the first time they would meet and he was eagerly awaiting the pleasure. He had heard of her beauty and her elegance and, most of all, her wealth. He had also heard of her dalliance with a certain Norseman from the wilds of Allerdale. Although this had shocked many of his fellow countrymen, he found it rather exciting. She must be a wild creature and perhaps rather more fun than many of the Norman maids he had exploited over the years. The King was keen they should marry and Roger was quite happy with this arrangement. His first wife had died in childbirth and he only had one son living, a weak and rather pathetic creature that Roger would rather forget about. Anyway, he was in Normandy with his cousins and, here in the north-west lands of Cumbria, Roger could find a new wife, new wealth and perhaps more heirs.

He stopped pacing as he heard the heavy door of oak open behind him. A small figure of a girl appeared, her head bowed and her black gown giving her the appearance of a little bird. Roger hoped this was not the famous Lucy. He need not have worried, however, as the small girl stepped aside and, behind her, appeared another woman, dressed also in a deep black but tall and with long, fair hair that fell to her small waist. She stepped forward with courage and with grace and Roger knew her identity immediately. He sucked in his breath at the beauty of her face with its huge eyes and tender mouth. They stood for several moments staring at each other. Lucy's expression gave nothing away but in her heart she was appalled. How could this happen? How had it come to this? She knew Roger's reputation and knew that he

211

was cruel and treacherous. But the King had commanded this match and she needed a husband in these dangerous times. And, most of all, she wanted to stay close to her beloved Anketil, here in the depths of Allerdale, and marriage to Roger would allow her to do so. He was to command the bastion at Carlisle and rumours abounded that the King intended to bestow considerable powers on this Norman scoundrel.

'Welcome to my castle of Appleby', said Lucy at last, drawing in her breath to force the words from her mouth. 'You are welcome in my house.'

'At last we meet', replied Roger, not taking his eyes from this beautiful creature before him. He could not believe his luck. 'I have heard of your beauty for many a year but these tales have not described it to the full. My lady, you are the most beautiful woman I have yet to see.' He went on slowly, watching her closely. 'You know the purpose for my visit. I wish to ask for your hand in marriage. Indeed, the King has requested this, commanded this union between us. I hope it pleases you.'

Lucy felt a wave of nausea rise to her mouth and she fought back the tears that wanted to well into her eyes. How could she do this? How could she betray Anketil and yet she knew she must. Sometimes, in recent days, she found herself wondering if in fact it had all been a dream. She had gone to sleep one night and dreamed it all. But, as she stood before this Norman suitor remembering the soft happiness of her short life in Bassenthwaite, she felt another presence in her heart, touching her soul. He was with her now, here in this great white castle, standing beside this ugly stranger. His presence assured her this was the course she must take. He would never leave her. Lucy smiled, quite suddenly, and Roger was taken aback. It was so unexpected. Her face was radiant as she moved towards him and put out her small hand in a gesture of friendship.

'I will marry you as the King has commanded, on one condition, that we live here in this place and within Allerdale. I have no wish to leave these lands. I have been happy here and wish to remain. Do you agree to this?'

'I do', Roger spoke quickly, unable to believe his luck.

'My lands in Lincolnshire you may have and my other possessions. But this castle, at Appleby, remains mine and here I will stay and, if God is willing, raise your children.'

Roger took her hand and pressed it her lips. Lucy no longer felt repulsed. She was not alone. Here, in Allerdale, across the fells and by the steep gorges of the racing rivers, she would be with Anketil. He would find her on the quiet roads within the forest. He would meet her at the ancient cross where once they had stood in the night shadows. He would touch her in the morning as she rode through the meadows of the summer and laugh with the warm breezes. Anketil was with her and she knew now what she must do.

CHAPTER FIFTY-EIGHT
The full moon, November 1092
Farewell

Hermod sat by the fire. It was already dark and the world beyond the village was settling down to its long winter sleep. It was a quiet night and the breeze that had blown gently across the fells earlier in the day was now also at rest. Lokin sat opposite the older man and gazed into the flames, occasionally picking up another log and adding to the orange glow. Ketel stood by the door and watched the night steal over the forest above them. The moon would be full and already its promise touched the eastern sky with little shreds of imperceptible light. A few hours yet but then the great yellow beast would climb from the forest into the November sky and reach for the furthest star above them. It was cold already and would get colder as the night walked across this land of Allerdale. Ketel shivered.

'Come and sit near the fire, Ketel. Keep warm for it is not yet time to leave. Try and sleep a little.'

Ketel turned and looked at the man by the fire, his older brother and the two small brothers who nestled beneath their covers, fast asleep. He was growing up fast, his mother dead, his father also. Lucy had left the village and returned to her world and to her new husband so the rumours told. Now, Hermod must also leave the forest and follow his father and brother back to the Land of Ice over the black sea. There was so much Ketel did not understand and so much he wished to know but Hermod had assured him all would be revealed in time.

'Knowledge comes as it wishes,' he had said. 'You cannot seek knowledge. It lives far away from this world and visits here only when needed. My father has lived many lifetimes and still has to wait!'

Ketel thought about these words now. He had only just discovered Sigurd's identity when Lokin had explained some of mysteries that lay across these lands. Imagine, Sigurd here in Bassenthwaite and Hermod, his son, and, of course, Siyulph, well, Rainaldo. It was all so confusing and yet it was beginning to make sense. Ketel felt comfort in the knowledge that he had been chosen to carry this secret. Lokin, Ketel, Bueth and Rikarth, four brothers, all with a different tale to tell, tales that would, without doubt, be told. Of this he was certain.

He moved across the room and sat beside his brother. Lokin turned and smiled and took his hand, boys for this moment, soon to become men. Hermod watched them. He knew as his father had also that the secret of Allerdale and the story of Sigurd was safe within these walls and through the lives of these brothers. Each would live out their life, short or long, and each would tell their tale. In a little while, Ketel and Lokin fell asleep, their faces close together. Hermod gently tucked a blanket of wool across their chests and touched them briefly on their foreheads. He then rose and moved silently across the hut to where Bueth and Rikarth lay. He smiled at the gentleness of sleep as it caressed their small bodies. He felt a sudden wave of sadness as he knew he now must go. He must leave this world and return to his own, awaiting him across the farthest shore. He must go but he would return.

Across the forest, little sparks of light touched the distant trees as the moon approached her moment of entry. She was hiding in the wings of this world, hesitating and teasing the night creatures who awaited her soft light. Hermod stood by the door and saw the wonder of the night forest. He, too, awaited her entrance. A little while later, the edge of a golden yellow ring appeared above the forest, unstoppable and resilient. The moon rose, slowly at first, then with a flourish and climbed higher and higher as he watched. She seemed to stop above the village and hang suspended in the night air. Hermod turned one last time to look at the sleeping boys and Radal lifted his head but did not move. Then, without looking back, the man ran quickly up the slope into the resting trees. A sharp whinny cut the night. Hermod raised his hand in farewell as Kugi stood watch over the village. He did not move.

'Keep them safe. I will return.' The little pony gently dropped his head in reply. The moon watched from her place in the heavens and poured her eerie light on to the paths beneath, showing Hermod the way through the darkness of the winter night. He followed the cascade

215

of silvery yellow touching the earth and knew the direction he must follow. As the moon continued her journey across the sky so, too, Hermod raced upon his path, sharing with her the secrets of the night. Many unseen eyes of this woodland world watched from the shadows and saw the tall figure leaping through the glades and across the fells. Hermod crossed Allerdale, north to the sea and then to his homeland. Behind lay the village of Bassenthwaite and the sons of Anketil who would awaken the following day to find an empty place by the fire. Far above the forest, they would see a great black bird, like a swan, but too far away to be certain, flying above their forest world, heading north towards the Land of Ice.

TO BE CONTINUED IN
THE TALE OF LOKIN